SHAPE OF SECRETS

46. ASCENDING

S. R. CRONIN

Dedication

This story is dedicated to my son,
with appreciation for the many ways
he encouraged my dream to write these novels,
my thanks for all the sparkly music,
and most of all my joy
at his having had the courage
to grow into the individual
he was meant to become.

Shape of Secrets is also dedicated
to the memory of Michael Ryan,
with my hopes of a future in which
the safety and well-being of all of our children
is considered far more valuable
than anyone's larger profit.

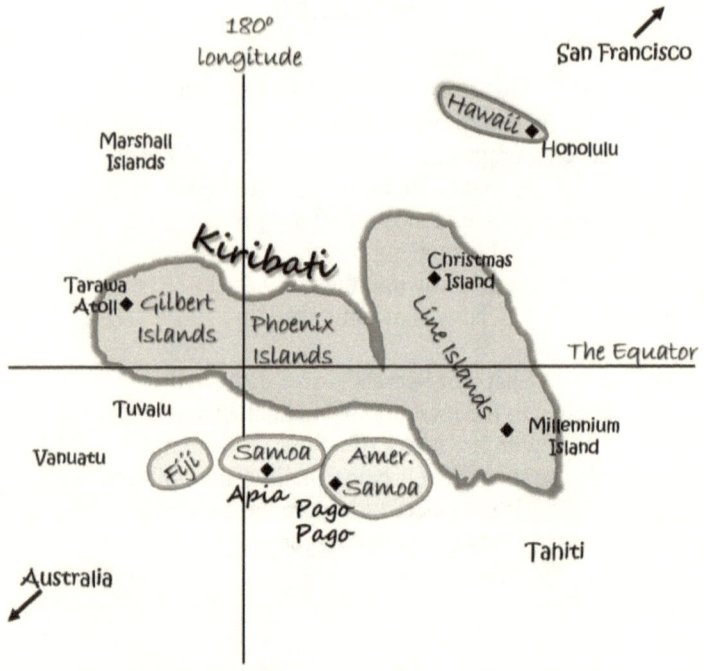

Map Toby drew for Joy: not to scale and only includes locations they were discussing at the time

Table of Contents

Kindling and Matches

Fire Dancing for Fun and Profit

y^1

y^1 is Why

Afterglow

Kindling and Matches

1. The Question

"What do you want to be when you grow up?"

Zane hated the question. He was about to turn seven and that seemed pretty good to him, so the truth was he wanted to be seven years old. But when he said this, the adults always corrected him.

He tried saying teacher and fireman. Those worked, but Zane didn't like lying so he kept trying new ideas.

It was Saturday morning and his daddy had brought him to the tennis court, so his mommy and little sister could have some girl time. Whatever that was. He'd spent most of the morning reading in the car and wiggling his ears and eyebrows in the rearview mirror. Now his daddy's tennis partner was trying to be nice and talk to him, and of course the man asked the question. Zane tilted his head high to look the tall man in the eye.

"A chameleon. I want to be a chameleon when I grow up."

The man sputtered out a laugh and Zane's dad gave a loud annoyed sigh. Too bad. Zane liked the chameleon answer, but he'd have to take that one off the list.

******

"He told my buddy Paul he wants to be a chameleon when he grows up!"

Lola tried to calm her husband while Zane listened from his perch at the top of the stairs.

"No, dear. He's confused. The boy *wants* a chameleon. For his birthday. He's so smart; you forget he's only six years old. He doesn't always understand questions. Don't be so frustrated with him."

But Alex was pretty damn sure Zane understood the question, and with Lola's defense of Zane his frustration went up a notch.

"A chameleon? How does he even know what one is? Why can't he want a dog? Like a normal kid. A pony. Even a snake. But for God's sake. A chameleon? This is exactly the kind of thing I mean."

Lola went to her soothing voice, which Alex hated, because it implied he needed soothing.

"The folks at the gifted and talented program warned us about this. Kids as bright as Zane and Ariel are going to be unusual. It's not going to be easy parenting them. We've got to stay flexible. I've been trying to find a good time to talk to you about this chameleon thing."

"Oh come on, Lola. You're not seriously considering getting him one?"

"Why not?"

"A pet is the last thing we need around here. We've got two working parents, children enrolled in every enrichment program you can find, a sink full of dishes, a yard full of chores, and a checking account that drops into negative numbers. You want to add a pet to the mix? Great. Good thinking."

Alex looked at Lola's expression and realized the chameleon was already a done deal. She hadn't been looking for the right time to discuss it with him. She'd been looking for the right time to tell him.

"Then that stupid thing is entirely your problem. Don't ask me to buy it food or clean its cage or whatever it lives in. I'm looking for ways to make my life simpler, not more complicated."

"Okay." Lola took a breath. "I'll make the chameleon my and Zane's responsibility. You won't even know we have one. I promise. Please Alex. Let's not fight."

"We're not fighting." He took a beer out of the refrigerator, picked up his bowl of chips and headed to the living room. "You're informing me of the new pet you and Zane are going to have. I'm watching the game."

******

It made Zane angry to hear his parents fight about him. Angry because they acted like he couldn't hear them, which he always could; angry because they seemed to think he didn't understand what was going on, which he always did; and angry because parents weren't supposed to fight. They were supposed to love you and love each other. That was their main job. His weren't doing theirs so well lately.

Zane stomped into the playroom he shared with his little sister. In truth, four-year-old Ariel was his best friend. She never made fun of him, was happy to play any game he made up, and she caught on fast. Better than that, she had this lack of fear Zane really liked. She'd try anything. No question—she was as good as little sisters got.

Zane didn't know why he walked up to her and kicked over the building blocks she was arranging into an elaborate structure. She didn't say anything, and all Zane could see was her bright red hair as she kept her head down and put the blocks back. That made Zane even madder. He kicked over more blocks.

"Stop it, Zane."

Now she looked up, glaring at him hard with those crazy light blue eyes. So he kicked over more.

"I said stop it, Zane." Ariel sounded just like mommy when she got mad.

******

Lola was loading the dishwasher and thinking about having to buy live crickets for pet food when she heard a high-pitched shriek from upstairs. Alex looked up from the television as Lola ran up three stairs at a time. The shriek came from Zane, who sat on the playroom floor holding his head in pain. Behind him stood Ariel, grasping a heavy three-ring binder full of paper in her little four-year-old hands.

"Okay. What happened?"

S. R. Cronin

"She hit me over the head with that. Hard." Tears of pain were pouring out of Zane's eyes.

"Ariel??? I can't believe you did that. Why?"

The little girl's chin jutted out with determination. "He told me to. He told me to do it."

"Zane?"

The little boy looked down and said nothing.

"Zane. Why would you tell your sister to hit you over the head?"

Ariel chimed in. "He was kicking over my blocks, Mommy. He kicked over almost all of them." Zane nodded in guilty affirmation.

"I told him to stop but he wouldn't. He said 'make me.' So I did."

Lola burst into a laugh. She knew it wasn't an appropriate response, but this was too funny.

"Okay Zane, I think you've learned your lesson without any punishment from me. And Ariel. You're not in trouble." Ariel's pale eyes widened in surprise. "I don't want you hitting people, sweetie… but if someone picks on you like that, well, that's exactly what you do. You make them stop."

******

Zane spent the rest of the day in his room because even though his mommy had only laughed, he thought he deserved to be in time out. He'd acted as mean as the kids he hated, and he didn't like knowing he could do that. He swore to make it up to Ariel, and promised himself he'd never be a bully again.

As Zane sat on his bed with the Ninja Turtle bedspread, he had a better idea. He could make up for what he did today by protecting people from bullies. That was a much cooler response. He, Zane Zeitman, could figure out how to use his odd brain and even odder body to become a real-life superhero, like Inspector Gadget or one of the Rainbow Brite kids, but way better because he'd be real and no one would ever suspect him.

As Zane declared to himself and the world that he would one day become a real superhero, he made himself whisper the words aloud. After the promise ceremony, as he called it, Zane felt better.

******

Lola waited until later that night to share the anecdote with Alex. Relaxing in bed, Alex laughed, enjoying the story even more than she had. She couldn't help thinking he was happy because for once his two overly cerebral children were acting like normal kids.

******

About a thousand privately owned companies go public each year, as control of the company is placed in the hands of stockholders. Peter Hulson Sr. was well aware of what he was giving up today as he offered stock in the pharmaceutical company he'd founded in 1972.

Peter Hulson Jr. stood with him, and that lessened the sting. His thirty-one-year-old son, with his dutifully acquired PhD in biochemistry and his easygoing nature, would succeed him someday at the helm of Penthes Pharmaceutical, even if his ascension would now need approval from a board of directors.

Next to Pete stood his own young son Joel, an awkward ten-year-old bored with the proceedings. Peter had no idea where the name Joel came from, and it irked him there was no Peter Hulson III, but the important thing was the boy already showed the promising bits of genius his father fell just short of having.

On the other side of Peter Sr., of course, was Neil. Armed with an undergraduate degree of his own in biochemistry and an MBA, Neil had befriended Pete in college and attached himself to the Hulson family, showing a zeal for profit-making which the Hulsons all lacked. It was Neil who'd pushed Peter into this IPO, persuading him public companies can raise more capital, attract better employees, and are valued at over fifteen times their earnings, while private companies are valued at more like five.

So Penthes Pharmaceutical became PNTH. Thanks to its previous two decades of success and Neil's careful planning, it was able to meet all requirements to be traded on the NASDAQ stock exchange.

******

A chameleon is a kind of lizard that can go from deep green to bright orange in a matter of seconds. It also changes its shape and manner of movement to better camouflage itself. It requires a large screened cage with small trees, a heat lamp, a continual water drip, and a variety of live insects. It needs to be taken outdoors for direct sunlight for several hours each week. In other words, this is not the ideal pet for a busy household.

But Zane had always been an easygoing little boy, never begging his parents for toys. He tended to his schoolwork and played whatever sport his dad enrolled him in without enthusiasm but also without complaint. His greatest passions were reading books, and making funny faces in the mirror. This chameleon was the first thing Lola had ever known him to really want, and she was determined to make it happen.

On Zane's seventh birthday, the Zeitman household gained a young male panther chameleon named Balthazar. Zane and Ariel were intrigued with his bug feeding ritual, sitting tight against Lola on either side, watching with fascination as Lola winced when she pinched the little cricket's legs so it couldn't hop back out of the cage before it got devoured.

While Zane preferred observing the dinner process, after a few days Ariel was willing to help pinch cricket legs to get the job done. After a week, Lola put her four year old in charge of Balthazar's dinner, and put Zane in charge of monitoring the heat lamp and the ice cubes that provided the water drip. *If I am going to have such bright kids, I might as well take advantage of it.*

Alex was caught upstairs in the playroom more than once, watching the creature snag its food with its foot long tongue.

Zane seemed to love his chameleon, and he held, touched and talked to his new pet each day as instructed. After a few weeks, Balthazar would lay calmly along Zane's palm and wrist and look at Zane with one eye. With so much care, little Balthazar grew bigger and thrived.

******

Balthazar was the best gift Zane had ever gotten, and he didn't care if his daddy didn't like the chameleon and thought he had a stupid name. Balthazar had been one of the wise men and Zane was sure this Balthazar was wise because he had these really cool eyes that could look at two different things at once.

When Zane got home from school, Balthazar always gave him a one-eyed knowing look while his reptilian skin went from green and brown to a spectacular bright orange. The change made Zane grin. He didn't know what orange meant with other chameleons, but he was sure it meant Balthazar was happy.

One afternoon, Zane took a deep breath as he watched Balthazar change colors, and he forced back his fear as he made himself remember *that time* last summer. Zane's dad had made him go outside and play, and he'd gotten stuck in a game of hide and seek with neighbor boys he didn't like. They did more mean things than most, so Zane hid well because he didn't want to be "it" with these guys.

As one boy came close to the bushes where he hid, Zane saw his own bare foot sticking out over the orange-brown soil. He dare not move it, so he thought hard about his foot and tried to flatten it tight against the ground.

The skin on his foot had started to burn and itch, and an alarmed Zane saw his foot was blushing. At least, it had turned an orange brown that mimicked the dirt. It had been his first inkling he could do more than make his body's shape twist and warp. Zane watched his orange brown foot in fascination while the neighbor boy ran by.

Every so often after that, Zane's skin would surprise him in the same way his muscles did. He could feel a color change coming, but didn't know how to control it. He figured he needed a wise teacher, like Balthazar.

"Can I learn to do that when I want to, wise one?" he asked his chameleon. He tried to make the feeling he felt when his skin did this. He concentrated hard on his arm. At first nothing happened.

Then, yes. He felt the feeling. He made the feeling. His skin went from its normal color to a tan orange.

"You and I are going to be great friends," Zane told Balthazar as his grin widened. "You can teach me ways to fight bullies and you'll be the only one who knows what I can do."

His second best birthday gift had been a book from Aunt Summer. It was a Dr. Seuss book, meant for way littler kids, but Aunt Summer lived far away and didn't know how well he read. He liked it because it said something he'd never heard before. It said there was no one alive more Zane Zeitman than him.

Zane wasn't sure why, but those words made him happy. Grown-ups always whispered he was different in a way that made different sound bad. Other kids, of course, just called him names. Brainy Zany. He's a pain-y.

But this guy, Dr. Seuss? He made being Zane Zeitman sound like a wonderful thing. So now, Zane had a new answer to the grown-ups' question.

******

"Our son has turned into a philosopher," Alex announced, carrying in the groceries he'd just bought. Lola looked up in surprise. "I ran into another teacher at the store, and she asked Zane what he wanted to be when he grew up. Of course. You know what he said this time?"

Lola prepared herself for the worst.

"He said he wants to be himself. Now *that's* a good answer."

Lola was relieved Alex wasn't annoyed. Zane, who'd heard every word from the garage, came in smiling.

"Doesn't wanting to be yourself when you grow up make a lot more sense than wanting to be a chameleon?" Alex asked his son while Lola glared at Alex to drop it.

"Sure daddy. Unless, of course, being yourself means being a chameleon. You know. Because yourself is a chameleon."

Both of his parents gave him a puzzled look as he grinned at them. He bounded up the stairs to check on Balthazar, who turned a cheerful shade of orange when Zane walked into the room.

December 1999

2. Y2K

There are hundreds of muscles in the human body, and by 1999 Zane Zeitman knew the name, location and function of every one of them. He kept his project secret because he didn't want people to think he was being a know-it-all again. He was just trying to stay awake in class.

In Texas history, he worked on his hands and arms. In his computer class, he worked on the muscles in his legs. Find them and flex them. In science, he concentrated on his torso.

He saved the human face, with its fascinating forty plus muscles, for English. While catching the necessary tidbits about literature, he tried subtle upper lip movements with his zygomaticus minor and amused himself by changing the area between his eyebrows with his procerus muscle. No question, his face was the most interesting to maneuver.

He tackled it in English, obviously, because that's when he was most bored.

******

While Zane struggled to flex his orbicularis oculi, a small but industrious segment of the world's population was working to avert chaos and doom. These computer programmers, mostly aging geeks, were hired by companies the world over to ensure the utilities, finances, government records, and communications now run by computers would not come to a grinding halt because decades ago well-meaning programmers like themselves told computers that years only had two digits.

In 1999, people wrote horrific articles about this problem, dubbed Y2K, telling of confused computers toppling modern society. As December neared its end, security forces the world over went on silent high alert.

December 31, 1999, was the big day, even if it wasn't really the end of the millennium. It was the day on which the odometer turned over and the nines rolled into zeroes. It was the day on which the world might end. It was the day on which everyone, including Zane, wanted to be somewhere special.

******

When your country is one of the poorest on the planet, you need to be clever about bringing in income. The Pacific Island country of Kiribati has fish, coconuts, ancient bird shit that makes good fertilizer, and beaches. Those resources don't make for a robust GNP. However, Kiribati was the beneficiary of a fortuitous manmade phenomenon.

In 1884, nations on the other side of the world decided the prime meridian ran through Greenwich England. This conveniently put the 180 degree meridian in the middle of the Pacific Ocean where the twenty-five countries making this decision didn't have to worry about whether it was Monday or Tuesday. Not so for Pacific Islanders.

When the Line Islands became part of the nation of Kiribati, they were on one side of the International Date Line and the rest of the country was on the other. In 1994 the I-Kiribati, as they call themselves, got tired of experiencing two different days of the week at once and redrew the International Date Line with a bulge so the whole country was in synch. Who could object to something so reasonable?

Then, the lucky I-Kiribati realized they had the easternmost piece of land on the planet. Caroline Island, about four-hundred-fifty miles north of Tahiti, would be the first land mass to experience the new millennium.

As 1999 approached, newswires picked up the story and travel agencies were flooded with requests for New Year's Eve lodging on Caroline Island. The only problem was there wasn't any. The island is an atoll about five miles long, less than a mile wide, and is all beach.

But the I-Kiribati would not let this opportunity pass. They changed the name of the island to Millennium Island. As the big day approached, the I-Kiribati assembled their seventy best singers and dancers and sent them, their logistical support, and a few dozen journalists over twenty-five-hundred miles by boat from Kiribati's capital through the wide-open Pacific to Millennium Island's flat uninhabited beach.

The yachting crowd was encouraged to attend the festivities by anchoring off of the island, and several yachts did. The news media established satellite connections while the dancers put on gold headdresses and bracelets, and lit flaming torches. The journalists double-checked their equipment. As the sun began to set, it was serious show time for Kiribati.

Friday, December 31, 1999, over a billion anxious folks of every nation on earth turned on their television sets to watch the performers of Kiribati dance into the midnight. There were no bombs. There was no apocalypse. The open beaches remained devoid of aliens, of vengeful angels, of aggressors of any sorts. All of the reporters' equipment, including their computers, appeared to function fine.

The first image of the New Year was that of a flaming orange torch being passed from an elder to a child. The first sounds were that of a beautiful chanting of farewell to the pain of the past. The first impression was given by healthy and happy young bodies moving with joy in a traditional dance to call for good luck.

Viewers watched with relief as midnight rolled its way without incident into New Zealand and eastern Australia and Asia, with television coverage of parties in Tokyo and Sydney. A few hours later the I-Kiribati greeted the first dawn of 2000 with a call through a conch shell and a song asking for love and peace.

******

Zane ate his cereal in front of the television set watching the taped footage of the dancers from Kiribati. He thought they looked as exotic as anything he'd ever seen and he wished he could be there, or anywhere more exciting than here.

Later that evening, his parents would go down the street to a neighbor's house for a party. Ariel was going to a friend's house for a sleepover and he was expected to greet the new millennium by watching his littlest sister. Nothing against her, but this was 2000. You were going to remember this night and where you were forever, right? You couldn't sit home and do nothing... how lame could you get?

So for the past few days he and his two closest friends had been planning to have a party somehow. They weren't clear how they'd manage it. Zane spent the day trying to coax them into coming over to his house, but Bhadra's parents refused to give her a ride, and Mei accepted a last minute dinner invitation with the family of a boy she liked. So Bhadra and Zane devised an alternate plan. At 11:55, they called each other.

Thirteen-year-old Zane held the portable phone between his neck and his shoulder while he fumbled with the cork on the bottle of exotic liqueur he had slipped out of his parents' liquor cabinet. It smelled vaguely like coffee and paint, neither of which Zane would ever drink. He hoped it tasted better than it smelled. His best friend Bhadra sat alone in her family's upstairs game room, talking to Zane as she stared at one of her father's bottles of beer.

"I can't believe they made me stay home by myself on the biggest night of the whole world's life. I'm going to remember this forever," Bhadra said as she opened the bottle.

"Yeah, well I'm here watching my little sister. So here's to outsmarting the adults. You don't have to be together to party together. Happy New Year, Bhadra." He raised the glass of noxious brown liquid high.

"Here's to a millennium filled with freedom for both of us." Bhadra closed her eyes and made herself take a swallow.

Zane coughed, and Bhadra gagged, but neither complained.

"I say the year two thousand deserves a second sip," Zane said. The second and third gulps weren't as awful.

"You know, a lot of cool shit is gonna happen in this next century." Zane was starting to feel more adult and philosophical.

"Yeah, this next thousand years, who knows what the human race is gonna do." Bhadra giggled as a giant burp escaped her.

The fourth gulp was easier, and by the fifth one Zane was starting to think he could enjoy coffee. Maybe even paint.

After another giant swallow, the mental image of him chugging a can of paint had him laughing out loud, which made the normally serious Bhadra start to giggle uncontrollably. Then they were drinking more and laughing louder and feeling very grown up and like, well, actually the truth of the matter was Zane was starting to feel like he was going to be sick.

He made his way to the bathroom, where he threw up for five minutes. With his head hanging over the toilet, he wondered why this was considered to be such fun.

******

Off the coast of Millennium Island, Peter Hulson Jr. took a few sips of the expensive champagne he'd opened to toast the midnight. Nikolas, who straddled the fine line between employed helmsman and invited friend, passed on the champagne.

Pete encouraged Nikolas to get off of the anchored 44-foot sailboat and enjoy the dancing spectacle on the island up close. An area cordoned off for guests beckoned. But with a night of sailing ahead of them, it was characteristic of Nikolas to decline, maintaining his energy and his focus.

Pete scratched his thick head of blonde hair which could have used a good shampoo, and thought it was to Nikolas' credit that he took the sea so damn seriously. The two men watched the dancers and the chanters and the torch passers from their boat with mild interest, each lost in his own thoughts.

Pete had half expected his wife Sylvia to join him at the last minute for this particularly well-publicized New Year's Eve. She may have considered it, but in the end she passed on even seeing him off in Hawaii, where they kept the sailboat docked. It was just as well; it made things easier.

It had been a full two week sail from Honolulu to Christmas Island and almost two weeks more to get here. Early in their marriage she humored him by spending weeks on the boat, but she had never really shared his love of the open sea. Over the last several months, they'd gone their own ways more often and they both knew it. Pete hoped Sylvia was doing something she enjoyed tonight. Anything she enjoyed. As for him, there was nowhere on earth he'd rather be than moored off of an island in Kiribati.

Nikolas had little family to be missing either, which was another reason he was here tonight. Nikolas seemed as happy as Pete to be on the ocean, and just as anxious for the Kiribati show to end so they could go back to sailing.

The waning moon finally rose, and as the beautiful orange crest lifted above the waves, the two men began their preparations for indulging Pete in his idea of sailing along the International Date Line on New Year's Day. They would spend January first letting the winds take them into the past millennium, then letting the waves push them forward into the future, over and again.

Pete loved the poetry of the image, even though he knew the current calendar system was arbitrary, the number 2000 held no special significance, and the International Date Line was a man-made artifice. The waters he sailed upon would no more be in two different millennia than water elsewhere. He didn't care. All those man-made conventions added up to a magic he could choose to believe in, and who couldn't use bit of magic once in a while.

So as the moon rose into a sky already radiant with stars, he and Nikolas headed away from Millennium Island. They smiled at each other when their navigation showed they had sailed back into the past, then they laughed as they re-entered the future. They couldn't have felt safer as they zigzagged along the date line. The eastern horizon began to glow faintly as the moon overhead looked like a grin in the early morning sky. Then the fun ended.

The search for their bodies and their boat would begin several days later, once they failed to reach Tahiti and it became clear no one had heard from them for days. Families and friends would seek information for years before they accepted the inescapable truth.

Fire Dancing
for
Fun and Profit

3. Selling Trust

Zane Zeitman spent nine months establishing that being a lab technician sucked. At least it did at Penthes Pharmaceuticals, a Chicago-based corporation known for its philosophy of stiff internal competition. The worst part was Zane understood the situation when he took the job. As he lurched along, holding on to a pole he shared with four other commuters on the full El train, he figured he had himself to blame.

Zane's six foot frame was shorter and rounder and his skin was pastier. His non-descript ash-brown hair was disarrayed and his khakis, one of three pairs of acceptable work pants he owned, had permanent coffee stains from long hours of trying to stay awake in the lab. How he had gotten himself into such a miserable position?

When he was handed his shiny bachelor's degree in neuroscience, his parents cried with pride. Their genius son. It turned out to be nice someone thought he was so special, because the job market in the summer of 2009 was less impressed. Zane knew he was in a field where a PhD was required for advancement, but the prospect of six years of, say, pulverizing rat brains in a blender and examining the results, did not enthuse him. He hoped a few years in the working world would help.

Penthes interrupted his desperate job search with an offer for nine months as a lab assistant, then nine in sales and marketing, so he could experience their two entry-level avenues. Tending to others' lab experiments and selling pharmaceuticals both sounded distasteful, but so did waiting tables.

Zane figured the lab work would be easy. Instead, it had been hell. Driven young researchers, fighting to impress Dr. Peter Hulson, Penthes' seventy-three-year-old founder, expected twelve hour workdays from Zane. Except for Britta, a college friend who'd also landed in Chicago, he had no friends in town and no time to make any. His life had devolved into tedious days drinking bad coffee in windowless rooms. It was no way to live.

As his mandated stint in marketing approached, he realized he was looking forward to it. He had no illusions about being skilled at acting friendly when he didn't feel like it, but any change right now was a good thing.

Vacation time was limited, but he managed to get a day off to go back to Texas for a long weekend before he began his new assignment. What he would have liked was several days in Cancun, but that wasn't going to happen.

His mom looked baffled when she met him at the airport. Zane realized it was his physical appearance. Damn.

As a teenager, he'd watched endless videos of shape-changing flounder, squid and octopi, learning how other creatures controlled their appearance and coloring. It wasn't magic; apparently it wasn't even difficult. Hell, cuttlefish could do it. But he was no longer a child avoiding trouble, or a boy in high school who benefitted from not being easy to find. Once he was in college, there'd been little incentive to alter his appearance. For the first time in his life he was surrounded by people who had no quarrel with him.

He'd kept quiet about his talents, even as a child. He was a loner, with no desire to show off and little desire for the attention lavished on the attractive. He liked being who he was. So no one, other than the now-deceased chameleon Balthazar, knew what sorts of physical transformations he could make his body do.

However, he often forget how his reflexes worked on his behalf without his conscious choice. Just like a cuttlefish's did. During his time in the lab, something in him knew appearing attractive would only bring him grief. You don't challenge the alpha dogs. So his body helped. He'd become a chubbier, shorter, dumpier-looking nerd with stooped shoulders and a receding chin. His whole body practically screamed, "Don't hurt me, I'm no threat." He'd hardly noticed the change.

But, of course, his mother did. The best he could do now was to take his time changing back, doing what he could get away with on the way home before he saw the rest of the family. His mom would think she'd imagined it.

The visit went well. His family was good in small doses. His dad's signature eggplant parmesan had improved, and his Mom was preoccupied with her own issues and for once held back on the questions. Ariel went out with him one night and got him laughing. Only Teddie, his fourteen-year-old sister, informed him with disdain that he was turning into an adult.

He supposed, with a bit of sadness, that she was right.

Zane laughed aloud the following Monday morning when he walked up to the receptionist desk in the marketing division. An attractive young woman smiled at him from behind a beautiful mahogany reception desk. Off to one side sat a large inviting decanter filled with water and floating orange and lemon slices. The carpet was lush olive green under his feet, and big office plants sat scattered around the waiting area, kept alive by the natural light which shown in through the ample windows.

"What's so funny?" The young woman was puzzled.

Zane was embarrassed at the honesty of his reaction. "Sorry. I've been working in research. The amenities are a little different here."

She nodded with understanding. "It's all about value here at Penthes." She sounded like she was reciting from memory. "The research people have the best lab equipment money can buy. Our job in marketing is to sell trust. And this," she gestured to the rich brown leather chairs and mahogany end tables, "this is our equipment." She smiled at Zane again, happy to have clarified the situation.

Zane remained dubious about how he could fit into a world of selling trust until he met Brenda, the head of marketing. She was around his mother's age, and a beauty-shop-coifed brunette. Her make-up, clothes, and jewelry made her as well decorated as her office.

Underneath her applied coat of gloss, though, she struck Zane as someone who'd fought hard for respect. Thanks to his own mom, Zane felt some sympathy towards that dynamic. He supposed that was why he didn't dismiss her, like many young males probably did. Brenda softened right away and Zane was sure this was going to be a more pleasant working relationship than the ones he'd had with his bosses in the lab.

"Your background is oriented to research, Zane, but Dr. Hulson insists all our bachelor-degreed new hires go through this department. I'd like to give you every chance to succeed here." Brenda jangled the bracelets on her wrist, sounding pleased with herself. "I think I've found the perfect project for you. You'll report to me, as this thing you're going to work on is a bit outside the normal chain of command." She wrinkled her nose a little to let Zane know she found the chain of command kind of silly.

Zane was shown to his own office, a small interior room with nice furniture and decent carpeting. Over the next few days he discovered he had normal working hours and time for lunch. More importantly, he had a chance to think for himself.

He also had data on every doctor in the greater Chicago area who could, would, or should prescribe drugs for mental health issues. Incredibly, he had data on which drugs they prescribed and how often, how their patterns had changed, and how often they'd been approached by Penthes representatives and in what way.

"Our database for tracking sales efforts is behind the times," Brenda said a few days later while she made little marks in her day planner with her bright turquoise pen. Brenda made the task of improving the database sound so sensible, and Zane was relieved to be assigned something he could do.

He rolled up his sleeves and began to think about making a killer tool for managing and improving Penthes' sales efforts. He was no programmer, but he was hell on wheels with data, and the logic behind such a design was exactly the sort of thing he did well.

******

Afi knew he was in trouble as soon as he noticed the small group of Samoan men watching him from an outside café a block away. He hadn't expected they'd have people looking for him, or would realize he was missing so quickly. His escape plan had been to get out of the facility, walk as fast as he could all the way to town, and then get lost in the crowds along the pier. Beyond that, he'd hoped to improvise.

He had a bit of luck on his side. There was an older, but well-maintained sailboat tied up to the main dock. Afi thought it might be a thirty-three-foot Hans Christensen, as he could see its beautiful teak wood peeking out of the cabin.

The owner, in defiance of good taste, had added a bright orange sun to his main sail and applied an orange stripe around the girth of the boat, adding to his visibility. It told Afi this sailor was more concerned with survival than style. Afi liked that.

The captain and crew seemed to consist of one wiry, well-tanned Anglo, probably in his forties, with older, lined skin but a healthy head full of dark brown hair. He was intent on overseeing the loading of the fruit, water, and fish he'd bought. This was good. The man was a single-handed sailor taking on provisions to head back out to sea. Afi gulped as he walked nonchalantly onto the public pier and ambled in the direction of the sailboat. He hoped to hell the man had a kind heart.

******

Toby was considering whether he should buy more pineapples. Samoan pineapples were tasty, but he didn't want more than he could eat before they spoiled. He was concerned he'd already bought too much fish, but it was too late to remedy that.

He looked behind him and saw a young man with straight jet-black hair and a Polynesian's round face with East Asian eyes. A genetic blend of the Pacific Rim, the young man was wandering along the dock near the back of his boat. He was thin and wiry for a local, and looked harmless as he took off his shirt and shoes as though he were thinking of jumping into the water. Toby glanced away, taking one last look at the pretty harbor with the older wooden houses framed by the fast-rising hills and dense trees. He heard a splash, and focused on getting the rest of his gear aboard.

He started his engine when he noticed three stout Samoan men wearing the traditional lava-lavas marching towards his boat. The oldest of the three waved at him and shouted. "Stop your engines.

We need to check your boat for a missing boy we saw head onto this dock."

"Oh, sure, I saw him." Toby pointed to a shirt lying on the pier as he yelled back "He jumped in. He didn't bother me."

"We'd like to make sure he's not on your boat," the Samoan said as the three men approached the craft. Toby shrugged. "Look for yourself."

There wasn't much looking to do on his vessel. Seating for up to six was above deck, and below was a cabin with a head and shower, a compact galley area and sleeping for up to five, depending on what was raised or lowered. The men boarded without further courtesy, which irked Toby. He was sensitive to people walking into his home. One man began opening each of his storage areas above deck, while another descended below and opened the door to the head. The small toilet seat had no one on it.

"I've been right here. I promise you, no one is onboard." Toby wasn't anxious to have strangers pawing through his possessions, legal though they were. "Please gentleman, I'd like to be on my way."

The man who'd opened the door to the head ignored him, opening the larger storage areas below deck, starting with those beneath the sleeping and sitting areas. One was filled with kitchen supplies, another held clothes and toiletries, yet another lifejackets. He shrugged to his cohorts.

"Guess he jumped in the water then. Radio back if you see him. He could be dangerous."

Toby's dark brown eyes widened. "Really? What's he done?"

"We don't know. He's one of the young men at that special school for troubled teens. These kids are lavished with good care and opportunities, but sometimes they don't realize what they've been given, and try to escape so they can return to their troubled ways. We help the school by returning these misguided ones.

"Well then, I hope you find him."

As he headed out into the harbor, Toby thought maybe the men had a point. He hadn't realized there were schools for misguided youth. Go figure.

He'd gotten past both reefs and was tacking under a nice slow breeze, heading northwest on a course for Fiji, when he decided to go below and grab some water. A movement caught his eye. The lid to one of the smaller storage areas was opening. No person could fit into it; it had to be an animal. Toby looked around for something to use as a weapon.

He grabbed a knife as the stowaway tumbled to the floor in a mess of ropes. A small young man in the briefest of underwear stood, shook himself, then turned to face Toby with apology in his eyes.

"I'm sorry. And sorry about no clothes. Please don't hurt me."

Toby took a deep breath and decided to hear the other side of the story.

Afi spoke English well enough as his words spilled out. "I'm twenty. Not a minor. Not a criminal. Don't do drugs. Don't steal. I promise. Just don't make me go back."

He hesitated, waiting for a response, but Toby waited in silence for more information.

Afi continued. "I tried to last there. I wanted my family to free me. The headmaster said that was the only way to get out. But it's been a year now, and I can't do it anymore. I can't watch what they do to those boys."

Toby was surprised at the last claim. When he raised an eyebrow, Afi explained.

"No, it's bad. They have this little cage they put you in when they think you aren't showing them enough respect. Two boys are, what is it, claustrophobic. They panic when they get put in. One instructor, he knows and he puts those kids in there every chance he gets. I can't watch it anymore. It makes me so angry." Afi was pleading now. "Please don't make me go back."

Toby lived alone on a boat, with limited email and a collection of DVDs. His interactions with other humans were almost all business transactions involving food, water, fuel and, once in a while, sex. These were more words than he'd had coming at him in a long time.

He walked over to one of his drawers and pulled out a pair of shorts. "Here. Put these on."

"Sorry." The young man pulled on the trunks.

"And stop apologizing."

"Sorry. I mean yes. Of course. Sorry for saying sorry."

Toby rolled his eyes. "Let's start over. I'll ask questions. You try to answer in a few words. Okay?"

The young man nodded.

"Good. What's your name?"

"Afi."

"Isn't that the Samoan word for fire?"

"Yes."

Well, the boy did follow instructions. Toby laughed to himself. "Are you Samoan?"

"No."

"Uh, Afi, you can add more words than that."

"Yes. Of course."

"What nationality are you?"

"I'm from Kiribati."

Ah, the giant island nation to the north that covered an area almost the size of the continental U.S. but had a total land mass about the size of Rhode Island. "Are you from the capital? Tarawa Atoll?

"Yes."

"Are you in legal trouble?"

"I don't think so. This school is for rich Americans. My father is an important man in my village, and the people who run the school belong to the same church as my family, so my dad got me in. Parents usually have their children kidnapped and taken there."

"Stop. Afi, rich American parents don't have their kids kidnapped and taken to boarding schools in the middle of the Pacific Ocean. That's ridiculous."

Afi shook his head. "These are kids who've gotten in some trouble. Minor drugs. A little sex. Bad music. Lack of respect. Things that embarrass or frighten their parents."

Toby laughed. "Sounds like half the teenagers in America."

"Yes, but these are the parents who won't tolerate it, the socially conscious, religious, or strict. I don't know, maybe some rightfully worried. It's a mix. Some have done nothing worse than have a nose ring or love hip hop; some wrote angry things in a private journal."

"Even then, parents don't send their kids off to be tortured. They really don't."

"Not knowingly."

"You think the parents don't know what goes on there?"

"They have no idea. They get told about tough love and time outdoors and it sounds so good. Then they get told it is important the kids don't contact them, so they can't whine for sympathy. The parents agree."

"Okay," Toby said. "So these spoiled angry kids can't turn to their parents for help."

"Which could be good." Afi surprised Toby by agreeing. "Except the people who run it don't care about the kids and some, I swear, like to cause them pain. I've seen kids not allowed to go to the can even when they begged, until they soiled themselves, and the instructors laughed at them and called them names until they cried. Then they forced them to wear the clothes for days to teach them a lesson. The last guy I knew who had to do that? He complained because one of the younger kids was covered in rashes from working in the heat all day in clothes they'd forced him to pee in. This guy, who was working hard to stay out of trouble, begged for the kid to be allowed to shower and change clothes. So they did the same thing to him. When he wore his stained clothes proudly? They locked him in that three-foot-square metal box and told him to smell himself and see how proud he felt."

"Okay." Toby held up a hand for Afi to stop. "You've got unsupervised adults. One crosses a line, the next goes further, and after a while unbelievable behavior is normal. I've seen it happen." He moved effortlessly to adjust the main sail as he spoke. "Look, I'm not sending you back. Even if you're exaggerating, the whole idea is disturbing." He paused to glance at the navigation equipment. "Plus, I'd promise not to send you back just to get you to stop telling me more stories like this. Yuck."

Afi gestured to the galley below deck. "I'm a great assistant. My mom taught me to cook. I'm good with boats. I know the sea." He looked Toby in the eye. "I don't need much, and don't expect pay. Make me your crew for a few months, then I'll find somewhere safe to go and promise you'll never be sorry you helped me."

Toby didn't want a crew. He'd come to like his life alone, but he recognized a desperate situation when he saw one. He had too kind a heart to take Afi back to Samoa, or even back to Kiribati to the family who'd sent him here.

"Let's start with a trial run over to Savusavu," he said. " I took on more food than I needed. You got any problem with visiting Fiji?"

Afi's relief was visible as he sat along the back of the deck. "None at all. I'll make you glad you did this."

"You don't have to Afi. Only a monster would do anything else. I'm not the nicest guy in the world, but I do try to stay out of the monster category." Toby settled back into his captain's chair and sipped his water.

Afi said, "So can I ask you a question? How does a man get to be so rich that he can have this nice boat and play all day long?"

Toby laughed. "You get one question a day, okay? If you talk to me too much, I'll leave you in Fiji." Afi looked nervous. "I'm kidding. But I am not much of a talker. And I'm also not rich. I'm a software engineer. Was one. From Northern California. Do you know what the internet is?"

For the first time Afi looked insulted. "I spent most of my childhood at the library on Tarawa. The internet taught me. It made me know a bigger world, and it gave me ideas. It helped me know myself." Afi looked wistful. "The internet is why I got sent to teen prison. My family didn't like the things I said after spending so much time online."

"Well, that's kind of a problem worldwide, I think. I guess in some odd way I'm responsible for your situation, because I'm one of the many people who helped turn the internet into what it is. I played a small but lucrative enough part in it, anyway. A few years ago I realized having more money wasn't going to make me any happier. Using the money I had to do things I wanted, would. So I bought this baby and sailed around the world. When I finished, I realized I was done working, but I wasn't done sailing. So here I am."

Afi nodded as if it made sense to him, which Toby imagined it did. It was only his own friends and family who couldn't understand.

"Now, I get to ask you one more question, and then we call it quits for today, okay?"

"That's fair."

"How the hell did you manage to hide in that storage bin?" This time Toby looked Afi in the eye.

"I guess you have a right to know. My body is unusual. How much do you know about an octopus?"

"If you fry them right, they're not bad to eat."

Afi laughed. "My mother says I'm the son of an octopus. Not really of course. In spirit."

Toby looked puzzled.

"You don't know much about them, do you? They can hide anywhere. Watch."

Afi crawled into the area under Toby's captain's seat, then began wrapping his legs and arms around his body, bending and squeezing his limbs together in a way Toby could never have done. In the end, Afi's skinny body was crammed into a space Toby wouldn't have believed a person could fit. Only his head and his clothes seemed to take up their normal space, making it clear why Afi preferred less clothes.

"I'll be damned. You're double jointed."

Afi began unfolding himself and shook his muscles as he stood back up. "I don't know what that is."

"Its real name is hypermobility. It's actually a disease, Afi. Your connective tissues have less strength in them. It can cause health problems as you get older, but all sorts of people including great musicians and illusionists have used this condition to their advantage."

"My people thought I was created weird," Afi said.

"Is this why they locked you up?" Toby asked.

"No, but it's how I got out. No one knows how well I can do this, except my mother. I'm trusting her to keep this to herself."

******

Joy Cabrini hung up the phone, wishing for once her mother could keep something to herself. Joy had spent two years running away from a relationship with a man her parents adored, and she didn't. Well, maybe she still wanted him on some level, but she knew the life she'd have married to Doug would be mostly miserable. Smart women don't marry attractive, rich, and charming men who cheat on them after they're engaged. Twice. Smart women know how to spot a pattern.

She'd gotten no support at home. *He's just getting it out of his system. Men have to do that, you know.* She'd gotten little support from her closest friends. *Honey, I'd take fifty percent of him any day.* Joy had gotten tired of it all and filled out an application for the Peace Corps. Then she'd headed out to spend two years teaching the small children of Fiji.

It had been lonely, difficult, hot, and not particularly exotic. She'd seen cockroaches bigger than pets back in Boston. Yet, it was the greatest thing she'd ever done.

At twenty-nine years old, she was ready to return as a new person. Self-sufficient. Mistress of her own mind and soul. She was looking forward to teaching and making new friends and living a life that brought her happiness. A life she chose.

Then her mother called to tell her she hadn't been able to keep from letting Doug know Joy was arriving back in the U.S. Doug had seemed so excited. "I think he's maybe forgiven you for running away like you did," her mother said.

Joy pulled on her thick, long, black ponytail in irritation. "I didn't do anything requiring forgiveness. His or anyone else's."

"Sweetie. You ran away from your engagement." Her mother sounded like she was trying to reason with a cognitively impaired child.

"We were not engaged. I broke it off with him."

"But everyone knows you didn't mean it. He said it was all a misunderstanding and he loved you way too much to let you go. It was so romantic. And then you left."

"Mom. Let me be clear. If he steps within five-hundred feet of me I will re-up for another two years in Fiji. I swear."

"Oh sweetie, don't be that way. He asked if he could come along to the airport to pick you up. I thought you'd be so happy. I can't say no, now. I already told him he could."

"Mom, forget it. I'm not going to be on that plane. I've got a little extra money and I'm going to travel for a bit. See more of the Pacific. I'll give you a call once I know my plans." For the first time in her life, she hung up on her mother.

What was she was going to do? She actually had almost no money, thanks to a bad habit of buying things for her students. It hadn't seemed irresponsible; she was planning to return to her folks' house for the summer, and had expected to be teaching and earning a salary come fall.

Meanwhile, her housing and living allowance here would run out in a few days. She thought her visa was good for a while but she'd better check. Except for a single credit card she'd sworn not to use, her only possession of value was her plane ticket home. It could possibly be turned in for cash, but that seemed like a bad idea. The problem was she didn't have a lot of good ideas to weigh it against.

******

Brenda sat at her desk with her hands wrapped tight around her first cup of morning coffee. A voice muttered something and she looked up to see Peter standing in her doorway.

Of course. For the last nine years there had been one set of circumstances that brought Dr. Hulson to her office. His visit was as predictable as clockwork. Well, this time she could give him an answer that would make him happy.

"How's my new boy?" he asked with an almost childlike hopefulness in his still sharp grey-blue eyes. "This one is a boy, right?"

"Yes," Brenda nodded her head. She knew he had an old man's preference for the male worker, and nothing in the modern world was going to change that. "My best one is Zane Zeitman. Ivy League. No pedigree, Texas born. Sharp as a tack and tearing into our database. He's full of ideas. A keeper so far."

"Keep me posted." The old man nodded. "Let's make sure some nice perks come his way. I don't have forever to find what I'm looking for, you know."

"I know sir. I'll give you updates and let you know if I need anything."

"Good, good," the man said as he left.

Zane Zeitman, Brenda thought. *Are you going to be the undiscovered protégé the renowned doctor has been searching for all these years?*

She gave it more thought.

Do you want to be?

4. On Fire

Joy spent her next few days trying to find the way home that would take the longest and cost the least. Her best option was to find work on a boat, so she scoured the internet for opportunities for a young woman seeking limited adventure, slow transport, and a little pocket money. Her computer chirped to let her know she had an email. Thank goodness. Maybe she'd gotten a response.

No, it was only her mother, writing from Boston. Her dad had left the previous evening for Fiji, would arrive today before nightfall and had a car waiting to take him to her apartment in Savusavu. Judge Cabrini had declared he wouldn't let his only child throw her life away in ill-advised acts of rebellion. Even if she was twenty-nine years old, she was coming home with him and that was that.

"You know how your father is when he's mad," her mother wrote. "I thought about not contacting you after you hung up on me like that, but you're my daughter and I forgive you. Besides, I thought your dad might be less angry if you were packed and ready to go." Joy felt like crying. "It's going to be okay, honey," her mother's email continued. "He's trying to look out for you. Please don't make a scene."

Dammit, how old do I have to be? The sad thing was she knew her father did love her, even if mixed up with his love was a sense of ownership. To Judge Cabrini, what she did reflected on him and his precious reputation. No other point of view occurred to him.

She fired back an email to her mom.

"Tell Dad not to bother. I won't be in Fiji by the time he arrives. He should have contacted me. I've found work aboard a ship leaving in an hour and am looking forward to the adventure. I don't expect to be home for a few months."

Then she added "I love you both."

She stuffed the last of her most essential possessions into her large backpack and accepted she'd have to leave the rest. Now, she had to go find a boat to work on. It was no time to be choosy about her future employer.

******

As June turned into July, Brenda noticed Zane was happier, better dressed and, she could have sworn, better looking. He sipped citrus water while he discussed his thought processes with her, and Brenda admitted she enjoyed her new assistant. He had a dry wit that was a welcome break from the intensity of the rest of the staff. Yet his insights into the sales database showed a surprising lack of naiveté. He understood exactly what the sales reps needed to know.

"I'm trying to do more than track what's been done," he said. "I want to design something to help us apply the right sales person, the most effective technique, and even the most influential incentives for each individual doctor."

"That's excellent," Brenda said.

"So, I have prescription data from all the pharmacies around Chicago. It amazes me people sell that information, but they do. I've got the DEA's secret coded numbers for every mental-health-related prescription and I have the decoder ring which the AMA sold us so I can match the doctors' names with the prescriptions they've written."

Zane paused. "Don't you think it's weird a group like the American Medical Association sells us doctors' DEA numbers so we can piece this together?"

Brenda laughed. "It's all about money. The AMA makes millions selling that information."

"Yeah. Okay. Well, I'm going to start by discovering which of our more loyal doctors have started prescribing lots of other company's drugs. That way our sales staff can be alerted to changing loyalties, or to a concern a particular doctor is having, and they can address those issues."

"Perfect. This is exactly the sort of results I hoped for."

Brenda knew Neil would be by her office to visit as soon as he was back from vacation. He always made it his business to know about the latest bright young thing his own boss was hanging his hopes on.

Over the years, Brenda and Neil had achieved an understanding. She knew she'd never come to run the company. When it came to women in charge, Peter Sr. was what he was. Rather than alienate herself by fighting it, she enjoyed the salary and the sense of importance within her own department, and left it at that.

Neil, in his own way, suffered from the same sort of problem. As Peter's COO, he ran much of the company these days. In the not-too-distant future, he'd likely run Penthes completely, at which point he'd have achieved everything he wanted in life except for the one thing he wanted most.

Brenda understood how much Neil wanted Peter to *want* to turn the company over to him. Not to do it because he had no better alternative or because the board of directors insisted. Yet, Peter never stopped reminding Neil how he was settling for him. Peter thought Neil was a guy who could run the business for a generation without killing it, but who could never take it to the next level of greatness.

For ten years now, the old man had waited for each crop of new hires, searching for a spark of genius. He wanted to find the protégé who could be trained while second-class Neil kept the company alive. Neil and Brenda both knew Peter hoped to still be alive when this rising spark took over the company.

Each year, when Peter checked in with Brenda, and with Raju, his head of research, they reported one or two names with high potential. Occasionally, Neil reported one as well. Every year Peter Hulson kept a close watch on those young people who had been recommended to him.

Every year for the last ten years, Neil also dropped by to visit Brenda to learn about the new hires being rotated through her department. Every year Brenda, in a spirit of cooperation, passed along the names of her best candidates. Neil was a good friend to have. Someday soon, he'd be a great friend to have.

Every year, her best candidate met with some change of fortune. One had personal problems which forced him to leave. Two got great offers elsewhere and quit. One became too ill to work and another flubbed up so badly they had to let him go. The others all made enough small mistakes to remove them from the list of those with high potential.

Funny. The guys from the lab and even the one or two candidates from finance ran into a similar list of problems. Year after year, not one new hire lived up to Peter's expectations. Were Peter's hopes too high? Neil would remind Peter they were all just kids, and kids today were less motivated, and less likely to have the qualities Peter sought. All those electronic toys, what did he expect? The kind of young man he was looking for probably didn't exist.

During these conversations, Peter would look sad. Sometimes he would nod in agreement. Then he would put his hopes aside until the next year.

"So what's this one like?" he asked Brenda as he sat on the edge of her desk like he was an old friend there to discuss lunch plans.

Brenda was annoyed. She enjoyed Zane, and she'd decided Neil was somehow facilitating the demise of her best candidates. She knew that sounded paranoid, and she wasn't sure how Neil could manage such a thing, but she had a bad feeling about it. She figured once every nine years she was entitled to a lie.

"Don't have one." She shook her head, tossing her curls for effect. "Got a beauty queen who doesn't have it upstairs, a computer nerd who's got no business sense, and a guy doing PowerPoints who's scared of his own shadow. A pretty disappointing group this year. I think HR needs some talking to."

"Well, that's too bad," Neil said in a way that sounded like it wasn't bad at all. "Not much this time around in my group either. Guess I'll check in with Raju."

******

The week-long trip from Apia to Fiji was an easy sail because Afi was as good a crew member as he claimed. He did cook well, he was competent at manning the sails, he cleaned and scrubbed the boat without being asked, and, as requested, he kept conversation to a minimum. Toby left Afi on watch many of the nights while he slept, and a full night's sleep at sea was a pleasant change.

When Afi wasn't sailing, he napped, found work to do, or sometimes just stared out at the ocean, often with a look of sorrow that wasn't hard to understand. Twice he took Toby up on his offer to watch DVDs.

As Miss Demeanor made her way towards Fiji's main two islands, Toby realized he was acclimating to having him on board. Perhaps he *would* let the boy stay a few months. In that case, he should learn more about him.

It didn't take much prodding to hear about Afi's chief hobby, participating in contests and performances of the Samoan fire knife dance. Afi had practiced every day before being whisked off to teen prison, and on occasion had performed for profit as well as fun. His unusual flexibility enabled him to perfect a few unique moves other dancers couldn't even attempt.

Years ago, Toby installed a high-end marine sound system on his boat, and it was one indulgence he never regretted. He prided himself on his immense collection of music. On this journey he'd played mostly classic rock, which Afi seemed to enjoy. Once he learned of Afi's love of fire dancing, though, he decided to find fire songs. He selected a few oldies from the fifties and sixties. Afi smiled in recognition at most of them, but when the speakers began to blare the Doors hit "Light My Fire" Afi grinned and started to sing along. Pretty soon both men were belting out the chorus. "Fie... errr..." drifted out over the waves of Savusavu Bay along with their laughter.

"What do you think?" Toby asked.

"I think you have a great sound system." Afi was honest. Toby waited.

"I think you found fire songs for me, which was nice." Toby waited more.

"I think your music could use a little updating?"

Toby laughed. He had been expecting that remark for days.

"We'll download more in Fiji and you get to pick the songs. Music is one supply I continue to stock up on, even if I don't need anything else."

The silence stretched on for a bit. "Afi, I think I should know what a fine young man like you did to get your parents to send you off to kid prison. It's hard to believe modern ideas would unsettle them so."

Afi looked down and fidgeted. His frustration was clear in his posture.

"That depends on what modern ideas you're talking about."

"Okay," Toby said. "Try me."

"The penalty for expressing gay sexuality in Kiribati is five to fourteen years." He paused. Toby looked uncomfortable but said nothing.

"The sad thing is I think my parents accepted who I was. They knew it, and they loved me. But part of the unspoken agreement was I remain secretive, with them and everyone else. Then I saw on the internet how things are changing and people like me don't have to be silent and afraid. Please understand. It's not that I wanted to make anyone uncomfortable. But a person gets tired of pretending."

"That makes sense."

"I told my parents this, because I thought they'd be happy for my new found courage. Not so. Our church has a particular problem with this issue, and my father is a deacon. I could see how troubled this made him. Then one day, not long after, I woke up in Samoa where I was told they were going help beat this demon out of me."

Toby tried to choose his words carefully. "Afi, you should know I left the U.S. before most of the changes you read about took place. I'm a little behind the times in my thinking." Toby looked nervously at the approaching harbor. "Is homosexuality illegal in Fiji too?"

"It is. I don't think the rest of the world understands most Pacific island nations have old-fashioned Christian beliefs. Until recently, most of our contact with the modern world was through missionaries and churches. Being openly gay is illegal everywhere that's not part of the U.S., Australia or New Zealand. The laws are only enforced if you draw attention to yourself, but secrecy is the requirement."

Toby shook his head. He hadn't seen this one coming. "Now we're two guys on a boat." Toby laughed at his own discomfort. "Okay Afi. One more question. That older kid who got in trouble at your school trying to help the younger one with the rash. What happened to him?"

Afi looked embarrassed. "He escaped and he's on your boat."

"Yeah, that's what I figured." Toby busied himself for a moment with the instrument panel while he gathered his thoughts.

"Look, you're going to have to put up with my awkwardness. I know damn well it doesn't matter that you're gay, and what you tried to do for that other kid was admirable. So, you're not going back. I'll hide you and I'll deal with my personal issues on the subject. Hell, it's probably time I did anyway. Furthermore, we'll find a way to get your friends out of there, too, although I haven't a clue how."

Without saying anything further, Toby turned his attention to the boat's engine. He ignored Afi's appreciative smile as he steered into the quarantine anchorage and paid the health inspector.

When he made his way over to the wharf, an immigration officer gave him paperwork so they could legally cruise the islands of Fiji. Toby persuaded the official to accept a bond instead of a passport for Afi, but his crew member's lack of identification was going to pose problems elsewhere.

It amused Toby that Americans thought of the Pacific as a wild frontier dotted with lush islands one could sail to. The ocean of the twenty-first century was divided into countries just like the land. One didn't cruise to an island any more than one wandered into Austria or Uruguay. One reported to customs and immigration, surrendered contraband and firearms, and secured permission to visit. Then, and only then, did one cruise around.

With permission to enter secured and the sailboat safely moored in a temporary loading area, Toby set off on a visit to the farmers' market while Afi stayed aboard to watch the boat. As he made his way, the noticed a young woman with a long, thick black ponytail and huge backpack leaving the market and rushing towards him. Her clothes and gear spoke of the States and of money, sensible yet fashionable. She was out of breath and kept looking back over her shoulder like she was expecting someone she didn't want to see.

"Please. Can I board your boat?" She was pointing to Miss Demeanor and as she got closer to him he saw she was a tall young woman, more handsome than pretty, with olive skin and dark brown eyes filled with a pleading, desperate look. "Like maybe now?" she asked. "I need passage off of this island really bad. I'm not in trouble with the law. I promise."

Another runaway? Had somebody put a sign on his back advertising his boat as an escape vehicle? Toby almost laughed at the image.

"I'll work hard. I cook. I sail. I clean. And you can drop me anywhere you are going next. Please?"

You don't grab strangers off of a pier as crew members, lady. What the hell is the matter with you? Toby reconsidered before he said his thoughts aloud. *What's the matter with me?* Another crew member could be what he needed while he became more comfortable with Afi.

"It's your lucky day, lady," he said. "Get yourself on that boat there. Tell the young man on board I said you could wait for me in the cabin. Talk to him. He should be sympathetic to your situation. I'll buy some supplies and be right back."

******

As July neared its end, Penthes invited Zane to attend a Cubs game, in one of the corporate boxes located behind home plate. He didn't like watching baseball any more than he'd liked playing it as a child, but he recognized the smart thing was to say thank you and show up. It sure beat his old schedule of working nights in the lab. Plus, it was being billed as a reward for high achieving new employees, and that struck Zane as a good group with which to be associated.

He arrived looking as well dressed as he could manage, and even with concentration he couldn't seem to stop his eyes from turning just the right shade of green to match his shirt. So he went with it.

It turned out Brenda was attending not only with him as her protégé, but also with a gorgeous young woman named Raven who had long tendrils of blonde hair, noticeably huge breasts, and a biology degree. She had been hired as a sales representative. Word was Raven had yet to be turned down for lunch by any male doctor when she requested the meeting in person.

Marketing was also represented by a nice but quiet guy doing something with PowerPoints, and a mid-level balding manager with thick glasses. The manager's name was Gil and he was planning the next big sales event, a symposium on treating mental illness in younger teenagers to be sponsored by Penthes and held at a resort location. Penthes had chosen to sponsor it late next winter when every snow-weary man, woman, and child would be dying to get out of Chicago.

"Is the Caribbean too ordinary?" Zane asked, trying to make polite conversation.

"It's been done a lot," Gill said. "It's more dependable than the Mediterranean for good weather, and easier to get to of course, but also easier to turn down. Brenda here thinks I should go totally exotic. Something in the South Pacific."

"Tahiti?" Jeez, now there was a destination for a conference.

"Could work, but some of our doctors have been there. It's better to find somewhere new, so they can't resist. I was thinking of Thailand, personally, but our boss Brenda says I need to look into Fiji." He winked at Zane. "I have a feeling I'm going to find Fiji is a great idea."

"Fiji should qualify as unique."

"Well, I'm glad to hear you like the idea," Gil said, and he lowered his voice to a conspiratorial whisper, "because the word I've gotten from Dr. P himself is he wants to make sure you are at this conference, helping out with logistics or something."

"Me?" Zane's voice rose half an octave. "Going to Fiji?" The research department all turned their heads in Zane's direction.

"Shhh." Gil chuckled, then added in his fake whisper, "This is entirely on the DL. If asked, I will deny having told you."

Zane noticed out of the corner of his eye that the Cubs had just hit a home run with the bases loaded. How his dad would love to be here. About half the Penthes group looked up in mild interest at the grand slam. The other half didn't even bother. They were too busy letting their bosses know how intelligent they were. In the corporate world, the savvy knew better than to waste good face time by actually watching baseball.

Before the evening wore down, Zane tried to engage Josh, the PowerPoint guy, in conversation. Josh appeared grateful for the effort, but it was like pulling teeth to get him to talk. After a bit Zane turned his attention to Raven, the beauty who had politely brushed off every male in attendance.

"I can't help but notice you're pretty good at making guys go away and feel good about it," Zane remarked and Raven smiled.

"The training comes with having equipment like this," she said looking down at her chest. "Unfortunately, I had to start learning at twelve years old."

"Well, it's good to meet another new hire. Can I assume taking doctors out to lunch is not your ultimate career ambition?" Zane asked it in a friendly fashion. "And, if not, I'm curious what your plan is."

Raven seemed glad to be asked. "They keep saying I have a degree in biology, but that's not true."

Zane raised an eyebrow. Did bra size substitute for a degree if one was in sales?

"What I have is a degree in botany, but that doesn't make me sound as qualified."

"Plants?" Zane asked puzzled.

"Yes. That would be botany."

"So how did you end up here? Interest in herbal medicine?"

He meant the question sincerely but Raven laughed, and Zane could see her small, fine white teeth, and then he noticed how much else about her was almost porcelain delicate. Once you got past looking at the huge chest.

"I ended up here because this was the only place I could find that was hiring. Except for Hooters. Or worse. No offense to the girls who work there, I've had friends who did. It's just not my style."

"Aside from the fact that you'd be an obvious hit, I can't say I blame you. But what's the plan for here?"

"That depends on whether you ask me or ask my mom."

"Okay." Zane laughed. "Let's ask your mom."

"Well," and Raven scrunched her face in what Zane could only guess was meant to be an impersonation of the girl's mother. "Beauty is not going to last forever, you know. I can't think of a better job than one in which a beautiful young woman meets doctor after doctor. Some of them have to be unmarried. Maybe the right one has to decide to become unmarried, if you know what I mean." Mom gave an ugly little chuckle.

"Hell," Zane muttered in sympathy. "Home wrecker. Now there's a career path for you."

"Exactly. And me? I'm trying to save some money to go back to school. My mom's a teacher and my dad disappeared long ago, so I've got forty-thousand dollars in loans to pay off before I take out more. Then I'll go back and study which non-genetically engineered plants are the most hardy. I'm really interested in tomatoes. They're kind of a passion of mine."

"Feed the world without messing with nature. It sounds great Raven. I hope you can do it."

Zane left the ballpark that night feeling good about himself. He'd made an effort to fit in, talked to some people he enjoyed, and felt he was being recognized for what he could do. It was like getting an "A" again. He was back to being Brainy Zany. Dammit, he missed that guy.

Hell, if Gil was reliable, he might even be going to Fiji. What a difference two months could make.

******

The woman's name was Joy. Toby liked the name. He'd guessed she was fleeing a nasty and possibly abusive boyfriend, but once he got back aboard he learned she was yet another run away from a controlling father. She and Afi seemed to have already bonded by comparing stories.

"I'm starting to feel like I run a theme boat here." He smiled at Afi. Then to Joy, "Where do you think your dad is right now?"

"He's probably been in town for the last hour trying to find me. Talking to neighbors, school officials, law enforcement. He's good at throwing his weight around. Offices are closing now, so he'll be getting lodging for the night, and tomorrow he'll be here in the harbor finding out what boat I left on."

"Then I guess you better leave on one. How about a sunset cruise, folks? I think I can find a beach we can moor off of for the night, and we will take it from there."

Any beach in Fiji is somebody's back yard. You don't just drop anchor and camp. Toby headed around to the southwest side of the island, looking for a place he'd been often so that formalities could be kept to a minimum. He dropped anchor and waded ashore, asking one of the inevitable inquisitive children watching them from the safety of the tree cover to please take him to the village chief so he could present the customary offering of kava root.

"He says to tell you there is no need to bother, Toby. He's too tired tonight, and still considers you an honorary member of the village from last time you were here," the child said.

"Tell him I thank him for his courtesy, Lela, and I will visit him in the morning." Sometimes it was good to know people.

Toby and his crew set about making a camp and a fire in the dusk. Joy was happy to cook. Afi unloaded the new provisions and hammocks to give them a night off of the boat.

"What's this?" he asked Toby, lifting a large bulky paper sack out of the dinghy.

"Tonight's entertainment," Toby replied. Afi's eyes widened as a single, almost forty-inch fire knife fell out onto the sand, its regulation fourteen-and-a-half-inch blade glistening. There was a fire wick and a small can of outboard motor fuel.

"It was sitting there when I walked into the farmers' market. The man was happy to sell it to me, and I figured you could use it to start getting back in practice."

Afi shook his head in disbelief and Toby thought he saw a hint of tears in Afi's eyes. "After dinner I want you to show me and our new crew member what you can do with this," Toby said.

So after food was finished, the knife and wick were prepared, and as the last glimmer of light vanished off to the west, Afi did a careful hand spin with the burning baton. Then he tried a slow figure eight. Then a cautious toss and catch, followed by a slightly more confident toss and catch behind his back, then a bolder under-the-leg throw. He was grinning now, and the muscle memory was coming back. Joy and Toby watched in wonder as Afi's hesitant movements transformed, until he was confidently moving the glowing stick to the beat of drums only he could hear in his head.

He began to stomp his feet as he moved, adding head movements in the Kiribati style. Toby and Joy gained a sense of the rhythm and Joy began clapping with the motion, adding a little percussion. Afi grinned in appreciation and she clapped more forcefully. As his movements sped up, her clapping sped with them, and soon the two of them were working together to create the performance.

Joy clapped. Afi spun the fire knife. Toby watched in fascination. By the end of the dance, Afi had become a whirling, glowing swirl of orange flame, powered by Joy's jubilant participation and by his own sheer joy in doing something he loved.

August 2009

5. Improvising

"Hey Mom. What's up?" It was late for his mom to be calling, so Zane hoped nothing was wrong back in Texas. Her question was not what he expected.

"What do you know about prescribing atypical antipsychotics to enhance the effect of common antidepressants?"

Well, this phone call was *about something.*

Last June when he was home, his mom confided she was having some issues after an accident, and a psychologist had recommended an antidepressant to help her through the experience. Zane had been happy to counsel his mom on the medicine's safety and encourage her to do what she needed to move on from the trauma. However, a short-term low dose of a common antidepressant was one thing and the kind of medication his mom was asking about now was another.

"I think it's pretty drastic," he said. "Surely they're not recommending that for you?"

"Actually yes. My psychologist thinks I'll get an uplift from it but I'm not sure I need to be uplifted."

"Well, you're trying to take care of yourself, and he is too. Let me poke around and see what I can learn. Stall, okay?" Zane tried to sound non-committal, but this sort of overprescribing was cause for worry.

"'I will. Get back to me when you can. I won't take anything new until I hear from you. Thanks."

Zane thought it might be a good thing to start asking more questions at work anyway. Ever since he had become Brenda's golden boy of the sales database, he'd sipped a lot of citrus water and assumed everything he did was for the greater good. Maybe that assumption needed verifying.

******

Toby's problems were multiplying. He already had an I-Kiribati crew member with no money, no personal items, and no paperwork to travel. This crew member was being chased by the staff of an unsavory school. Now, he'd added another. She'd thankfully boarded with a valid passport and a well-stuffed backpack, but she was almost as broke and was being hunted down by a controlling father described as someone who could and would make trouble.

Toby had limited funds of his own. He had a huge desire not to draw attention to himself, a personality unsuited to sharing space with others, and a thirty-three foot boat. This was not a situation that was going to work well for long.

After years at sea, Toby approached life's problems like the sailor he was, so he set about trying to chart the best path for him and his crew. The first leg appeared to involve tacking into the wind, figuratively speaking, by spending days wandering around Fiji's more remote islands waiting for Judge Cabrini to move on. Joy would have to tell him how many days that would be.

Then, he'd return to Savusavu where he already had the correct entry paperwork. He'd take on more supplies, and get Afi a comb and toothbrush, and collection of his own swim trunks and t-shirts.

The next step would be to sail a thousand miles northward to the Kiribati capital of Tarawa, where he could look up an old friend and see what could be done for Afi, paperwork-wise. Toby would radio ahead with a couple of creative ideas.

He was mulling things over as Joy waded out to the boat with a heavy armload of gear. She'd taken to wearing swim tops and running shorts, and it was hard not to notice her lean body. It wasn't diet-a-lot skinny and it wasn't work-out-a lot muscular. It was the strong body of someone who used their muscles to do stuff, and over the last few days Toby was finding himself noticing her body more. Come to think of it, that was another thing needing a remedy.

Their little group had enough issues without anyone lusting after anyone. He promised to treat himself to some serious adult shore leave once he got these two kids safely on their way.

******

"I'm just saying that woman seems to like him, which is one strike against him," the girl next to Raven was saying. "He looks so geeky in his badge photo, which means he's somebody my grandfather will love, too. So no, he's not my idea of a potential friend. But thanks for the invite."

Zane had particularly good hearing, and he heard every word of the conversation as he approached the back of his new friend Raven in the coffee bar. She was listening to a tall young woman with light-brown hair cut short and spiked in the way only a good salon could. Her hair and the almost boy-like skinniness of her back was a sharp contrast with Raven's curves and long feminine tendrils. The two girls stood close, looking out of the floor-to-ceiling window of the coffee bar on Penthes' marketing floor, and they spoke like old friends.

"Hi Raven." Zane felt he should say something to let them know he was standing behind them. Then to the other girl: "Didn't mean to interrupt."

"No problem." The tall young woman smiled in a friendly way. "I'm Chloe, another new hire, although, as you'll find out soon, I've been around here for years. So welcome." Then she added to Raven: "There are so many new people this year I can't keep track anymore."

Raven seemed to feel the need to offer Zane an explanation. "Chloe and I lived in the same dorm freshman year, across the hall from each other. We both had horrible roommates and talked each other out of contemplating murder more than once."

Zane nodded with sympathy. "I had a similar thing my freshman year."

"Dorm life is an experience to survive, isn't it?" Chloe laughed. "Listen, I need to go, but the three of us should go out for a drink one day after work, okay?"

"How about tonight?" Raven said.

Chloe looked puzzled. "Thought you had plans? To go out with this Zane guy."

Zane looked puzzled. "She does. I'm Zane."

Raven looked puzzled. "I thought you knew this was Zane."

Chloe looked puzzled. She squinted at Zane. "You don't look anything like the photo on your badge. No way you're Zane."

"Life in the lab was bleak," he said. "I'm taking better care of myself these days."

Chloe shook her head in disbelief. "I guess. Okay, Zane guy. Drinks for the three of us it is."

Zane was surprised by Brenda's reaction to the question "Who's Chloe?"

She bristled instantly. "You mean her highness?"

"She's a friend of Raven's." Zane tried a tactful response.

"Yes, I know she is. I try not to hold that against Raven. I think we'd have hired Raven anyway, given her rather remarkable credentials." Brenda rolled her eyes. "This business is what it is. But why do you want to know about Ms. Hulson?"

"Oh." *Well that explained a lot.* "She's related to Peter Hulson?"

"Yes. She's his granddaughter. Fresh out of school with a journalism degree and she's been hired as our new communications manager. Go figure. The rationale is she's been interning here every summer, but honestly this kind of thing would only happen here if your last name was Hulson."

Zane could understand the resentment. "She seems nice enough."

"She's been taught manners."

Drinks after work were at the trendy, overpriced place located half a block from the office and frequented by Penthes employees. Chloe seemed to have forgiven Zane for his association with Brenda. Raven and Chloe talked while Zane listened, but after a while he felt he should make some effort to join in.

"So does your dad work at Penthes too?" He was met with surprised and disapproving silence. So this wasn't a good question?

"Zane." Raven was shaking her head and making how-could-you eyes at him.

"Somebody needs to learn to do more googling before they take a job," Chloe said.

"I'm sorry." Zane was a little annoyed. "I looked up stuff. I guess not enough. Your father is…"

"Dead," Chloe said. "Look, it was ten years ago. I was thirteen and we weren't close. He died doing something stupid and my mom has never forgiven him for it. Neither has my grandfather, which is what makes dad's death one of the most taboo topics around the office."

She gave Raven an it's-okay look before she continued. "Honestly. No one ever brings it up around here. Grandfather was certain dad would someday take over this company. My dear Aunt Paula wasn't up to it, as spending money, not making, it is her talent. So poor grandpa has been searching for a substitute heir-apparent ever since. Everyone falls short, by the way, myself included, in spite of the nice job he's given me. So he keeps on looking."

"I'm sorry Chloe. I didn't know, and didn't even know I needed to know."

"I said don't worry about it. You should know," her tone was softening "because solving grandfather's issue is pretty much what this place is about. My grandfather's old patents, which made all this money twenty to thirty years ago, are running out. Raju, our head of R&D, basically combines, renames, and remarkets our old drugs for new ailments, gaining us the occasional new patent to reset the clock."

Chloe paused for a sip of coffee and hesitated a second before she shrugged and continued. "For fifteen years now, we've yet to come up with the next big thing. So along with Raju's skills, we have to keep relying on Neil's clever marketing tricks to increase sales. After all, it's those quarterly profits that keep the shareholders happy. Meanwhile, what keeps my grandfather happy is his never-ending search for a rising star he can use to replace my dad. It's pretty sad. Even sadder is the cutthroat culture he's managed to create trying to ferret out this wunderkind."

"Thanks, Chloe." Zane appreciated the girl's honestly. "I'll try to keep my head down and stay out of trouble."

"That could be difficult." Chloe laughed without humor. She really wanted to dislike this guy but he was so damn not full of himself. "My whole point here is your boss Brenda has pointed you out to my grandfather as the smartest thing to walk in the door in a while."

"Me?" Zane's voice rose in discomfort and disbelief.

"Yeah, well, don't be so flattered. It's a pretty low bar to cross. We have a lousy reputation for how we treat our new hires, so it's not the best and brightest waltzing across our threshold. Someone shows up here with an actual ability to think for themselves and they end up on grandfather's short list."

Raven started to object, but Chloe cut her off. "Let's not play games with him, Raven." Then to Zane. "Once people are on this list, Zane? They have a short corporate life expectancy here. The variety of misfortunes that befall them are amazing. Some are serious. So watch yourself."

Great. Just when things are going well, I find out it's bad at this place if things are going well.

******

The South Pacific is known for its friendly people. However, they have rules. They need to discourage the arrival of pests, diseases, waste materials, and people with no means of support. They have the added challenge of needing to be highly self-sufficient thanks to their extreme isolation.

Over the years, Toby had learned which ports and officials were overly strict and which were easygoing. Either way, he tried to respect the system, remembering he was a guest. Their place, their rules.

Fortunately, among the almost 50,000 I-Kiribati living on the Tarawa Atoll, Toby had friends with influence. They knew him to be a respectful I-Matang who seldom asked for a favor and always returned in kind. Furthermore, the I-Kiribati tended to have a less rigid attitude towards official documents than the U.S.

As they were enjoying the luxury of fish grilled over a fire on the beach, he broached his plan with Afi. The young man was horrified at the idea of returning to Kiribati, but Toby persuaded him to reconsider.

"You must have paperwork to be able to stay on my boat, or for that matter to go anywhere else. I need a reason to be involved on your behalf. My story is going to be, well, I thought I'd tell my friend that I married you two at sea." Joy's face shot up from her careful picking out of the fish bones. "You what?" she asked.

"Relax. I'm not going to actually marry you, Joy. That's ridiculous. I'm just going to say I did and I want to file the appropriate paperwork in Kiribati, with the add-on that Afi, a bona fide citizen of Kiribati, wants the marriage to be in the new name he has chosen to use, and he wishes to secure a passport in that name as well. He has picked a name meaning fire dance in the tongue of those who have taught him and this is how he wishes to be known point forward.

"I think my friend will work with me on this, and if we're lucky Afi will end up with a legitimate passport and be harder to trace. You can either ignore the whole thing or if it makes you nervous just annul it when you get back home. It's a small favor."

But Afi was even less happy with the plan than Joy was. "Toby, I have promised myself I will not live a lie. This would be the worst of untruths."

Toby understood that point, but he still thought the marriage idea was brilliant. Besides justifying the name change and rushed passport application, it would signal to the school that Afi need not be recaptured. If Joy was willing to take the charade further, it could open up Afi's options for relocation. Toby asked them to at least stay open to the idea if a better one wasn't found.

Joy looked over at Toby, who seemed happy to have thought of a way to help Afi. *This guy is kind, in spite of the fact that he likes to think otherwise. Clever, too. How often do you find that combination in a man?*

******

Neil was not happy with Brenda. "I thought we had an understanding."

"We do," she insisted. "After I talked to you, this kid's work took off. Peter happened to come by so I mentioned it. I was going to come find you, make sure you were in the loop and then I got busy on this stuff with Gil."

"Brenda. Don't bullshit a bullshitter. My working theory is you're developing latent maternal instincts here. Go sign up for a foster child, okay? This boy is not yours to protect. This boy is a threat. Peter has gotten increasingly goofy about not having an heir. He's capable of latching onto some random youngster and doing something irrational like turning half the company over to him. Part of my job as Penthes COO is to protect us from that. I can't do my job if the people working for me don't do theirs. Right? And your job is keeping me informed. So we won't ever have a conversation like this again, will we Brenda?"

Brenda shook her head.

"I didn't think so. Now, why don't you give me details on this conference I hear you and Gil are getting set up in, where? American Samoa? Tahiti? Fiji? It's all over the coffee bar."

"Samoa and Fiji. We couldn't firm plans up until we were positive Penthes would get the patent, so we're running late but I think we're okay. We'll fly the doctors into American Samoa, spend the night, then sail them over to Western Samoa in real yachts. The second night is in Apia, a charming town in Samoa. We'll go on a half-day visit to a local school for troubled kids while we're there.

"Later, we tie that visit into the idea of helping youngsters. You know, medication could've prevented the need for this. It'll provide a positive framework for our product and give us a justification for the exotic locale."

Brenda was happy to see Neil nodding in agreement. She continued.

"Now, here's the good part. I've found a small, older, cruise ship that only does charters. They're available and way more reasonable than you'd think. They take up to sixty guests, which is perfect, because this is going to have to be a wives-invited thing and we're targeting thirty of our most influential doctors. Get this. We'll cruise the whole group from Samoa over to Fiji across the International Date Line—everybody loves that idea—and we'll do a light seminar schedule aboard ship during the three days at sea. We dock in Fiji. For the last day of presentations, I've got a couple of reliable Aussie doctors who are great. So, seven nights in paradise, all expenses paid."

"And we get a core group of physicians fired up about preventing families from experiencing the heartbreak of a rebellious teen by using the new cocktail drug Raju designed and will have patented by February," Neil responded.

"What do you think?" She smiled sweetly.

"I think this is you using those brains I know you have," Neil replied. "Keep using them."

******

Toby, Afi, and Joy sat on uncomfortable folding chairs in a stuffy modular building waiting for Toby's friend to see them. Determined to live a life of honesty, Afi had nixed the idea of a fake marriage no matter what the possible benefits to him. Fortunately, Toby's friend Tiemti had agreed anyway to rush documents so Afi could travel freely under his chosen name. When Tiemti finally came out to greet Toby and usher them into his office he looked troubled.

"You have no problem with my name change?" Afi asked as he introduced himself.

"No, I don't," the man said. "You want to be called Afi Siva, dance fire? It's your choice and it's done." His words were blunt but in no way unkind.

"So what's your concern?" Toby asked his friend.

Tiemti surprised them all when he turned to Joy to answer. "I'm worried about you. Your father, a Judge Cabrini, has contacted every country in the Pacific offering a sizable reward for information on your whereabouts. He claims you've either been taken somewhere against your will or have lost the ability to make rational decisions. It appears to me you are lucid and here by choice. Is that true?"

"It is." Joy rubbed her left temple, trying to stave off the headache she felt coming on. "As you might guess, it's my father I'm avoiding."

She looked at the Kiribati official, certainly a father himself, and her eyes pleaded for understanding. "He has other plans for my life and confronting him directly over many years has not gotten my message delivered. So I'm trying another approach."

The man nodded his head in sympathy. Joy could see that across cultures, gender, and age differences, he understood.

"Sad, but this happens. He's offering a lot of money to have you detained in any port, while he makes arrangements for your return home. It's money I'm happy to forego, of course, as you're a friend of Toby's, but I fear not everyone you encounter will be so principled." He looked at the door. "Not even everyone here in Kiribati. It *is* a lot of money."

Tiemti turned to Toby. "This is a small island country and we know each other's business. I know why Afi's father sent him away. I think it was unnecessary and I've heard bad things about that school on Samoa, so I'm not going to make it my affair to send the boy back and neither will others. But this young lady's freedom is in danger, and in her case, the people here have no loyalty to her."

Joy had been afraid her dad would try something like this. What could make the locals want to aid her instead of her powerful father? The only buoy she could think to grab onto was, well, the boy sitting next to her.

"There is more you should know," she said. "We had another request to make of you, but held back because we'd already asked for so much." She swallowed hard before she went on, hoping Afi would forgive her.

"I want to marry this man. As soon as possible." She tried to catch Afi's eye as she searched for reasons to give the official. "We've become close. We have much in common. He is willing to look out for me, to see I am free and happy." She looked hard at Afi. "I, at the same time, wish to see him living a life that makes him happy, too."

Toby's mouth dropped open.

"That sounds like friendship, not marriage," Tiemti remarked.

Afi understood Joy's words were driven by her fear. He would never do this thing to make his own life easier, but he would do it for the safety of another. He gave Joy a small smile.

"I don't think I've asked you properly. Will you marry me?" Then, because he had to say it: "For the time being?"

Joy smiled her thanks at him. "I will, and you should know divorce proceedings can begin whenever either of us wishes."

"That is sweet of you, my dearest."

She looked at the I-Kiribati official. "Please. Marry us. Then send word around Tarawa and to my father and to every port that I am married to a man of these islands and enjoying a glorious honeymoon which only the most heartless would interrupt."

Tiemti nodded his head. He in no way liked the idea of making a mockery of marriage, but he understood the girl's desperate plan.

"Okay. Things like this aren't generally done here. Planning a marriage takes months, even years. But if you give me a day, I think I can assure your safety while the ceremony is arranged. As an added favor to Toby, I'll circulate your wedding photos around with my assurances of your desire to embrace our world as your own. After that, if you avoid trouble, I think you'll be left in peace. I'll also let your father know you requested photos be sent to the Honolulu paper."

"Thank you so much." Impressed by the man's shrewdness, Joy said it from the bottom of her heart.

"Oh, but I do have a favor to ask in return," the official added. "There is a woman, a friend of mine, and a relative of my wife's. She is from a far edge of Tarawa, but she can be here by tomorrow morning. She could be sad or happy. My favor is Afi choose happiness for her."

Afi looked puzzled. The official went on. "You don't know me, but I know your mother, Ruti. She's my wife's second cousin. I know the school hasn't told your parents that you are gone, which is disturbing in itself. I know your mother loves you, and was bothered by your father's solution. She'll be baffled by your marriage to this woman, but she'll assume the best, and if she attends she'll keep her own counsel as to your whereabouts, at least for a while. To see you, and to be at this little fake wedding, would bring her more joy than you could know. In exchange for my help, I ask you let Ruti attend."

Thus, Joy found herself preparing for her wedding day, smoothing out the one sundress she had stuffed into her backpack. Tomorrow she would exchange vows with a likeable boy nine years her junior, and meet her new I-Kiribati mother-in-law.

******

Neil hid from Brenda the cold fury her little deception caused. Better not to let the glorified bimbo know how frustrated he was with her. Damn, her finest quality had always been her blind cooperation based on the fact that he'd been the best friend of the lover she still pined for. What made a woman stay in love with the memory of a man ten years after he was gone? Ten years, and he was sure she'd barely dated since Pete died. How pathetic was that?

Neil knew Brenda would have been with Pete aboard the ship that night, if Pete had wanted her there. Pete was capable of dissuading his wife Sylvia from joining him, and capable of discretely inviting his mistress along instead.

He'd chosen not to, and that piece of information told Neil the love affair had been over as far as Pete was concerned. Neil guessed Brenda had ignored the telltale signs, making excuses for Pete's growing distance. Now, Neil bet the woman still believed Pete would have left Sylvia for her and would have married her, if he'd lived.

Neil prided himself on being a man who could seize an opportunity. You could plan all you wanted in life, he believed, then life would deal you cards you never expected. The trick to winning the game was being able to adapt to your cards.

Life had unexpectedly dealt Neil a college friend who could open doors. Wonderful doors. So he jettisoned plans and embraced the new possibilities. Almost twenty years later, life took that friend away. Neil couldn't have anticipated either event, but he was astute enough to see how his friend's death provided opportunities as well. For the last decade, Neil attempted to play those new cards as well as they could be played.

Now he was examining a new hand. Dr. Hulson was becoming more desperate to find a protégé to replace his son. Brenda was becoming increasingly untrustworthy. A kid named Zane Zeitman had strolled into the drama raising hopes all around.

How could that be useful? There were many possibilities for a man who was able to use all circumstances that came his way.

******

Most of Zane's knowledge about the pharmaceutical industry, came from the medical profession. He knew it was filled with those who wished to help people, but he was also smart enough to know it had a bias in favor of its own approaches. Like all institutions.

As Zane thought about Chloe's warning, he decided he wasn't comfortable with everything he'd seen going on. How did Penthes keep increasing its profits without any actual innovation? Why would anyone propose putting his relatively healthy mom on antipsychotic drugs to give her an uplift? It was time to do some research.

The internet put him in touch with a drastically different point of view. Ranging from disillusioned former medical practitioners to people who thought they had been abducted by aliens, critiques of modern approaches to mental health ran the gamut from the well-informed to the kooky. Yet, even the ragged edge had a few compelling points to make. The more Zane read the more disturbed he became.

He'd viewed the database he was creating as a benign sales tool, a way to help his team sell more widgets in a world where all widgets were the same. But all medications were not the same. Some were more addictive, or had worse side effects, or mixed poorly with other common drugs. Some were harder to stop taking, or more expensive. Yet he was designing a database to guide doctors to Penthes drugs based less on their patients' needs and more on Penthes marketing. In fact, he was helping guide professionals to choose medication when perhaps therapy, diet, or behavior changes would provide safer or cheaper relief.

The argument was all the other drug companies were already doing this, and poor little Penthes would be overlooked by busy doctors unless Penthes got out there and marketed their products. Okay. Zane understood. That's why they had a marketing department. But some things about this whole arrangement were beginning to feel wrong.

******

Later, Joy would remember little about her wedding to Afi. The decision happened so fast, and once she was outside in the fresh air she realized how the threat of her father's actions had scared her to her core. It was the first time she understood he would choose to ruin her life rather than relinquish control over it. Her body shook as she thought about it.

Afi would remember little as well. He'd accepted he'd never be able to return to Tarawa, to the land he cherished and felt almost flowed in his blood. He never expected to see his family again, and the sheer unfairness of that pained him more than he could fathom. But here he was, one day after their arrival in Tarawa, standing in a small park looking at an official understandably annoyed at the request to rush a wedding.

The one thing Joy would remember was the sight of Afi hugging his mother. A surprisingly tiny, Southeast Asian-looking woman sobbing with emotion, Ruti hugged Afi for over a full minute when she arrived. Neither spoke a word.

What a sad story. What a loving son. He's been so generous to help me. I must be as good to him as I can.

The one thing Afi would remember was the look of sorrow on Joy's face as his own mother clung to him, and how Joy had joined in the hug at the end, greeting the woman with respect and affection. Afi realized he wasn't the only one who had been unfairly exiled from his family. Joy might never experience such a reunion with her own mother.

How sad. This is a good woman with a good heart who has been forced into sad choices. I must be as good to her I can.

So, rather unexpectedly, it happened. Love, of sorts—in one of its more unpredictable flavors—was born that day in Kiribati while the ocean breeze strengthened and the sound of the waves crashing into the reef mixed with the sounds of the marriage vows.

September 2009

6. The Laws of Nature

Zane took another long weekend to visit Texas at the end of the summer. Saturday morning when he saw his mom sipping coffee on the porch, he joined her.

"Is work any better these days?" she asked.

Zane shrugged. "My company's supposed to be providing relief to the sick people of the world. Do you know what the problem is with sick people?"

"They're sick?"

"No." Zane had to smile. "There aren't enough of them." He took a long puff on his cigarette, which he could tell his mom tried to ignore. "Seriously. Not enough of them to grow profits and meet the expectations of Wall Street. You have to find more customers."

"Right," his mom said. "Only it's not like you're selling video games and need to convince more people to start playing them."

Did she realize he'd spent the entire day yesterday playing old video games instead of going through the stuff in his room? How did she know? "Exactly. You either find more sick people or convince more people they're sick."

"So we get commercials about how our acid reflux is more damaging than we think, or we're more depressed than we realize."

"You got it. Along with this advertising, which, by the way, is only legal in the U.S. and New Zealand, pharmaceutical companies push doctors to use newer, more expensive drugs, and to use them for things they haven't been approved for. It's called off-label use."

"That's what they're offering me. What's so bad about these atypical antipsychotics?"

"Well, they up your chance of hyperglycemia and diabetes, but the main thing is someone like you doesn't need something so drastic. My guess is your doctor is getting pressure from some sales rep to try this. Tell him you want to stick to the oldest, safest stuff. If you're firm, he'll listen."

"I'd do that," she said "except I decided I didn't need medication at all and stopped taking it last week."

"Mom." Zane knew it was a bad idea to do that on one's own. "This is serious stuff."

"I know. I gave it serious thought."

Luckily, she seemed fine. Actually, compared to last June, she seemed better.

"So what is it that's bothering you?" she asked in that gentle way that seemed to always get him talking in spite of himself.

Okay. It was time to talk about how he should have put more thought into where he was going in life.

"I'm not stupid." It fell out of his mouth. "I mean, I know how hard you and Dad worked to make this college thing happen. A private university wasn't in your plan, but you found a way. And now… I don't like the field I'm in. I don't think I can find anything in it I want to do. I never was excited about getting a PhD even though you guys and every teacher I ever had thought I should. But just because a person learns easily doesn't mean that's all they want to do, you know? But if I change fields now, I pretty much piss away everything."

His mom didn't even open her mouth for a few long seconds, which was pretty unusual for her. Finally, she found what she wanted to say.

"You're not a screw up. You're a twenty-three-year-old trying to figure out what he wants to do. That's normal. We're happy you even want to find a path in life."

Yeah right. Like she'd ever say anything else.

"No, I'm serious. And, there are solutions. You don't want to wash test tubes for the rest of your life? Understandable. Just because you have the brains for years of scholarly research doesn't mean you have the interest."

At least she got that part.

"You've encountered things that are making you question the business side of the pharmaceutical industry. That doesn't mean there aren't decent people and worthwhile careers there."

He started to object but she cut him off.

"Look. If you just plain don't want any of that, fine. There are connected industries, and related degrees that wouldn't be hard to get. Or, go be a history major. There are cheaper schools, and loans, and what you've learned goes with you no matter what you do. A degree might be wasted, but education isn't."

"I suppose."

"Come on. Your dad and I didn't make sacrifices so you'd be trapped in a life you hated. We happen to love you. What the hell kind of love would that be?"

She paused. Zane knew plenty of kids in far shittier situations with their folks, and he felt lucky to not be one of them.

"Thanks, Mom." It was little more than a whisper, but he meant it.

She gave him the hug he knew was coming. He hugged back, giving her what he hoped was a big, appreciative smile in return.

******

Toby had taken on crew before to help with the upkeep of his boat and provide temporary company, but he didn't think he'd ever found better than the two strangers who were aboard now. Afi was a capable seaman with a wonderful disposition. The more Toby saw of Joy, the more impressed he was with her as well. She was neither as good a cook nor as good a sailor as Afi, but she was sensible and helpful. She was even cheerful in a quiet way, particularly considering her situation.

Under other circumstances…

But this wasn't other circumstances. The current situation included the reasons why Joy and Afi were the worst of crewmembers. Joy had a thousand New Zealand dollars from cashing in her plane ticket. She had nowhere she wanted to go, and no way to get there. Afi's mother had slipped him some personal items and a hundred Australian dollars, probably a fortune to her.

Afi had only places he wanted to avoid and the clothes Toby had bought him.

Sooner or later, Toby needed them to move on. It looked like it was time to head to one of the ports where he'd be allowed to do charter work, and to let his crew earn some money.

American Samoa would work well. Once they were finished, they could make the long sail up to Hawaii, where Joy could get Afi entrance into the U.S. The newlyweds could find work, make a life that suited them, and eventually go their separate ways, each seeking their own happiness.

Toby watched Afi showing Joy some of the finer points of sailing, while she laughed and tried to imitate the technique he was demonstrating. Under her hand the boat turned too far and picked up more speed than it should have. She stopped her laughing and got the boat under control, without panic. Afi stood still and let her do so. Well done by both, Toby thought. When they reached Hawaii, they would cease to be his problem.

******

Joy had learned to sail as a child, the same way she'd learned to play tennis, ride horses, and play piano. It was expected of her. She hadn't particularly enjoyed the sailing; others knew how to handle the boat so much better, why should she endanger them as she fumbled about trying to remember which ropes did what. Her mother also declined to take the helm, except when absolutely required to do so by her dad. Joy wondered if her mother felt the same way.

It surprised her to discover how sailing Miss Demeanor was fun, with Afi and Toby encouraging her and not wincing at every mistake. Her confidence grew with their trust.

Her affection for Afi grew as well. Over the first few days of their marriage, the two of them became comfortable with friendly physical contact. Being able to lean against Afi, or rest her head in his lap, made the small boat seem larger and made her feel less lonely. Go figure. He made a surprisingly good husband, in all areas except for the obvious one. In that regard, there was a mutually accepted lack of interest. So she sometimes found herself noticing the muscles under Toby's shirt, or the strength in his capable hands as he performed tasks on the boat.

Get a grip. This is no time to get fixated on the only interested male within arm's reach.

Joy was sure the friendly dynamics of any functioning trio, including theirs, would not be improved by having two of the people rolling around together on a beach. Besides, Toby had to be at least in his mid-forties, and she wasn't attracted to older men. Then, as she watched his body as he pulled the boat into shore for the night, she acknowledged it didn't look old. It looked good.

******

When Zane returned from Texas, he had an email asking him to contact Dr. Peter Hulson's personal assistant to set up an appointment. Shit. This sounded exactly like the situation Chloe and Raven warned him about. On the other hand, he didn't have a lot of options. An employee is never too busy to meet the CEO. Never.

So he found himself taking the elevator up the remaining three floors to an opulent foyer that made sales and marketing look like the mid-rent district. His department's nice carpeting was replaced by a beautiful dark cherry wood floor and several ornate oriental rugs. In place of the live plants were a collection of old Asian vases Zane suspected were worth a fortune. The foyer was bounded on one side by a wall of floor-to-ceiling windows revealing an expansive view of half of Chicago's downtown skyline and the highways that reached like tendrils out into the western suburbs.

The eastern view on the other side would include glimpses of Lake Michigan in-between the buildings. Zane understood that view was reserved for Dr. Hulson's private suite.

It was hard not to like Peter Hulson when one met him in person. In spite of his age, he had a liveliness about him, and his sharp, bright blue eyes were probing but not unfriendly. He shook Zane's hand, gestured him onto a soft green velvet-covered settee and offered Zane water or coffee. Zane passed, although he wasn't sure if it was ruder to accept or to decline. He allowed himself an appreciative peek at the surprisingly unobstructed view of Lake Michigan.

"I'll get right to the point, young man," Peter began, drawing his attention back. "It's well known I'm seeking bright new young people, and I like to mentor them myself. I get a fair amount of grief from my VPs about it being beneath my pay grade, but the fact is I want my company to thrive for a long time. The way I see it, that only happens if I can hand the reins over to at least two more generations of focused and brilliant successors."

A swirl of sorrow came and went from his face so fast Zane thought he might have imagined it. The older man kept talking.

"I'm finding these brilliant successors to be in short supply. But, you've landed on our doorstep with excellent grades from an exceptional school, and managed to get yourself in a position reporting directly to my director of sales and marketing. Word is she thinks you have excellent potential."

Zane tried to smile appreciatively.

"Excellent potential." Peter repeated the words for emphasis. "I don't think there are two finer words in the English language. So I'd like to personally do what I can to encourage you."

Zane tried to make the smile even more appreciative because he had no idea what to say.

"Would you consider a trip to Fiji to be encouragement?"

Okay, he could answer this one.

"Yes. I think most people would."

The older man chuckled. "Good, good. Brenda and Gil are in the process of putting together an important conference for us and I've told them to spare no expense. We believe we can save families huge amounts of grief by providing a treatment to guide young people into making more mature and acceptable choices. Mind you, the drugs aren't new, but the combination and the approach are. This conference in Fiji will introduce our new product in the most favorable light possible, so its success is important. I've okayed sending Brenda to Fiji late this month to do a recon and I want you to go with her. Help her with travel and logistics, but also keep your eyes open and your brain on. Help us find ways to make this symposium better. Have ideas for us, Zane. Think for us. Will you do that?"

Shape of Secrets

Of course Zane said yes. He said it sincerely and shook the man's hand and thanked him. Because Zane wasn't an idiot.

But on the ride back down on the elevator, Zane kept seeing his fourteen-year-old sister Teddie's face. She had anger. She had issues. More than he'd had at that age, for sure. But she also had a huge heart and a creative streak a mile wide and Zane really wondered if both Teddie and the world would be better off if some doctor was convinced to medicate her now.

******

Neil knew Peter would like Zane. Brenda already felt protective towards the boy, which was unfortunate. Worse yet, Zane had become friends with a college chum of Chloe's, the new girl in marketing with the big tits. As a result, Zane had Chloe as well as Brenda in his court, adding a new layer of difficulty to his removal.

Of course, it couldn't all be as easy as it was with Raju's group. Neil needed to do pitifully little to keep Peter from finding a potential heir within the research department, even though it would have been Peter's natural first choice. All he had to do was to encouraged Raju to deal with the lab's twin problems of non-innovative performance and poor morale by laying off the bottom twenty percent of his employees each year. The idea of keeping the best appealed philosophically to Peter, so the yearly slashing of a mandatory number of researchers was part of Penthes' culture.

It had left a cutthroat environment in Raju's domain in which everyone worked together to sabotage the most successful. Researchers with more tenure discouraged their younger colleagues, lest they find themselves replaced by them. Information was a closely guarded currency. Eventually, lone achievers got run off and the group turned to devour one of their own. It wasn't a pretty process, but the end result was a group of people who worked so hard to survive that they accomplished almost nothing.

Of course, once Peter finally accepted the inevitable and retired, Neil would start to change Penthes' corporate culture. There would be seminars on interdepartmental cooperation and communication. There would be field days with outdoor exercises to build trust. There would be a moratorium on lay-offs and a much better documented process for firing with cause. Everyone would find themselves with more vacation time and flex hours to achieve a better work/life balance, both of which were trends Neil repeatedly counseled Peter to eschew.

Yes, Neil would singlehandedly bring Penthes into the new millennium, albeit a decade past the date. The changes at a company so well-known for its ineffective ways would garner Neil favorable write-ups in many a fine business publication. That would certainly raise the stock price, at least for a while. Success and better conditions would attract better people who could do better things. Later, if not sooner, the old man would have to admit that Neil, of all people, was perfect to run the company and had been all along. He hoped the old goat would live for decades and have to watch him succeed.

Neil sighed. This was a complicated, difficult life's work he had set for himself, requiring more patience than most people had. As with all complicated tasks, he needed to take one step at a time.

His next step was to get an annoying child named Zane Zeitman out of his hair. Neil would stay alert, watching each hand as it was dealt for that unexpected card he could use to his advantage. It would get dealt sooner or later. It always did.

******

Toby knew the few dozen or so other boats making their permanent home in his part of the South Seas. As opposed to the wide-eyed explorers who sailed through living a dream, this group of permanent expats depended on good relations with every island nation in the region for their food, water, and a welcoming port in a storm. In a loose sense, they depended on each other for occasional aid and information. So Toby put out word that he could use a little work anywhere local rules allowed, then he sailed around the eastern islands of Fiji while he waited.

Word came back that another boat had run into problems and had to pass on providing transport for two businessmen from some U.S. company who were flying into American Samoa. They wanted to travel over to Samoa by boat and then on to Fiji. Toby knew the stop in Samoa would make Afi nervous, but it paid well. He radioed back that he was happy to help out by taking the job.

A week later Miss Demeanor arrived in Am. Sam., as the locals called it. Toby was told plans had changed somewhat and he needed to be ready to sail back out before dark. His passenger hoped to be on south side of Upolu, Samoa's main island, by early the next morning. Passenger? He was surprised to find a boy about Afi's age waiting for him on the dock, with a duffle bag and a general air of confusion about him.

"You're the two American businessmen?" Toby laughed. The young man laughed also and took Afi's offered hand to come aboard. Okay, maybe he was a little older than he looked.

"Zane Zeitman." The young man introduced himself, then explained. "My boss twisted her ankle the morning we were supposed to leave, and she was still at the emergency room when our flight left. She sent me on ahead. It is a pretty bad sprain, but she'll meet me in Fiji. I thought if we could sail to Upolu tonight, I could handle the business there myself, and then we could make it to Fiji in time for me to meet her plane." He shrugged. "I'm new and was supposed to be along to help her, you know, so to be honest, I'm faking it as best I can here."

Afi and Joy both studied Zane with interest. He looked out of place in his brand new khakis, short sleeve dress shirt, and role as advance man for some group. "Are you finished with your business here in Pago Pago?" Toby asked.

"Completely. I've been over the hotel arrangements and now I'm supposed to trace the intended path for the group. That means I need to sail to Samoa, experiencing a day at sea in a small boat, and report back as to whether it is going to be a crowd pleaser or a barf fest. No offense."

"None taken," Joy said. Afi added, "We're all voting for not-a-barf-fest."

"Me too," Zane assured them. "Apparently I'm the lab rat being used to decide if we go by sea or fly. Anyway, then you guys are supposed to sail me over to Fiji to give me an idea of what that is going to be like, even though our group will be on a larger ship. There, I meet up with my boss and go back to following along." He rolled his eyes. "At least, that's the plan."

Toby laughed. "It sounds like a good one. Why don't you get yourself into some shorts, and let my capable crew here get you settled? It'll be a sunset dinner and a night at sea. Let me know if you have any issues. We do have meds for that."

The oranges, corals, and peach colors of that night's sunset would have made a travel brochure cry with envy. Conversation was light as they shared the simple dinner on deck. Zane realized he learned more about the geography and history of the Pacific Islands over supper than he had come across in his whole life.

As the colors of the sky turned to darker blues and violets, Toby suggested Zane get some rest below deck. With a last look at the western sky, Toby reached for one of the small battery-powered lanterns. As he fumbled for the on switch he said, "The dispatcher said you wanted to make landfall on the south side of Upolu? Why? You do know there's no port of entry there?"

"I do. But if you can get me in close, my company has arranged special permission for me to be taken ashore by my hosts for the day. They'll take me over to a school there for troubled teens called Tropical Retreat Academy. I'm supposed to assure these guys that allowing our group to visit next February is no threat and might even result in additional referrals for them. Apparently they're a nervous bunch. I'm supposed to assure them we're partners in the business of helping youngsters."

Toby's hand froze on the light switch as Zane's explanation was met by a long dark silence. "So you're in the education business?" Toby asked from the darkness behind the unlit lantern.

"Oh no, not at all." This group did not appear to be big fans of education. "I thought you knew. I'm in the pharmaceutical business. I work for a company called Penthes. We're about to release a new medication designed for troubled teens." When the silence continued, he asked "Is something wrong?"

In the odd light cast by the last streaks of indigo in the sky, Zane could have sworn all three people, who had been so warm and friendly moments ago, were now giving him an icy stare. Toby spoke.

"Get some rest, Zane. We will let you off tomorrow at eight as requested, and then we'll take you over to Fiji as agreed. You seem like a nice enough kid. On the way to Fiji, there'll be time to talk."

At 6:48 a.m. the next morning, the surface of the earth moved deep under the ocean between Samoa and American Samoa, causing a 8.1 magnitude earthquake. It would turn out to be Earth's strongest, though not deadliest, earthquake of 2009. A whole lot of water moved up a few inches, an unimpressive feat unless one considered the power required to move that much water at all.

Toby had decided to keep Miss Demeanor far from shore, hoping to ease Afi's mind while the group ate breakfast. He planned to hide Afi below deck before he went in closer and the boat from the school pulled up alongside. He wasn't happy with his plan, but it was the best he could do.

He was about to call his crew for breakfast when he felt an odd rippling in the water and saw both Afi and Joy sit up. They felt it, too. He looked in toward shore, and even from this distance he could see the waterline of the ocean retreating out to sea, far from the tree line. *Shit, shit, shit.* The power of all that water rising a few inches was about to be converted into the power of far less water rising far higher.

If this had happened an hour later, Miss Demeanor would have been near land and thrown ashore by a three-story wall of water. Any of the four of them would have been lucky to live through the ride. As it was, Toby could only watch helplessly from his boat as the laws of physics were obeyed.

The wall of water rushed the shore, pounding its force into the trees and buildings it found, meeting resistance from the air and the slope of the land. After it had traveled inward as far as its energy could take it, it sloshed way from the shore before throwing its remaining power into a weaker second wave. This wave charged onto the beach, mixing with pools of water left in low spots and dissipating most of the remaining energy as it pushed against the sand, trees and rocks until nature was satisfied.

There were no people or animals visible on the beach, but the shore was now strewn with debris, and Toby heard sirens beginning to wail everywhere in the distance. He decided to find another cove where people might be hurt or in need of rescue and where Miss Demeanor and her crew could offer emergency assistance. Whatever Afi's fears and concerns were, and for that matter whatever Zane's business plans were, they would all be dealt with later.

******

It was lunchtime in Chicago when the earthquake struck, and by the time Raven was back at her desk it had made internet news. She called Chloe, who called her grandfather, and by late afternoon all of Penthes knew about the missing new kid from marketing who was supposed to have been on the south side of the island when the tsunami occurred. There was no death toll given yet, but it was assumed it would be high. He would have been exactly in harm's way.

Brenda, at home with her leg elevated, rejoiced over her own incredible good fortune at not being there and rubbed her swollen ankle thankfully. Then she worried about Zane.

Peter Hulson sat dejectedly in his office, staring out at the spectacular view of Lake Michigan and thinking of how much he hated the sea. Neil, in his office down the hall from Peter, wondered whether it was realistic to hope he could possibly be so lucky.

******

In Texas, Lola Zeitman searched out Samoa in the news after she kept getting the oddest sensations about Zane. She read of the earthquake, and she forced herself to sit calmly at her desk and think of her son. Lola had learned over the past few months how to push her mind to do unusual things. Today, she felt certain she would know if Zane were injured, or worse.

Breathe slowly, she told herself, forcing relaxation and concentration. *There. Breathe again. You know he's not dead. Keep breathing.* She waited for more information to come.

October 2009

7. Believe

Zane worked as hard as he ever had for the next few days, as he and Miss Demeanor's crew sorted through debris, helped push stranded cars to dry ground, removed rubble from roads, and otherwise provided whatever aid they could. Although the Samoans responded with food, shelter, and appreciation, the small villages of the southern coast of Upolu were a difficult environment for Zane. After life in Chicago, the temperatures were stifling, and the lack of power tools and communication devices was frustrating. All three people from the boat earned Zane's respect as he watched how well they accepted the hard work under rough conditions with little complaint and occasional humor. It appeared he'd regained their respect as well.

One-hundred-ninety-two deaths were reported. In the midst of the second day's clean-up, South Sumatra in Indonesia experienced a 7.5 earthquake in which over a thousand were killed. The tragedy further tied up communications in the South Pacific, so it took a day before Zane could text Raven he was alright and to ask her to let the office know he would call when he could. He sent a similar text to Ariel.

******

Raven received the text from Zane after she got home from work. She was relieved he was okay, but wasn't sure what to do with the information. She called Chloe, who called her grandfather. Dr. Hulson was quiet for several seconds.

"Chloe, could you and Raven keep this information to yourself for a day or two more? Better yet, why don't the two of you take tomorrow off and go shopping. I'll clear the absences and your first purchase is on me."

Chloe was happy to help. A Friday off together shopping along Chicago's Magnificent Mile was not a gift to be declined.

The next day in Penthes' office, Gil argued with Brenda that too much time had passed and they needed to contact Samoan authorities. More importantly, they needed to open a dialogue with Zane's next of kin. Brenda argued for waiting until Monday. Neil, meanwhile, was talking to the company's chief counsel about Penthes' liability and how best to lessen it. Peter watched.

******

Ariel had her whole family reassured seconds after she heard from Zane, and everyone but Lola breathed a silent sigh of relief at the news. Lola, for her part, was relieved she could stop *pretending* to be worried about Zane, who she was fairly certain was having an interesting and even somewhat enjoyable week.

******

By the end of day three no more emergency aid was needed. Toby brought the four of them together as the sun set, suggesting they camp on the beach rather than accept another night of local housing in a fala. Joy offered to prepare the fish so Toby and Afi could talk to Zane. It was time.

Afi did most of the talking, Toby passed around brandy, and Zane listened. At the end, everyone eyed Zane, waiting for a response.

"Okay. I get these people I've been sent to visit here in Samoa are creeps. But what I don't get is why?"

Toby responded. He'd given the situation a lot of thought.

"Obviously abusing kids isn't the goal, but making money is. They hire cheap help and once the staff isn't being watched, things gets out of hand. I think the genius is they've convinced parents not to monitor what's going on. They make it sound like part of the program's philosophy, but removing oversight lets these guys run a dangerous program. Then they charge five thousand dollars a month for it."

"Five thousand a month?" Zane was incredulous. Even his Ivy League education cost less than that.

"Yeah. I did some research," Toby said. "These schools help parents take out loans and get second mortgages. Their most adept employees appear to be their sales force."

"The kids respond like any human would to finding themselves captive in a boot camp. They're resentful and uncooperative, which brings on the extreme punishment," Afi said. "Then they convince parents to keep kids there longer, often past their eighteenth birthday."

Toby looked at Afi. "Forcibly enrolling an adult has to be illegal."

"Dinner." Joy hated to interrupt but she was hungry. The group gathered round to help themselves to food. They kept talking while scarfing down the seared local tuna and cooked green bananas.

By the end of the meal, they agreed to sail to Apia the next day to make proper entrance into the country so Zane could try to visit the school. He would go for his job, but also to keep his eyes open on behalf of Afi's former schoolmates.

"I'm not sure what we can do for these kids," Toby said. "but more information is better. Ask a lot of questions, Zane. See if they'll let you take a photo. Better yet, take some even if they won't."

Zane didn't mind observing, but he had concerns about turning this into a pseudo-espionage attempt. He was barely older than some of the students. If he were caught spying, they could keep him there or even move him to another of their schools where Penthes or his family would never find him. This could be serious trouble.

Toby agreed, and offered to go with him, posing as a substitute Penthes employee.

"They aren't going mess with two of us. You focus on being the pharmaceutical guy. Keep them occupied with your questions, and I'll pretend to be a last minute addition who isn't all that interested and can't wait to get to the beach. Once they start to ignore me, I'll focus on looking around."

After a bit more brandy, it sounded like a brilliant plan. The group offered to leave Afi in Apia, so he wouldn't be anywhere near, but Afi didn't want Joy alone on the boat in case of trouble.

As the coals began to die out and the orange embers glowed, Afi brushed the coals apart with the shovel, making a narrow rectangle about four feet long. A few little flames erupted as he split apart and redistributed the coals.

"We've made a pact," he said with ceremonial solemnity as he worked. The group looked puzzled. "Let's cement our agreement with a spectacular demonstration of our allegiance." Then he smiled mischievously. "I suggest we finish the evening off by walking through fire for each other."

Three people looked at him with expressions saying *no way*. Afi laughed. "My new friends, I would never want to bring harm to you. Allow me to demonstrate."

He stood up, and bowed first to Toby. "I dedicate this fire walk to the man who rescued me, with deep thanks." Then he bowed low to Joy. "I also dedicate it to the fine woman who has temporarily become my wife in an effort to make both of our lives better. May we always be friends." Finally, he turned to Zane. "And I dedicate it to my new friend Zane, who I thought was evil itself, but who turns out to have a pure heart, and who will visit hell on my behalf. To all of you."

With that Afi turned and walked onto the path of hot coals. He walked straight down it without changing his expression or his pace, stepped off of the far edge into the sand, and bowed again. His three shipmates stared at him in silence.

"This is generally a crowd pleaser," he said. "I often get applause for it."

"Did you put something on your feet?" Zane asked.

"No."

"Can you do it again?" Toby asked.

"Yes." Afi smiled and retraced his path gracefully back to his original place.

"Did you hide cool rocks in it when we weren't looking?" Zane asked.

"No."

"I'll do it," Joy said. She put out a hand to stop Toby's objection, kicked off her flip-flops, and without further hesitation walked over the coals at the exact same steady pace Afi used. When she got to the far side, she bowed low. Afi was grinning.

"Damn, lady. You are nuts." Toby shook his head.

"No," Joy said. "I took a self-defense class once. The final exam was breaking a board in half. You want to know the secret to doing that?"

"Strong hands?"

"No. Believing you can. The board could care less what you believe, but if you think your hand will go through, you won't slow it down to prevent injury. You hit it with enough force to break it."

"Based on that, you just walked over hot coals?" Zane was baffled, but Afi was nodding.

"She's right," he said. "Nothing mystic about it, although I understand seminars about getting in touch with your inner power do give this as the final exam."

"Okay." Zane stood up. He was less convinced but curious.

As he stepped forward, Afi reached out his hand and took Zane's. "You're not sold on this," Afi said. "Let me walk next to you on the sand. Keep pace with me and do what I do. Alright?"

"Alright."

Zane squeezed Afi's hand and walked alongside of him, calm on the outside although his heart was pounding. Left foot, right foot, left foot, right foot. The coals felt hot under his feet, but he kept moving, and in four steps he was back onto the sand. He laughed.

"I have no choice, do I?" Toby said as he stood. "How does this work?"

Afi confessed. "These coals are from wood. Their outside is not so hot because wood doesn't heat through like metal. If you go too slow, it is hot enough for your foot to get burned. If you go too fast, you push your foot deeper into the coal and you get burned. But if you believe you can do it, and you walk over them just right, you will feel their heat but be fine."

"Not too fast, not too slow. Believe in yourself. Good advice,"

Toby said. Then he brushed away all helping hands and took four well-paced steps through the middle of the coals.

******

When Zane called, the Headmaster at the Tropical Retreat Academy was not happy Zane still wanted to visit. He was making excuses when he was interrupted, and Zane found himself talking to a different person.

"Mark Hadley here. I'm the director of the Pacific-wide Turn Your Teen Around in the Tropics Program. With whom am I speaking?"

"Zane Zeitman. With Penthes Pharmaceuticals. I had an appointment with your headmaster Dick Stafford on Tuesday before the earthquake hit."

"Oh yes. Of course." The voice was polished and professional. "Please don't misunderstand Mr. Stafford's reticence, he's overwhelmed with focusing on the welfare of these youngsters. Our entire program of fourteen schools, and still growing, considers itself partners with those in the medical profession. We welcome a visit from you and eventually from the doctors attending your conference. With sufficient notice of course."

"Could I and a colleague drop by tomorrow, to introduce ourselves and assess the feasibility of transporting twenty-five or so doctors there to visit next winter?"

"Tomorrow morning would be perfect, Mr. Zeitman." Zane winced inwardly at the title. "I'll be here to personally meet with you. You do understand you can't tour the facility, right? These boys don't do well with distractions and their welfare has to be our biggest concern. But you and I can discuss logistics. Can you be moored on the south side of the Island at nine?"

Mr. Zeitman said he could.

The next morning Toby offered to be Mr. Zeitman, but Zane brushed him off. "No. We'll both respond to the name and they'll know something's amiss." Then he added in a mumble to himself "I can handle this."

As Zane changed into his best dress clothes below deck, he concentrated on aging his face. A few minutes before nine, a canoe with a small outboard motor came out of a cove and approached Miss Demeanor's port side.

The sailboat had dropped anchor and Joy had the helm. Afi was below deck. Toby had donned his cleanest shorts and only collared shirt, the best he could do. Zane, in his khaki pants and dress shirt, looked like the guy in charge. He saw Toby and Joy notice how he seemed to have put on a few pounds and his face looked older. Maybe they'd decide those fine lines were from a week of sea and sun.

The Samoan man lowered the throttle on his tiny engine, then introduced himself as Va'iga, an assistant headmaster of the school. He helped the two men into the little transfer boat and after a short ride they climbed out onto a small dock concealed by shrubbery and made the short walk to the school's office. Zane noticed the state-of-the-art burglar alarm as they entered.

Mark Hadley greeted them. He was an attractive, well-groomed man with a full head of silvery-blonde hair, and a smile that turned off and on in an instant. He liked to gaze straight into a person's eyes while asking rhetorical questions like "Don't you think we have no greater asset than our youth, our hope for tomorrow?" After a few such questions to both men, he focused on Zane as the decision-maker, and the one most likely to answer "Absolutely, no question" to Mark's every utterance.

Toby embraced the part of the accompanying aide, while Zane grew into his own role. He knew he not only looked older and fuller, but also a little taller. Hopefully Toby would attribute it to dress shoes and standing up straight.

The meeting was short, and the tour even shorter. Mark spoke with pride about how he'd personally built his chain of academies from nothing over the past ten years, helping hundreds of youngsters. He had great plans to expand in the next decade. Toby thought the man sounded like a walking infomercial.

They met Dick, the headmaster, who turned out to be a short, stocky American with a military haircut and a curt demeanor. They were allowed to see the eating facilities while not in use and to view a few students from a distance. Toby tried to memorize everything he could about the place while Zane engaged their host.

After a final exchange of platitudes, during which Mark announced he would see to it he was there to show the visiting doctors around in January, they were taken back to their boat. Toby could tell from fifty feet away something was wrong. Joy was sitting at the helm crying. Va'iga left them off without comment and Toby hurried to Joy's side.

"I couldn't stop them. They came aboard. They kept insisting someone named Barantiti had boarded this boat in Apia, and they had to find him. I didn't know what to do. They came on board and they looked everywhere."

"They took Afi?" Zane was sick. If Afi was forced back into that place because of him...

"No!" Joy sounded almost hysterical. "That's the problem. He isn't anywhere on this boat. They searched every inch, and I insisted they stop, but I had no way of making them. I can assure you Afi's not here. He's not in the water. He didn't go to shore. I'm... I'm afraid he swam under the boat and, rather than be taken, he stayed there. Too long."

Toby didn't believe that. He went to the back storage bin with the ropes. Sure enough, buried deep under the bright aqua braids he saw something that was part of Afi. As Toby watched in wonder, a human back and arms wriggled and the hands and arms moved out of the tiny space first, followed by what looked to be a twisted shoulder and neck, and then hair. The rest of Afi more fell than stepped out of the storage area. He shook himself as he walked out onto the deck in the skimpy men's underwear he favored, and gave his three friends a big grin.

Joy, who had seen the whole process, was speechless.

"I'm sorry Joy. I should have told you I can do this. I was going to, I just hadn't gotten to it ... and then when I heard you crying I didn't know for sure if they were gone ..." Afi was trying to apologize when he looked over at Zane wondering if he needed to offer Zane an explanation as well. But Zane's appearance took him by surprise.

"What happened to you? You look like you're forty years old."

"You do," Joy agreed through blotchy eyes.

Zane sighed.

"You explain first," Afi said. Zane nodded as he took a seat.

"I seem to have more of reflexes for camouflage than most

humans." He shrugged. "I don't know why. It started when I was little. I'd love to be able to tell you what it is in my brain or muscles or skin cells that makes it happen, but I've been trying to find out since I was five and I still don't know." Then as an afterthought: "You know, I've always managed to make excuses when caught. You're the first people I've ever told this to…"

Afi smiled in understanding.

"So what exactly was it you were doing in with the ropes?" Zane asked.

Toby broke in. "I say we set sail and put some distance between us and that school. You two can talk this through to your hearts' content on the way to Fiji."

******

Zane and Afi were sitting together out on the bow of the boat as it sped along, each with an arm held out. Afi, still in his barely there underwear, had his thumb bent back so far it could touch his wrist, and Zane's hand appeared to be a shade of grayish blue. As near as Toby could tell, they were engaged in a game of "that's cool but watch this."

Joy came up behind Toby and put her hand on his shoulder. "I'm sorry I lost it back there. I really thought Afi was dead."

Toby shook his head. "We should have warned you. I knew Afi could hide like that because I've seen him do it. "You've no need to apologize for anything. You've been a remarkably stable bright spot these last several weeks."

She knew he meant it and was glad. It was a little scary how happy she found herself as a refugee on a small boat with almost nothing, as opposed to how miserable she'd often been as a girl with her own huge room in a well-furnished house.

She watched the two young men out on the bow for a minute, then turned to Toby and laughed. "In some ways, doesn't this feel like the weirdest double date ever?"

"Speak for yourself," Toby said. Joy's mouth opened in surprise. "I'm joking, Joy, I'm joking." Then, because she still wasn't laughing, he gave her a playful hug from the side, which led to the two of them sitting with their arms around each other saying nothing and enjoying the warmth.

******

Zane noticed Joy and Toby becoming preoccupied with each other. Interesting. Meanwhile he and Afi had inched closer during their comparison of skills, and he found himself increasingly compelled to touch Afi's fascinating body. But when he leaned forward to touch, his mouth moved instead of its own accord to brush a soft kiss across Afi's lips.

Afi pulled back with surprise.

Oh please tell me I didn't misread this one.

"It's all right." Afi reassured Zane. "I was just surprised. I come from a world where that sort of thing doesn't happen."

"First kiss?" Zane asked incredulously.

"No, but close. It would be fair to say opportunities for exploring my sexuality have been extremely limited."

"Hell, I thought it was tough growing up in Texas."

Afi leaned in to return the kiss, to let Zane know the interest and affection were returned.

"Welcome to adulthood."

"I think it'll take more than a kiss to do that," Afi replied, playfulness in his eyes.

"I guess it will. You know, I can do some pretty unusual things with my body."

"Fascinating," Afi said. "So can I."

Now this could be good.

******

By late-afternoon Friday, Peter knew it was time to end his little charade. He'd watched much of his staff in action and learned what he needed to know.

He shared the happy news with everybody that his granddaughter had received word Zane was alive and well and regretted he'd not been able to get word to the office sooner. Zane had been busy generating goodwill by assisting in rescue operations. Peter suggested the barely-limping Brenda get to Fiji, where the important conclusion of the conference would be held, so she could assume responsibility for finalizing arrangements best handled by someone more experienced than Zane.

Peter also asked Brenda to reassign the database maintenance duties to someone more appropriate in IT and to put Zane on a new marketing endeavor when he returned. Peter wanted a review of the database for himself, before the end of the day, in his office, with Gil and a couple of IT's best to look at it with him.

When Neil suggested Peter hardly need concern himself with something so trivial, especially so late on a Friday, Peter ignored him like he hadn't heard. That irritated Neil more than anything else could have.

******

By the time Brenda and Zane returned from Fiji a week later, Zane had achieved a sort of hero status around the office. He tried to downplay it. He didn't enjoy the attention and he found the office chilly and claustrophobic after three weeks in the tropics.

Brenda, however, was inclined to milk the favorable attention for her department. After all, Zane had been her brilliant protégé.

Neil watched. Peter's quick involvement in the database the previous week was unprecedented. As a result, Peter now had his own copy, and IT's on-the-spot assessment, making any future sabotage of Zane's work obvious. Such sabotage had been one of Neil's plans of last resort, but he could forget that avenue now.

Worse yet, Brenda was lost as an ally for the time being, her momentary vanity having trumped her good judgment. Fine. No need to make a fuss. The situation with this kid and Peter was turning more serious, so Neil had to be careful. It would probably be better to do without her help at this point.

Heroes always garner resentment. Neil looked around the office, to see who might be annoyed by Zane's sudden celebrity status. A new ally would surface. One always did.

******

After a few days back in the office, Zane came down with a

head cold. He rarely got sick, attributing it to his strong mind-to-body connection. This time around, he had a disgusting runny nose and avoided people as Brenda moved him on to another project for the marketing group.

Zane didn't like the new project. Brenda wanted a tool for doctors to use to write articles about their experiences prescribing Penthes' medications. The goal of this "doctor's little assistant" was to enable the busy medical professional to spend a minimum amount of time on the article, while making it sound like the doctor had written all of it in his own words, and while making sure it conveyed the message Penthes wanted.

Using common office software, this tool would scan previous articles penned by the doctor looking for common word and phrase choices. It would then graft these choices onto a skeleton article in which Penthes had already supplied the facts and conclusions.

Zane shook his head at the possibilities for misuse. How liable was he for an uninformed doctor prescribing a Penthes medication on the basis of another doctor's review? Shouldn't uninformed doctors do more research? Shouldn't Penthes medications be better choices? Shouldn't new hires be faced with fewer moral dilemmas on the job? Zane thought so.

The last bit, of course, was a touch of self-pity, which Zane admitted was born of spending too much time thinking about how he'd rather be feeling the slosh of the waves under his body and the touch of the breeze on his face while sailing along on Miss Demeanor with his friends. Damn. That was living. This was not.

During his goodbye to Afi, Joy, and Toby after the sail to Fiji, he'd suggested he take time off in February after the Penthes conference, to join them for some more time at sea. Toby had agreed, announcing he would keep his crew on through then if they liked, and adding he would look forward to a reunion for some light fire-walking and possible random rescue work.

Which meant, of course, that Zane needed to still be employed at Penthes come February. So his automated ghostwriter had to progress. He turned back to his screen with resignation when a soft chime informed him he had a new email.

It was from Dr. Hulson's personal assistant. Dr. Hulson would like to meet with him next week. Would he be available

Wednesday morning at 8:30? The question, of course, was rhetorical.

******

Except for a small cut to cover gas and mooring fees, Toby passed the Penthes payment onto Joy and Afi in New Zealand cash. Zane had been dropped off in Suva, to meet with his coworker with the bum ankle. They'd all said goodbye on the dock, and Toby recognized how the little group had bonded in less than two weeks. He was sincere about keeping Joy and Afi on board for a few more months, and he wanted to find a way to make the February get-together work. He took on ample supplies in Suva, and proposed a change of pace to his crew.

Years ago, he managed to rent part of one of the uninhabited Phoenix Islands from the nation of Kiribati. He kept a permanent structure there with extra provisions. The building was the closest thing he had to a permanent home, after Miss Demeanor.

"I'd like to sail over to the Phoenix Islands," he proposed. "Any concerns?"

"Happy to go, but it's a long trip and there's not much there," Afi said. Joy shrugged but made no comment.

"You'll like it, I think," Toby said, knowing all three of them needed something to dissipate the sense of having lost a welcome crewmate. "While we're there, we'll see what we can find on the internet to help shine a more discerning light on the activities of Mark Hadley and his billion-dollar Turn Your Teen Around in the Tropics empire."

"You think we're going to find internet access good enough for research anywhere in the Phoenix Islands?" Afi laughed.

Toby smiled back. "I know we will. I put it there."

8. A Secret Entry

Peter Hulson had two glasses of ice water with orange slices waiting on the silver tray in his office. They gave Zane the impression this visit was important to the old man. At Peter's gesture, Zane seated himself on the soft green little sofa.

"Do you know why people go to see therapists?" Peter asked.

"I always wondered."

"Sometimes it's status. Look what I can afford."

This sounded like dangerous ground, so Zane kept his eyes fixed on the low, grey clouds over Lake Michigan and said nothing.

"Other people want the therapist to fix them. They think it's like taking their car to a mechanic for a new alternator." Peter cleared his throat and then was silent. Zane concentrated on the three distinct colors he could pick out in the cloud layers.

"I see you have the good sense to not say something stupid to fill the silence. You'd rather wait and see where the hell this is going, wouldn't you?"

"I would."

"You're a smart boy. You keep proving it. My IT people found the various ways you tried to make your sales database tamper-proof. They also discovered you made an unauthorized copy of it, which they couldn't find in your office. They thought perhaps you were planning on selling it."

Zane's heart started to race. This was not the conversation he expected.

"Sell it? No way. Besides my own ethics, which I do have, I'm well aware I'd likely get caught and ruin my life faster than I could imagine. I'm not—"

"Stupid," Peter finished. "I know you're not. So why did you bother with safeguards and a backup copy? Honestly."

"Okay." Zane figured he didn't have much to lose now. "I've never seen a group of people as cutthroat as they are here. Even the pre-med kids at my college worked together better than this."

"So you were protecting yourself?" Peter asked.

"Exactly."

"That's what I was afraid you'd say. Zane, I believe people talk to a therapist so they can discuss personal matters with someone who isn't emotionally involved, has the obligation to be discrete and the training not to say something stupid. Most of us don't have someone like that we can turn to. "

"Are you thinking of seeing a therapist?"

The old man gave a sad smile. "I've never had therapy, so it would cause speculation, and now's a bad time for that."

"Why?" Zane had found that single word to be the best response when none other seemed appropriate.

"Because I'm dying, Zane. To my frustration, I've learned that after creatively blazing my own path in life, I'm about to become a stupid cliché in death. A seventy-something rich guy with cancer too far along, who only wants the good health all my money can't buy. Fortunately, this particular model comes with enough brains to not put himself through months of chemo to stave off what my own research shows is inevitable. My choices are to live a little longer and be very ill, or to use my remaining strength and time to put my house in order. That's where you come in."

If ever there was a time for a wise response, Zane thought this was it. But no wise words came to mind.

"I'm sorry for your situation." At Peter's quizzical look he added, "Because you do seem like a decent guy. You should have more time and a better end."

"Well, I think so too. My dear wife Darlene died in 1998, after thirty-nine years of marriage. She was only sixty-one. I loved her every day, although I didn't always have the good sense to show it. You've no doubt heard how my only son died at sea in 1999. No one in the office ever mentions him because they think they're sparing my feelings. My daughter Paula and I interact in superficial ways, big showy hugs and all that. It's been years since we've had a serious conversation and I don't know if she even likes me. She appears to spend most of her time thinking about herself and how she looks. I can't honestly say I'm terribly fond of her.

"My two granddaughters tolerate me, lest they get written out of my will, although I will say Chloe and I have had a few exchanges that might approach affection. Maybe. My employees at work and at home defer to me and my business associates all know how to behave, so no one treats me poorly. Yet I don't think I have a single real friend. The morning after I got the news, I woke up and realized there was no one on the entire planet I wanted to tell."

Zane finally got it. "I'm your therapist."

"You have no emotional attachment to me. You seem to have the ethics not to sell my story to a magazine and the good sense to not say anything stupid. So, yes, this morning you're my therapist, though I'm hoping to hire you to do more than that."

More?

"I asked you up here to make a business proposition. You realize I have every possession I want, and what I do yearn for you can't get for me. My loved ones back, my health, the successors I'd hoped to find and train. Yes, you could've been one, if I'd found you sooner. but there's no time left for it now. We'll let everybody think that's why I'm meeting with you so often, though."

Zane nodded his agreement and Peter continued. "No, there's only one reasonable thing left for me to want. At least I think it's reasonable, but it doesn't matter whether it is or not. It probably won't matter to you either, because I'm going to offer you a million dollars."

Zane felt his own eyes widen.

"That's right. A flat rate and don't ask for more. I'm pretty sure you'll spend it wisely." Peter paused. "You do seem wise for a young guy. So let me ask you. What is it you think I want before I die?"

Zane let himself think aloud. "You've ruled out love. And hope. Peace?"

"Peace is good. You've sort of got it, because I want things that will bring me peace. I want information about my company and my life. I want to stay powerful and involved up to the end. The end is all I have left."

Peter took a small sip of water and continued. "Which is a problem, because I understand I'm going to be in a good bit of pain soon, and it's only going to get worse. I'll be on medication, and my judgment will be clouded and my powers of observation weaker. I'm going to be sick. I hate that idea. Right now, at least, I hate it more than I hate the idea of dying.

"So, I want to hire you to be my stronger body, my still highly functioning brain, my eyes and my ears. I want to rent you Zane, pure and simple. I want to be able to ask questions and to get answers from someone who has nothing to gain by lying to me. That will bring me peace." Peter finished and waited.

Zane knew he was going to say what he really thought. It had been his downfall so often, and it would be his downfall here.

"Sir, I understand your wishes. They're a little odd, but they make sense to me. They actually do. I could be good at doing this, too, but part of what you're asking for sounds like you want me to spy on people for you. I'm not well suited to that. I'm not good at misleading people and I don't like doing it."

"I know." Peter smiled for the first time since the visit began. "You're a particularly bad liar. That's the reason I believe I can trust you. You don't have to lie to anyone. Just keep your silence. You're good at that. And for the next six to twelve months give me all the truth you can. Good, bad, indifferent. I want it all and I'll know if you're holding things back. Do this for me, and your check for a million dollars will be with my personal attorney, predated and accounted for so it doesn't get mixed up in my estate."

"Are there particular things you'd want me to look into?"

"More than I can name." Peter chuckled. "For starters, I didn't like what I saw when the staff here thought you were injured or killed in the earthquake. Tell me more about the people who work for me. While you're at it, I want truth about the products I've spent my life creating. I want you to go to the Penthes website and tell me how much of it is bullshit. I want to know what the members of my family are really like, not what they pretend to be to me. I'd like to know more, if there is more, about how my son died. I'll pass along to you the contents of the whole ugly investigation that followed. Money brings a lot of craziness in its wake. And, I'd like some idea about how my company is likely to change and how it will fare once I'm gone.

"I'm going to get you off of this ghostwriting project Brenda put you on. We shouldn't be writing articles for doctors anyway. I'll have you moved to things that will allow you to poke around at will all over the place. Go be my eyes and ears, Zane. Be my brain. Ask questions and draw conclusions and pass along to me everything you learn and even what you suspect."

What could Zane say? He could respect a man's search for the truth. He could certainly use the money. And, given his odd abilities known only at this point to a dead chameleon and a boatful of people in the South Pacific, he could be way better at gathering information than Dr. Peter Hulson suspected.

******

Different latitudes have different reputations in the Pacific. Sailors avoid the wild and dangerous forty-degree band known as the roaring forties and in the even higher waves and stronger gales of the furious fifties. The equatorial region is the opposite, known for light winds and an occasional absolute calm.

Toby kept fuel on board to help with these doldrums, a sailing word more widely used to describe depression. As Miss Demeanor headed north towards the equator, progress slowed and he used fuel to propel them forward in search of breeze.

The threesome worked together with a soft, easy rhythm. Although Toby was in charge of his boat, he gave reasonable orders with ample explanation. In one area of command, he relinquished control completely. He knew he'd never enter the third millennium tune-wise if he didn't let somebody younger serve as the boat DJ. Joy took over and days were spent listening to 2010's top dance club songs, which she'd downloaded in Fiji.

Toby knew he was enjoying the camaraderie of his crew. Would their loyalty be as strong if they knew more about him? He tried to remember how he'd left things at his place. What was lying around? Would his crew even recognize the evidence of the other life he led? Most likely not.

Nervously cleaning up once they arrived would only make him look dodgy. His best bet would be to open the place up to them and count on his new friends to ignore anything personal.

******

The way Zane saw it, he'd been offered an impressive sum of money for his discretion, his powers of observation, and his ability to produce a final report on a complex subject. This was something he could do. There were no guarantees he'd ever see the money, but he couldn't imagine why Dr. Hulson would cheat him. What would be the point? So he assumed the agreement was legitimate, and started with the easy stuff.

How much had Dr. Hulson's work helped humanity? His mom's situation had already pushed him to consider the opinions of those less approving of pharmaceuticals. Zane decided to give that path a second look.

A recent blog by a natural health doctor praised modern medicine's ability to help the deeply depressed, but decried the astonishing increase in the diagnosis of depression. It suggested that rather than encouraging more of the nation's despondent to stop hiding their misery, advertising dollars had instead worked their magic to convince an extra 10 million Americans experiencing life's normal ups and downs to go on medication. The article concluded that depression, a real disorder, was being exploited by consumer marketing in a profit-driven medical system.

Does having the local pharmaceutical rep take you out for nice lunches make you more willing to accept a patient's advertisement-driven desire to go on antidepressants? What if the company is paying to send you on an educational jaunt to an exotic resort?

******

Joy became concerned when Toby became more nervous as they approached his island property. She guessed he'd never had friends over to his house before.

He's lived a solitary life. He's showing a lot of trust bringing us here, If it's a horrible dump of a shack, I need to be careful. It's his home and he cares for it.

Afi noted the change as well, but he wondered if Toby had something to hide. If so, what?

They approached the small island and Toby took them through a barely visible break in the island's surrounding reef. While they dropped anchor and began the process of getting supplies into the dinghy, Afi noted the man had never built a dock for his own convenience. The better to keep his place hidden?

As the dinghy touched ground, Toby jumped into the shallow water and gave his companions a hand disembarking before he pulled the little boat ashore. He walked across the beach towards the small shrubs.

Like the other islands in the area, this was a low-lying atoll, made from the remnants of a volcano worn down and covered by the carcasses of ancient corals. The soil was poor at best, and the atoll barely rose a dozen feet above the sea.

The scant dwarfed shrubbery spoke of sparse rainfall. Even the hardy coconut trees looked to have seen better days. Afi guessed there was no fresh water to be had and less than a square mile of land total. This island would be of no use to anyone. He wondered how much the Kiribati charged for its rental.

Toby headed toward a dense part of the vegetation, dropped his supplies, and began digging into the sand. He uncovered a cement paver attached to the shrub above it and moved them both aside. Afi looked closer. The shrub was plastic. Behind it was a low door. Toby looked a little embarrassed.

"Yeah, it's a secret door. My security system."

After unlocking bolts, he stooped down to pass through the four foot opening and Joy and Afi followed, wondering what to expect. Steps went down to a floor dug a couple of feet into the ground. The ceiling sloped upward at the same rate, leaving the three of them standing comfortably in a full sized entryway. It was stifling hot but rather nice.

"Let me cool things off a bit." Toby started to raise metal shutters, open thick plastic louver blinds, and turn on fans everywhere. The house seemed to extend for several rooms back into the atoll.

"No AC, but the solar provides all the fans you could want. It'll cool off quickly, I promise."

Joy noted with relief the full screens on all the windows, and the thickly caulked crevices everywhere the cement floor met the cinderblocks that made up the first four feet of the walls. In fact, there was enough caulk and reinforcement to look like it kept out the water and the horrible insect pests for which the Pacific Islands are famous.

"You have solar?" Afi was impressed.

"And a rainwater collection system. And a small desalination set-up. And a satellite dish. Some hydroponic gardens, which is why I have to get back here every few months." By now Toby's embarrassment was turning into pride.

"I told you I was pretty successful for a while. This is where most of my money went. I love sailing, but I'm a project person. Not that my dear Miss Demeanor isn't a project, too, and a fine home. But I don't think I'd have enjoyed my life at sea as much if I hadn't had this place to build and make better. You don't stop being what you are just because you run away from your life, you know."

"Wherever you go, there you are," Joy said.

"Exactly," Toby said. "You're in a house built by a bored geek who once had money, plenty of time to transport materials, and nothing better to do. Let me show you around."

******

The human brain fascinated Zane. It was amazing that art, music and literature were all created by chemistry; that philosophy and even love had their roots in substances traveling in-between neurons. It was incredible it worked at all, much less as well as it did.

Zane knew different brain chemicals deliver different kinds of messages about thoughts and feelings. One messenger, serotonin, likes to blab about mood. The theory behind antidepressants is that serotonin is linked to a person's happiness. When people are depressed, maybe they don't have enough serotonin running around inside spreading joy.

Zane knew the problem with a theory like that is no one gets to do experiments on a live human brain. Thankfully. Dead human brains don't send chemical messages, and we can't tell if the sorts of animals accepted for grisly lab experiments are depressed. So, no one knows whether depressed people have less serotonin in their brains, or how much serotonin a joyful person has. Can one have too little? Or too much? A few antidepressants lower serotonin levels, and they appear to work as well.

As Zane's housemate Britta left for work, she asked Zane if he could make some time that evening for them to talk. Zane suspected the conversation was going to be about pitching in more on the housework, and he was ready to acknowledge his shortcomings and promise to do better. But as his usually lighthearted roommate stood in his doorway that evening, he sensed something else was wrong.

"You're upset with me?"

"Yes. You left your laptop out on the couch and, well, I couldn't help noticing what website you were on."

"Okay." What had he been looking at?

Britta looked down at the floor and when she raised her eyes, there was anger in them. "It bothers me you read the lies put out by those horrible people."

"What horrible people?" Zane was confused. Hadn't he been doing research for work?

"Those people who claim antidepressants are evil. Crackpots."

"Oh." Time to tread lightly. "Actually, my boss asked me to do that. He wanted some information about the other side of the PR picture."

Britta took an audible breath. "Oh, okay. That makes more sense. Good idea to track what stories these idiots are making up. I'm sorry. I shouldn't have doubted you."

"Britta, do you take antidepressants?"

She came all the way into his room, shut the door and seated herself on his floor."

"No."

"Does your boyfriend?"

"No." Then, with a hint of an apology, "My mother was severely depressed. She came from the kind of family that didn't believe in help for that sort of thing. She killed herself when my twin sister and I were four. It's not a story I share."

"Oh Britta. I'm so sorry."

"Everyone always said Elsa, my twin, looked like my mom. We're fraternal twins, and I guess she did. By the time Elsa was fourteen or fifteen, she acted like my mom. I was running around involved in everything and Elsa could hardly get out of bed. Thankfully my dad wasn't going to screw up a second time. He had her on antidepressants before she was sixteen and now I still have a sister and she still has a life. I don't have much use for the naysayers, Zane."

"That's understandable. But not every story is as clear-cut, Britta. You must know that?"

She nodded. "I still think if my mom's world had been more open to treating her condition as an illness, she'd be alive today."

Zane was searching for what to say next when his cell phone rang. He picked it up to turn it off but Britta reached out and touched his arm. "It's okay. Take your call. I'd rather this stay a short conversation."

As she closed the door behind her, Zane adjusted to the sound of his Aunt Summer's cheery voice. He liked his aunt, but they almost never talked, relying on his mom to pass information both ways. Aunt Summer must have called for a reason.

"Zane. Your mom tells me you work for a company that makes antidepressants, and you're having some scruples working for the marketing group."

"True." *Oh dear. Another testimonial?*

Aunt Summer proceeded to tell him what an awful mistake it had been to take antidepressants. She'd hit what she called "a real low spell" about a year ago, when her doctor talked her into trying medication to help. Later, Aunt Summer heard stories about the doctor having frequent lunches with a gorgeous sales rep. Zane thought of Raven and her army of beautiful sisters regularly dispatched with generous expense accounts by all the pharmaceutical companies.

"The problem, Zane, and I'm going to be blunt here, is they give you this giant list of side effects nobody reads. I know I didn't. So I didn't happen to notice, well, you've got medical training so don't be embarrassed, I didn't notice decreased libido is a common side effect."

"Decreased libido?" Zane hadn't known that.

"Yeah. You know. You don't particularly want to do it, but, your spouse still does. I want you to know the damn stuff nearly ruined my marriage, which frankly was the best, least depressing thing I had in my life. Ironic, huh?"

"Aunt Summer, I'm really sorry to hear that."

"Don't be. It's okay, everything's fine now. But I thought here you are, my godchild, and you're trying to make these big decisions about your life. I can't keep back information that would, you know, help you see the real picture. Zane, stay true to yourself. These big drug companies can be greedy evil bastards.

"Oh, and don't you dare tell your mom about this. She's a West Texas girl with no use for these kinds of meds." His mother, of course, had already made Zane swear not to share anything about her own use of antidepressants. Great.

Zane did his best to thank his aunt for her concern and as he hung up, Zane remembered Aunt Summer's gift to him as a small child. He went to the box of keepsakes in his closet. Yes, it was still there. He laughed aloud, thinking how the little book had helped him get through his childhood.

To this day, he still believed Dr. Seuss' words, that there was no one alive more Zane Zeitman than he. He thought about Britta and Aunt Summer's conflicting testimonials, and wished being true to who he was could solve every dilemma.

******

Neil poked around the research department to see if Zane had made mistakes, or maybe enemies, in his earliest days at Penthes. Nothing of particular use surfaced. He spent time getting to know Josh, who was fast becoming the marketing department's go-to guy for attractive PowerPoint presentations. The young man resented the attention Zane was getting, but in spite of Neil's frequent requests for information and Josh's growing dislike of Zane, Josh had yet to produce anything helpful.

It was time to try another tactic. Placing the names of promising new employees with a headhunter friend had gotten more than one problem child removed in the past. Had he used that one too often? Probably. How about a family emergency? That had worked well once before, but it might be suspicious a second time. Maybe something else having to do with Zane's family?

Neil had worked before with a discrete private detective. He was expensive but particularly good at finding dirt on the most upstanding of citizens. Neil didn't know anything about Zane's upbringing, but surely this guy could locate a thread somewhere in the Zeitman household, that, if pulled hard enough, would force Zane's future at Penthes to unravel. Neil gave the man a call.

******

Toby's nervousness subsided after a day or two, as it became obvious Afi and Joy appreciated his home and respected his privacy. Toby was sure Afi sensed he was hiding something, but once they found a more-or-less clean place with no arsenal of guns or bizarre lab experiments, Afi and Joy relaxed into enjoying the amenities of his bungalow.

Now that the three of them had more privacy and space, Toby was even considering the appealing idea of trying to seduce Joy. He thought Joy shared his attraction and there was little doubt what would follow would be wonderful. A younger Toby wouldn't have hesitated.

He was pretty sure there had been physical intimacy between Afi and Zane, removing an unspoken taboo aboard ship. He was surprised to find he had no vestiges of disapproval. Rather, he was happy for Afi. After all Afi had been through, he deserved some affection and pleasure.

But, in the case of him and Joy, there was the aftermath to consider. What were the odds of a fun encounter with no emotional baggage to follow? It wasn't like he and Joy could avoid each other on a small sailboat if things got awkward. Toby sighed. Sometimes he wished he wasn't so mature.

He focused instead on the care and upkeep of the water, food, and power supply he relied on to work in his absence. He steered Joy and Afi to using his internet to learn more about Mark Hadley and his alternative education empire. It didn't take long for them to find two surprising facts.

Mark Hadley seemed to have emerged around 2002 with no traceable background in education. In fact, the man had no traceable background of any kind. They theorized about trouble with the law, maybe even prison time or a religious conversion. It was plausible the man had moved on from a troubled past.

The other surprising fact was the man had made a ridiculous amount of money running these schools. The amount charged to the parents seemed almost criminal, and it was hard to believe real people could be induced to fork over that much cash. But they did. Ironically, Afi would never have been able to attend if he hadn't essentially received a full scholarship.

No one website listed all the schools, and the connection to Turn Your Teen Around, Inc. was not easy to find on any of the individual school's websites. But it was there if one looked hard enough, and it appeared Mr. Hadley had at least a dozen of these schools operating in the Pacific.

Toby also had trouble believing there were so many youths in need of such dire intervention. The more he studied the materials Joy and Afi found, the more he understood there probably weren't. The problem with Mark Hadley's business model was there weren't enough people in need of his services for him to make the kind of money he wanted to make. So Hadley had turned to a tried and true American solution. He'd used advertising to convince people they needed his services when they didn't.

Toby had to admit the advertising was slick. Better to intervene in your child's life too early than too late, it claimed. Who could argue with that? It looked like Hadley targeted those who belonged to stricter or more conservative religious and political groups, where relatively harmless teen rebellion would be least tolerated. Good marketing.

Toby was willing to guess that by the time the typical young person was dismissed, most parents wanted to believe they'd gotten something for their huge investment when, in reality, their teenagers were now scarred, angry, and scared. In the best of cases, the family listened and worked together to achieve healing. In the worst, the financially broke parents had a child who was broken, perhaps a time bomb of repressed anger waiting to explode. Or perhaps a time bomb of deep depression waiting to implode.

Nothing unites people like a common cause. By the time they had amassed all the information, Toby, Afi, and Joy agreed they had to find a way to bring Mark Hadley down. They were in Toby's office, brainstorming ideas, when Afi asked the one question Toby had been hoping he wouldn't hear.

"What is y raised to the power of one?"

"It's y, isn't it?" Joy chirped out the answer, sure she'd learned in algebra that any number raised to the power of one was itself. Afi and Toby looked at her like she'd missed the point of the question.

Toby's fears were confirmed when Afi added "Yes, I know who you are and I know where I am." Toby didn't know what to say, so he replied with a helpless shrug and said nothing.

y^l

9. The Best Christmas Ever

Zane liked to blend in. It was why, in his own way, he was a rather good actor. He sounded more Texan in Texas, more East Coast at school, more educated on campus, and less educated in a bar. He could carry himself like a preppie, gesture and stand like a rodeo kid, and walk like he was from the inner city. He didn't choose to mimic people; it just happened.

Although there was nothing magical about him, he knew the results of what he'd learned to do with his body would have astounded his friends and family. He also knew there was one major difference between his skills and those of the male cuttlefish as it turns its skin from brown to white to warn approaching males it's going to fight. The cuttlefish, as far as we know, doesn't give the process any thought.

Zane, however, had a human brain, and making choices was one of the things his brain had evolved to do. So while changes would occur without conscious choice, like a reflex, he still controlled them. He stopped changes he didn't want, he undid changes he didn't like, and, over the last few years, he'd gotten better at learning how to instigate changes of his own choosing. That last part turned this into more than a reflex. It was no longer a quirk. The things Zane's mind could make his body do were a gift.

Certain things, of course, couldn't be altered. Clothes, obviously. Zane often carried a second shirt in his backpack in case he wanted to disappear. Hair of any kind was a problem, because it was made up of dead cells with no ability to respond. Zane kept his medium brown misbehaved mop cut short and wore hats a lot. Sometimes he took alternate headgear with him.

His size could be altered some, but not as much as he would have liked. Zane guessed maybe plus or minus ten percent. He'd learned to modify his shape somewhat. He could make his chin recede more or his shoulders appear broader, but he couldn't make himself have a third arm coming out of his back. At best, he'd managed to produce a short lump looking like a tumor between his shoulder blades. He kept working on it, though.

He'd always been good with color, as long as it involved pigments contained by his cells. There was no turning turquoise, but it was sometimes convenient to change ethnicity, and occasionally helpful to turn his skin toward the color of his surroundings if he could manage to get the clothed parts of him otherwise camouflaged.

Afi had asked him if he had ever tried modifying his texture. He hadn't, but he liked the idea and planned to work on it. He smiled at the memory of Afi, a little surprised by how much thinking of Afi made him smile.

Tonight would be the first time Zane contrived ahead of time to use his gift to purposefully mislead someone. He knew another person might have gone there years ago and done so often. What an ability for a con artist to have. But to Zane, misleading was lying. It didn't feel comfortable. He had neither the need for nor the interest in it.

Tonight, though, he was armed with dual justifications. He'd convinced himself Peter Hulson's quest for information before he died was a noble cause, so he'd resolved to make his reports accurate and frequent. If a little subterfuge was needed, he was going to be okay with that.

Then a second incentive presented itself. Earlier in the week, Chloe invited him to join her and Raven for drinks after work. He was looking forward to it. Then yesterday, she postponed the outing. "Raven will be having drinks without us," Chloe said, "doing what a girl's gotta do."

"What's that?" Zane had been puzzled. Chloe rolled her eyes.

"When the great and powerful COO of a company wants to take a lowly sales rep out for a drink and stare at her tits, she goes. I just hope he's content with staring and doesn't try to strong arm

Raven into more. She's had trouble saying no to powerful men before. I think it's daddy abandonment issues."

So Zane brought a backpack into work containing a shirt he'd never wear out in public, and a hat that classified as the same. He was thinking he'd go for being a little smaller and tanner, with Asian features. He planned to go to the bar and try to sit as close to Neil and Raven as possible. Given his good hearing, he should be able to listen in fine.

What if Neil started to pressure Zane's friend who was easier to push around than she should be? The time for assertiveness training for Raven would be later. If he heard anything he didn't like, Zane was planning to find a way to accidently knock an ice cold drink on Neil's lap.

The bar was as noisy and crowded as usual, but a lone seat was available at the bar not too far from the little table occupied by Neil and Raven. Zane kept his back towards them. One of the downsides of being twenty-three is that you are always carded, and Zane's ID looked, unfortunately, like Zane. So he ordered a drink before he morphed, hoping the staff and patrons would be too occupied to notice or care.

Once the drink came, he slouched over and stared into his mojito, willing the change. A process like the one he had in mind would take a couple of minutes if he concentrated on one thing at a time, which worked best. He started with the skin around his eyes, feeling the familiar itch as the flesh moved.

Next, the iris. Zane figured everyone in the world knew without looking if their own index finger was curled or straight, even though he suspected not one human could adequately describe the difference in sensation. There was a time when Zane had to look into a mirror to change the color of his eyes, but now he knew what brown eyes felt like. It was as clear as the difference between a curled and straight finger. Zane made his eyes dark brown. His skin should go more golden. Natural tones were easier to acquire and to hold. He made the feel of golden brown skin.

The last part of today's transformation would take the longest. It would be achieving what he had come to call "a sense of shrinking self." It sounded so Zen. He was about to begin the process when he felt a tap on his shoulder.

"Zane?" A smiling Raven withdrew her hand, startled as he turned to face her. "I'm sorry. I thought you were a friend of mine." She gave the strange man with some of Zane's features a funny look. "So sorry."

******

Raven was relieved when the conversation with Neil stayed on banal pleasantries, peppered with a few subtle innuendos. By the end of the evening's drinks, Raven was pretty sure Neil had no real interest in her career, or any sort of relationship with her. He would be perfectly happy to use her friendship with Chloe in any way he could and equally happy to have sex with her if it was convenient and didn't affect his life in any way once they were finished.

******

By the end of the evening's drinks Neil figured out Raven was brighter than he expected and was considerably more loyal to Chloe than he would have thought. Also, she was in no way attracted to him.

That meant she would have to be coerced into sex. No problem. He'd save that fun for later. It was enough for now to pressure her into getting drinks and being seen together. She wasn't going anywhere, and watching her accept the inevitability of his eventual success was going to be half the fun.

******

After the first few days on the island, Joy knew Toby's dwelling was more than a storage area. She thought it was an ingenious self-sustaining home, and found herself considering seducing the home's clever designer.

There was no denying her growing attraction to the man. Afi slept out on the boat, Joy preferred slumber in a hammock hung perfectly to catch the sea breezes, and Toby enjoyed the nighttime privacy of his own bedroom. There was opportunity, and plenty of motivation. Joy didn't think Toby would turn her down, and she thought what followed would be pretty damn good.

Then Afi's cryptic comment and the confusion that followed forced her to reconsider.

She'd watched as Toby hadn't denied anything while Afi explained how he'd figured out this place was the well-hidden headquarters for an organization called y^1, a somewhat secretive philosophical organization. As she listened, Joy realized she didn't know Toby at all. Seducing a stranger who ran a mysterious organization maybe wasn't so wise.

Over the rest of the day, Toby tried to answer her questions and gave her access to his site. She learned he'd founded y^1 years ago, after his time at sea left him hungry to find others with whom he could have intelligent discussions. At first, y^1 was no more than a few dozen souls who liked to get online late at night and converse about economics and philosophy, two of Toby's passions. The group had grown by orders of magnitude and given the subject matter, it now included many powerful people. Toby had tens of thousands of followers who read and appreciated the work he posted online.

Joy was baffled when she heard this. What could an isolated sailor have to say that would interest so many? Then as she read, she understood. Toby was less a man running away from a civilization and more a man determined to spend his days in the ways he chose. His number one premise was that the currency by which anything should be judged was not the money it produced, but the joy which resulted.

He wrote "The idea that one's pursuit of happiness is largely interconnected with one's freedom of choice is such a common premise today, and yet we still judge our own success by measuring the extent to which we get to tell other people what they can and can't do." He attracted disagreement from all points on the political spectrum, and as Joy read their lively discussions she realized these worldly philosophers were Toby's true friends.

Toby told her he named his group y^1 as a way of celebrating the individual, for anything raised to the power of one always equals its own joyous self.

"Why y?" Joy asked.

S. R. Cronin

"Because we like asking why," Toby said. "And sometimes, we like asking why not."

The whole thing seemed harmless, and the more Joy learned the less she understood why anyone would feel the need to be secretive about it. What could be safer than geeks talking economics?

She resolved to find out. Then, maybe she would understand this other side of Toby. Then, perhaps, seduction would follow.

Afi turned out to be almost as surprising. In Tarawa's odd mixture of traditional island life and modernization, Afi was driven to learn about a world he was likely to never see. When he discovered y^1 he lurked on its website, becoming a silent admirer of its philosophy. It was how he acquired the background to identify Toby as the founder.

Working at Toby's desk, he'd seen notes and articles another would have ignored. Afi was curious, thinking he and Toby were like-minded fans, which would have been a wonderful discovery. But the office and computer had far more about y^1 than made sense for any fan. Afi finally connected the dots. Go figure. He'd run onto a random boat looking for help and been rescued by his own online hero.

Once he was sure he knew the truth, he hadn't been able to resist posing the question that Toby ran as a banner across the top of the site. "What is y raised to the power of one?"

Toby didn't appear to hold Afi's detective work against him, once he discovered the sincerity of his admiration. After a day of intense discussion, the two made their peace. The conversation returned to stopping a man from making masses of money by inflicting misery on young people.

"We could start by just rescuing the older ones," Toby said. "I think we're guilty of kidnapping if we take those under eighteen. How many of the boys do you think are legal age?"

Afi shook his head. "It's hard for me to judge. I know two boys were nineteen because their parents signed something special so they could be held. At least six of the boys were only fourteen or fifteen. One said he was kidnapped on his fourteenth birthday."

"How about we go at this the more obvious way," Joy said. "If most parents wouldn't leave their kids there if they knew what was going on, why don't we pass along the facts."

"Who's going to believe us?" Afi asked.

"Anyone who sees the photos and views the videos," she said. "We go back and capture information from a distance. There's some serious video equipment here. I think we could produce a hell of a CD. Individual families will recognize their own, and see the pain they're in."

"How are you going to know where to send them?" Afi asked.

"Break into the office and get addresses," Toby said.

"Or find a way to get near each kid and ask him?" Joy said.

Afi shook his head.

"I think our recon mission with Zane established none of those will work. But, you know, there is one way to get every student's home address." Afi was pleased with himself. "Not only are the students not allowed to talk to their families, but the families can't send the students care packages. They make two exceptions: the student's birthday and Christmas. Everybody gets a box at Christmas, and the day they arrive is one of the few joyful moments there. Last year, those packages came in on the weekly supply truck. You know what every box had?"

Joy nodded. "A back address."

That was enough for Toby. "We're going to Samoa. I bet we can put together a CD worth sending to every parent. "

With that plan, they began to close up the y^1 headquarters to set sail to the southwest.

******

Zane had a meeting with Peter once a week now. Peter's admin labeled it as "mentoring" on both of their calendars. She was a kindly older woman who took her role as gatekeeper seriously, and Zane wondered if she had guessed anything yet about Peter's health.

Peter made a wide variety of documents available to Zane so he could carry out his work learning to be Peter's eyes and ears. Zane read about Dr. Hulson's postgraduate work, his brief time as a professor, and his original research back in the sixties. The seventies brought brilliant breakthroughs, FDA approvals, and the patents that launched Penthes. Soon after came lawsuits against imitators, lawsuits from the dissatisfied, and lawsuits against and from employees as the company congealed. It seemed Penthes had a sort of belligerent "so sue me" style about it from the beginning, but the scrappiness was more charming in a new company fighting for its existence.

Zane found old newspaper society write-ups on the Hulsons and biographical information on children Pete and Paula as they passed through their teen years and married. There were dozens of local tributes to Peter, and to his company. By the time Zane made it through the first ten years of Penthes' existence he was bored. Time to change tactics.

He went hunting for news of Pete's death at sea, and discovered a goldmine of information. The incident received a fair amount of press in Chicago, not only because of the family's local prominence, but also because of Pete's idea of sailing around the International Date Line on New Year's Day.

An employee named Nicolas cared for Pete's boat and had disappeared with him. There had been no distress call and no one deemed the men missing until a couple of weeks later when they didn't arrive in Tahiti, a thousand miles to the south.

Family members compared notes and realized no one had received a message since New Year's Eve, but it was normal not to hear from Pete when he was at sea. Both men were excellent sailors, neither likely to be drunk or careless, and the boat was large, well equipped, and highly sea worthy.

Search and rescue teams combed the open sea between Millennium Island and Tahiti for weeks, with frequent reports making the local papers. In the end, both U.S. and local authorities gave up hope and the Hulson family financed additional searches. All nearby deserted islands were checked multiple times. About a year later, the main body of the yacht was found floating near the equator, where prevailing winds had carried the dilapidated vessel and left it drifting at sea, covered in barnacles.

Zane read through all the speculations. Those who wished to consider the whole unfortunate business an act of nature settled on a rogue wave or a large sea creature catching the twosome off guard, perhaps while they were making a risky repair or maneuver. There were a few who went with a midnight swim and sharks.

Meanwhile, those of a more suspicious nature blamed the employee Nicolas. He was a divorced man with few ties in Chicago, and he'd received three large sums of money over the couple of years before the accident. His family, involved in shipping, had means of its own, and said the money came from his now deceased grandmother in Greece who'd handed out large sums to her favorite grandchildren before her death.

The more suspicious thought Nicolas had blackmailed Pete, or someone else in the Hulson family. Pete was rumored to be in a relationship with the female director of marketing at his firm. *Really?*

These more cynical folks went with the theory that Nicolas had asked for money one time too many, leaving room for plenty of scenarios. A fight combined with some sort of natural emergency? An accidental death of either man, combined with remorse or panic and problems at sea? Perhaps Pete had tired of paying and threatened to expose Nicolas for the blackmailer he was. In that case, perhaps murder *had* been involved, followed by Nicolas' unsuccessful attempt to take the boat and start a new life.

Another theory held that Nicolas managed to steal the money from Penthes, and Pete might have confronted him on the trip. To no one's surprise, the Hulson family preferred the idea of theft over blackmail, but an army of accountants was at a loss to figure out how the deed was done.

The widowed Sylvia Hulson finally acknowledged in an interview that she knew of her husband's affair, and he knew she knew. While no one was happy with the situation, blackmail made no sense. She begged for the public to leave her alone.

Although neither man's body was found, the wreckage did include shreds of blood-soaked cloth tangled in with the ropes. Perhaps the cloth was used as bandages? The sun and sea had deteriorated it to the point where no analysis was possible.

There was speculation one man or the other had survived, and, due to the nature of their falling out, had elected to hide. That possibility was intolerable to Peter Sr., and he spent considerable money searching the South Seas for years for any sign that either man lived.

In the end, Dr. Hulson was advised by not one but three private firms that the chances of either man eluding detection had been reduced to nothing. In 2003, Dr. Hulson called off the search, and focused his energy elsewhere. The story never made it into print again and Dr. Hulson's employees began to pretend like Pete had never existed.

Only one small article printed near the end of the final search effort contained something surprising. It was a fluff piece comparing the Hulsons with other prominent families who'd suffered multiple tragedies. Zane found the sensationalist tone of the article offensive, but it did mention a trio of tragedies occurring in each family. A trio? What else had happened?

******

The Samoan Tropical Retreat Academy could only be accessed by land with a demanding hike. It was tricky to find by sea. If Zane hadn't led the Miss Demeanor crew there earlier, they couldn't have found it from shore. Toby didn't want to leave his boat anchored close to the school so he planned to leave it with friends and rent a small sailboat to get there. His old-fashioned walkie-talkies would suffice where cell phones were problematic and could leave a trace.

Also, this time Toby would come armed. Not with guns, they had to be surrendered upon entry everywhere in the Pacific, rendering them largely useless. The years had taught Toby what he could get by with: fishing knives, heavy steel bars used as boat parts, aerosol sprays that blinded, a first-aid kit with at least three items that could render a man unconscious in seconds and another that would leave one vomiting uncontrollably, duct tape, and several small stun guns which doubled as flashlights. He armed his crew, and discussed with them how to use every weapon available.

Thanks to the tropical climate, much of the school was outside, and Afi would take off on foot to capture anything useful from a safe distance. Moving solo, he could remain undetected while he spent up to three days on his stealth mission, relying on the water and food stuffed into Joy's backpack. Toby gave him a small GPS device and asked him to secure it well.

Meanwhile, Joy and Toby would intercept the weekly truck bringing supplies. Typically, the school had the boys hike the three miles out to meet the truck and then carry the goods on their backs over the steep terrain back to the school. The boys were bound together loosely by their wrists for the hike, ostensibly to promote teamwork. It also discouraged escape.

This particular day, the truck would be a little late because Toby and Joy would be sitting in the road, looking for help.

When the truck stopped, a large Samoan man got out. Toby was lying on his side moaning. A distressed Joy said it must have been either the food or water they'd taken on their hike, and could they please get a ride back into town. The man let Toby lie down in the back of the truck, while offering Joy a seat up front. As soon as the back door closed, Toby set to work on the addresses. Up front, Joy made conversation and soon had learned all about the Samoan man's family.

The boys were waiting at the usual meeting point, backpacks empty in anticipation of being filled, but the excitement of receiving something from home was lightening the mood. Joy stayed in the truck, discretely photographing the boys strung together like criminals. As the boxes were offloaded, she hit the record button as the three accompanying school officials tossed the boxes around between them, over the bound boys' heads, joking about breaking the contents and laughing they would confiscate anything good to eat before the boxes were distributed. "Don't worry. We'll leave you the underwear and socks," they laughed. "The sweets from mom, those are our reward for looking out for the likes of you."

Joy noticed at least two of the boys blinking back tears at the men's jokes. Hell, a box of anything for Christmas might have been the only thing to look forward to for weeks for these kids. In the end, there was a box for every boy save one, an older teen who shrugged like he didn't care.

As the truck driver unloaded the last of the other supplies, he asked Toby if he was doing better. "Who are you talking to?" The school official in charge of the group was suspicious and headed to the back of the truck. "Who is that?" he demanded to know.

"Some tourist sick and needing a ride," the truck driver said. "Don't worry. He doesn't have any idea where he is. I'm just taking him back to town."

The school official shook his head. "Stupid tourists."

When the driver finally dropped off Joy and a still doubled-over Toby, Joy thanked him and offered to pay for gas.

"You've had enough trouble for one day," the man said, shrugging off the money and leaving his two passengers standing outside of a nice little resort where they were not really staying.

Once the driver was gone Toby stood up straight. "Let's get one of those motorbikes they rent here and get you back to the boat so you can sort through what we've got. I'll see if I can raise Afi on the walkie-talkie. If he's got anything at all, we're good to go. There's no sense in him spending any more time out there."

Once they were on the scooter, Toby turned around to face his passenger and kissed her on the lips.

"You were wonderful back there," he said, and then he turned forward and headed down the road. He looked in the rear view mirror and was glad to see Joy grinning in delight.

A few hours later a relieved Afi was climbing onto the back of Toby's rental scooter, happy not to be sleeping on the ground that night after all.

"How much stuff did you get?" Toby asked before he started the engine. "Don't worry if it's not much. I think what Joy and I have will work fine."

"Not as fine as what I have," Afi said. "I hadn't realized they only let good boys go on the weekly hike, because it gets sympathizers out of the way so the bad apples can be dealt with appropriately. You know, for their own good."

"In that case," Toby said, "our information should be plenty eye-opening."

******

Zane was so engrossed in his research he barely got packed in time for the flight to Texas. His dad met him at the airport because his mom was in Nigeria for her job. At least his dad thought she

110

was; no one had heard from her for days. According to Teddie, there were issues about which Dad was not being forthcoming.

In spite of that, Teddie seemed less defined by her adolescent anger than she'd been last summer. Was something better? Or were love, time, and common sense all working their slow magic to ease Teddie into adulthood?

Ariel arrived the next day and Zane took her out for a birthday drink. "What do you think is happening with Mom?" he asked. "Dad doesn't even know when to expect her. Do you think they're having problems?"

"No." Ariel shook her head with more certainty than Zane felt she was entitled to have. "They're not and Mom's fine. But there's something odd. With you too," she said.

Yeah right. Zane wanted to tell Ariel about Afi and the surprising way he stayed in Zane's thoughts. He wanted to tell her about Peter Hulson and the weird drama at Penthes past and present. He wanted to describe the rhythm of the waves as he rode in a boat over the Pacific Ocean and tell her of all his oddities and moral dilemmas. But it was so much. He didn't know where to start.

"We're a weird family," he said. "How's college going for you?" She smiled with understanding.

Zane's mother made it home Christmas day and his relieved father insisted the whole family meet her at the airport. She looked exhausted as she exited the secured area, and Zane was afraid she was going to cry.

"Group hug!" Teddie said, jumping into the awkward moment. They all obliged, arms around each other laughing and walking and hugging and exchanging greetings and not caring how odd the whole thing was.

Yes, every family has its own definition of normal.

As the happy huddle moved over to the baggage claim carousel, Zane thought he rather liked the sense of normal he'd been given.

******

Miss Demeanor only made it as far as Fakaofo Island before the winds turned stronger and came from the north. Toby was concerned and headed in toward the island's coral shelf. He dropped anchor, pulling down the sails while complaining there was no passage through the reef for them to take better shelter. In half an hour the sky went from cerulean blue to a fuming dark grey. The wind wailed like an indignant cat stuck outside while large raindrops splat hard against the boat.

They gathered below and Toby pulled out his better tins of food while Joy made something to drink. The three of them celebrated Christmas rolling with the sea, eating canned shrimp lo mein and drinking lemonade made from a powdered mix.

They'd been too busy planning the escapade at the Samoan school to think of gifts. With the possibility of days of storm ahead of them, followed by a week of sailing, they opted to use a single lantern and no other electronics.

Toby pulled out a deck of cards and they played cribbage as they finished off their meal with roasted cashews. As Joy watched Toby's weathered hands deal out the cards, she thought it was the best Christmas she'd ever had.

January 2010

10. Avoiding Trouble

Right after the holidays the marketing department at Penthes was filled with anticipation of the big event. Twenty-three doctors, eighteen wives, and one husband were scheduled to attend. Brenda had hoped for a slightly better turnout, but her strategy of an exotic location had paid off in the way that counted most. Nearly all of the most influential doctors had accepted.

Raju and his group were relieved to have done their part as the new patent was received on time. Penthes was poised to be a leader in the emerging field of treating anger and rebellion issues in adolescents. Of course, marketing had begun work months ago to ensure several of Penthes' more dependable doctors provided testimonials indicating the drug showed evidence of lessening the feelings of alienation and hostility sometimes experienced by young people as they made their way through the early teen years. Anecdotes of domestic anguish being replaced by happy family moments were interspersed.

Chloe finished reading one of the more heartwarming articles and threw the magazine down in disgust on the table in the break room as Zane walked in to grab a cup of coffee.

"If this shit is so good, why the hell don't we put it in the drinking water at every high school?" she asked.

"Seeing as the product has already been proven to alleviate sadness, why don't we put it in the city's water supply, too? That way mom and dad can be happier."

Chloe looked hard at Zane. "We're in the wrong profession, aren't we?"

Zane shrugged. "I think I could get behind developing drugs to help people with serious mental issues, but there's not enough money in doing that. People would rather pay me to market what we have."

"Not enough crazy people." Chloe laughed. "Some days, the evidence seems to the contrary."

"Yeah. Look Chloe, I'm not cut out for this any more than you are."

"Then it's too bad my grandfather has latched on to you."

Zane was surprised she knew.

"Zane, everybody knows," Chloe said when she saw his surprised expression. "You meet with him once a week. Raven tells me even Brenda isn't sure what he's got you working on. Neil hates you. Everyone knows he's been turning over rocks looking for someone who knows a way to hurt you. The people in research all hate you, too, because you managed to weasel your way out of being their serf and into traveling to Fiji and having weekly chats with the president of the company."

Chloe filled her mug with hot water. "I come to work every day expecting to find you've been fired or hospitalized, or your body's been found in the dumpster. Yet so far nobody's touched you. And you, you just show up every day with that calm demeanor of yours, do your job, make a few cynical jokes, treat people well, and apparently go home and get a good night's sleep. It's rather charming. I think there might be some sort of betting pool going on in finance about how long you're going to last."

Zane laughed out loud at Chloe's tirade. "What else should I do? Quit?"

"No, keep on being you," Chloe said. "But put more effort into watching your own back."

"Oh believe me, I already am." He wondered how much more he would need to watch it once he had tomorrow's conversation with Dr. Hulson.

******

Joseph Cabrini spent three days in Fiji in August of 2009, and he was still angry about it. How could a man be thwarted by his own daughter?

Joy wasn't even the family he'd hoped for; he'd wanted lots of children Then his wife Gina turned out to be sickly. She had headaches. She had backaches. After Joy was born, his wife sought the priest's permission to use birth control for health reasons. Joseph had thought he'd always have the Roman Catholic Church on his side when it came to this issue, but in the end the Capuchin friars failed him and the little girl became his only child.

While she was never pretty in a classic sense, she was sweet, smart and obedient, and as her father saw his own career peak as a judge, he realized there was one useful career for which Joy was well suited. For while she had the brains for law or medicine, she lacked the ambition. She wanted to help people. She wanted to teach children. She was exactly what one wanted in the wife of a rising politician.

So Judge Cabrini did his best to discourage Joy's interest in the parade of unacceptable young men who sought her attention. Then he found Doug. The nephew of an old friend, the boy was charming and full of ambition. He was already working in investment banking, with excellent family connections and a sense of how to use them. Doug could easily be the son he never had, and maybe, dare he hope it, the son-in-law he could help elect. He just had to help these two young people understand they had so much to offer each other.

Joy and Doug began to date. Although Doug seemed to grasp the possibilities, something in Joy resisted loving him. Joseph could feel it. Then Doug worked at charming Joseph's wife. Good instincts. Before long the older lady adored the boy, and that nudged Joy closer to Doug as well.

Then Doug showed his first bit of bad judgment. Joy caught him in bed with some bimbo. Stupid on the boy's part, but he played the contrite suitor, and after enough flowers, gifts and apologies there was talk of an engagement. The young couple looked at rings.

Then Joy went out drinking with girlfriends and ran into Doug and some woman entwined around each other in a corner booth of a bar. What was with this concept of a girls' night out, anyway? His wife had never needed to consume alcohol in public without him.

This time there were no tears, but a more frightening silence. Within the week, Joy announced she had applied to the Peace Corps and intended to go halfway around the globe. After a month in Fiji, Joy broke her mother's heart with an email saying she didn't love Doug and never would. Gina cried for hours.

Joseph Cabrini, however, knew love could come and go and come again. He also knew spending two years in the Peace Corps was pretty useless, unless you cared about public opinion. Then it was admirable. It was, in fact, the perfect thing for your wife to have done.

Joseph bided his time, assuring both Doug and Gina that when Joy came home he would see to it she regained her senses. Then Joy refused to come home.

So Judge Cabrini had traveled for two days to have an important talk with his daughter. Once there, he discovered she'd abandoned over half of her possessions and left on a boat with complete strangers, running from him like he was the devil himself. Would she really rather remain penniless than let her father reason with her?

When he responded by trying to find her, she did the one thing that had always severed daughters from their father's control. She married. In this case it was a man she found on some godforsaken atoll in the middle of the Pacific, and she had pictures sent to the newspapers. An angry Judge Cabrini knew no amount of annulment, contrived mental breakdown, or other spin could undo the damage. Joy was no longer the ideal political wife. Doug knew it too, and he moved on. Gina and Joseph grieved as if their only child had died.

True, she emailed them from an untraceable location a few weeks before Christmas, telling them she was safe and happy and hoped someday they would accept her decision. Joseph suspected Gina responded to the email, even though he told her not to bother.

******

Dr. Hulson looked forward to Zane's 8:00 a.m. Wednesday mentoring appointment, even though every week, true to both his assignment and his professed preference for honesty, the boy came to Peter's office armed with uncomfortable questions and disconcerting facts. He was doing the job he was asked to do, even if it made Peter feel oddly like a man sitting in judgment of his own life. Yes, that had been a good idea. No, that had worked poorly.

The process of information exchange and evaluation was giving him something better than closure. It was giving him a sense of power as the cancer in his liver moved outside of his control. He couldn't make the wildly multiplying cells of his own organ behave, but he could assess what he'd accomplished, and no riotous tumor could stop him from doing so.

The first Wednesday after the holidays, Zane came with one of the questions Peter had been dreading. "Why does nobody ever mention Joel?"

"Right. Joel."

Zane noticed Peter was starting to lose weight. He wondered how long it would be before the man's changing health would be noticeable to everyone.

"Among other things, I was curious as to how long it would take you to find out about him and how much you'd be able to learn. You should know one of the reasons Brenda has maintained her position at this firm is the fine job she did of minimizing the publicity about Joel over a decade ago. It saved me a lot of personal pain, and, of course, was the best thing for the company." Peter's voice had dropped to almost a mumble.

"He was your grandson?"

Peter nodded in response. "Yes, Chloe's older brother. It was April, and he'd turned sixteen a month earlier. She was thirteen, and she was the one who found him."

Zane gulped. It had not occurred to him his friend could have played such a traumatic role in what looked to be the family's best-kept secret.

"I'm sure you found out first how my wife died from a staph infection in early 1998. Minor surgery gone bad. She was only sixty-one. It happened so fast. We were all in shock."

Yes, Zane had found a variety of articles praising Darlene Hulson for her work with charities and mourning the loss of a lady who used her wealth, free time, and influence to try to do good.

"I made the money, but she was the emotional center of the family. She kept everyone talking to each other, behaving well, it's hard to explain. After she died, things fell apart."

The sorrow in Peter's eyes was fresh. Zane wished he'd not needed to bring this up. But Peter kept talking.

"Joel was a funny kid. Really smart but kind of, I don't know, skittish. Easily upset. Pete and Sylvia did okay with him, but he was really close to my wife. He turned fifteen a few days after she died, and that's when he started to have these panic attacks. Out of nowhere, he'd be gasping for air and couldn't breathe. It was embarrassing. For him too, I guess."

Zane tried to imagine the boy, his agitation level rising around his demanding grandfather as he fought an oncoming attack.

"Here I was, head of one of the premier pharmaceutical companies devoted to mental health. And here was my grandson, in need of help."

"You put him on one of Penthes' drugs?" *Okay, this was starting to make sense.* When the man said nothing, Zane pushed. "One that wasn't approved for adolescents?"

"Yes. I did." The old voice was sharp now with anger and defensiveness. "I did it because I wanted to help him, damnit. Nobody told me about these drugs causing young people to commit suicide. It was barely a statistic back then. Some of our folks had heard of the problem, but I had no idea. I'd have watched him like a hawk if I'd known."

"Was he suicidal before? Depressed?" Zane tried to steer the conversation back to the facts.

"No, nothing like that. Just a nervous kid. Apparently some small percentage of the time, and we don't know why, this type of drug pushes an otherwise non-suicidal young person to take his own life. It's not the classic cry for help, but more like a genuine desire for death, because they go straight to a successful method. No one understands why."

Peter now had his head in his hands. "After a decade full of lawsuits, the medication now carries a black box warning. The doctors, parents, and kids all know about this quirk of the medication. Everybody's alert. It hardly happens anymore because it's so closely monitored."

"*Hardly* happens?"

"Yeah." Peter had caught the emphasis on hardly. "You can imagine how it would've looked for one of the major mental health geniuses of this century to have been responsible for his own grandson's death, right?" Peter sounded like he was asking for forgiveness. Or understanding.

"So you and your marketing department did everything possible to hush up Joel's death?"

Peter nodded. "It was intimated there were medical problems and the boy died from complications. No details were ever released. Brenda knew lots of people. Neil was effective. My money bought cooperation. The story circulated was that the death was so similar to, and so close in time to, his grandmother's demise that the family did not want more public sorrow."

Peter had tears in his eyes. "There were six people at his funeral. Six!"

Zane didn't respond, but Peter was waiting for something. Finally, Zane understood. He was supposed to guess.

"The six people. They were you, Joel's dad Pete, Joel's mom Sylvia, and his sister Chloe. His aunt Paula and a chaplain? You didn't even let anyone from his mother's family attend?"

Peter nodded. He liked it when Zane solved his little puzzles.

"I heard Sylvia's people did something private at her parents' house. They haven't been too fond of the Hulsons since. His school agreed to pass on holding a memorial service. At first they insisted on it, saying his friends needed closure. But we couldn't risk the press coverage. I had to donate a whole damn building to keep them from holding anything."

"There was a short obituary in the paper," Zane said.

"Very short."

"So to protect Penthes' good name, Joel was only mourned in absolute private? The circumstances around his death became the most unmentionable subject in the company?" Zane couldn't imagine what such secrecy could do to the grieving process.

"That's right. Until a few months later of course, when Sylvia was still barely speaking to any of us, Chloe seldom spoken at all, and my now disturbed son Pete turned to Brenda for comfort. I don't think that worked out so well. Then he disappeared at sea and *his* death became the most unmentionable subject in the company."

"Was he on antidepressants too?" Zane asked. Peter got the implication.

"No. He was old enough, of course, to not be at risk, but he refused to take medication and refused to let Chloe do so either. I know Paula was heavily medicated for years. I don't know what Sylvia does."

"How about you?" Zane asked, suddenly curious. "Do you take your own medicines?"

"I don't need them," Peter said.

******

Barantiti's mother Ruti loved her church, loved her husband Biribo, and loved her three daughters and her two sons. She thought that much love should be big enough to cover all possibilities, but it turned out it wasn't.

The best thing about her husband Biribo was he was a man who didn't like trouble and no trouble was a good thing. The down side of this was Biribo often had the opinions of whomever he spoke to last. When he talked to her, he acknowledged their son Barantiti was different, but added that a parent had to accept that.

When he talked to the other elders of the church, though, he sang a different tune. Some things were not to be tolerated. Perhaps something needed to be done.

Then had come that horrible day when Afi, as Barantiti insisted on calling himself, decided he wanted to be open with his parents. Ruti had known no good would come of that.

For honesty meant Biribo would have trouble. He'd face conflict in the community and the church, and while Biribo was basically a good man, Ruti knew he couldn't deal with so much trouble. So when others in the church suggested the school on Samoa, even Ruti had been happy. Afi loved Samoa. Maybe they would teach him more about fire dancing at the school?

She and Biribo had little money, but Afi qualified for some scholarship. The school wanted to have a boy from the islands to provide variety in the brochures. Biribo signed a release form so they could photograph Afi as much as they liked.

Ruti was excited to tell Afi the news but when she went to find him she discovered he'd already gone. Without saying farewell? She was assured this was how the school worked. They were told they wouldn't hear from Afi for a while, but not to worry. Then they heard nothing from Afi for many months.

One day her cousin told her to hurry over to the town of Bairiki. Afi hated the school and had escaped. He'd arrived in Kiribati with I-Matang friends who'd helped him. He'd fallen in love with a girl on the boat and was going to marry her. A girl?

Ruti was confused by every part of this story, but she made her way to the cousin's husband's office where she'd cried and hugged her son. Ruti watched the quick ceremony, which had none of the beautiful Kiribati tradition about it, and felt sad, but she wished her boy and the girl well. Wanting to give him the best chance, she gave him all the money she could get from her cousin and then kept her silence so he and his new wife could escape.

After the New Year, the school sent word through the church that Afi had disappeared and they'd been unable to find him. They assumed he'd returned home. Ruti could no longer hide what she knew, so she told her husband her story.

Biribo was angry with her of course, but not as angry as another man may have been. If she'd spoken up, there would have been trouble all around. Now, with the marriage done and the boy gone, Biribo's life stayed simple. He could be sad at the turn of events, and happy his son had run away from school to marry a girl. That part of the story he would tell many.

Ruti had a mother's sense that her son was no more interested in marriage to a woman after attending the school than he would have been before. She thought perhaps he was trying to help this Joy person. Afi had a tender heart for those in need.

A week after she told her husband of the marriage, her cousin came to visit. Her cousin could read, while Ruti could not, so the cousin read her an email from Afi telling his parents he was safe and happy now but the school had been more horrible than they could imagine. He was sorry about the rushed marriage but he was trying to help a friend. She was a good woman, and he hoped they would accept his decision. He would try to write again soon.

Ruti could not read the email, or recognize her son in the printed typeface. But she took the piece of paper and held it tight against her chest and cried, hoping somewhere and somehow her most unusual child was finding happiness.

******

Zane liked to go to thrift stores to find clothes no one would expect Zane Zeitman to wear. The orange-flowered Hawaiian shirt worn by his East Asian-looking alter ego was one such acquisition. Now that Ying, as Zane thought of him, had been at the bar near Penthes several times, always in the same easy to remember shirt, he was recognized by most of the staff and not carded. It made things easier.

Ying liked to drink alone while playing handheld video games, and he often found himself seated near employees of Penthes. Because Zane had looked through the ID photos in the employee database many times, he knew most of his coworkers whether he had met them or not. He knew their departments and what aspects of the company they would know about. It was nice his ability to memorize was turning out to be useful.

Ying was amazed by how unhappy Penthes employees were. Some were well paid. Some had made friends at the company in spite of the culture. Some even enjoyed their particular professional niche in the grand scheme of things. But over and over, the only ones who didn't dislike their job worked for a few people. Zane noted with interest that Gil's direct reports made up one of these contented groups.

Zane decided a manager could make a surprising amount of difference in the lives of others. Sure, everybody bitched about their boss sometimes, but there was a small group of supervisors who looked out for their staff, and their commitment translated into happier employees. The ironic thing to Zane was that this group of bosses tended to have short careers in management. Those who remained there for years seemed to be those who looked out for themselves.

******

Neil expected competence from the people who worked for him, and he had little patience with anything less. Today he had to let Harold, the private detective he hired to look into the Zeitman family, know how disappointed he was in the man's final report. Basically, Harold hadn't been able to find anything of use, in the background of this kid, his parents, or his siblings. Neil didn't believe it. Everybody had secrets, or at least awkward moments in their history. Everybody.

As Neil read the correspondence from Harold in more detail, he found Harold to be adamant about the Zeitmans being above reproach. Neil also found it odd that Harold had only charged a minimum fee and elected not to turn in his usual well-padded expense report. Strangest of all, Harold was going on an extended vacation and wouldn't be available for other work for some time.

Okay. Neil recognized evasive maneuvers when he saw them. Someone had gotten to Harold and this someone had to be even more persuasive than Neil. And Neil could be quite persuasive.

He hadn't expected the Zeitmans to have a guardian angel. How annoying. Neil was curious about it, but it made no sense to pursue the issue now. There were other avenues for dealing with Zane, and using any of them would be easier than fighting whatever boogeyman had spooked Harold.

Neil went back to his list of approaches. Which one to try next?

******

After five days the weather cleared and the trio began the week-long sail to Toby's island, where he had supplies and equipment to prepare packages for the families with a son attending the Samoan school. This time the winds stayed strong, and the crew made good time. After days of waiting out the storm, they were glad to be on land.

Joy knew how to edit and present the material well, and dove into her work. Toby tended to his home and his group y[1] while Afi searched the internet for students of other Turn Your Teen Around academies.

Toby knew they needed at least two weeks to sail back to American Samoa. Once there, Toby planned to take a commercial flight to Honolulu where their packets would go out securely. With the storm's delay they were cutting it close, given Toby also had minor repairs and supplies to see to before they picked up Zane in early February in Fiji.

Joy wanted to re-enter the U.S, so she volunteered to make the trip to Hawaii instead. It would give Toby more time to deal with his boat and she could look into the paperwork needed to bring Afi in as a spouse. Toby was happy to accept Joy's offer.

Afi sorted through his email and was delighted to find a warm message waiting for him from Zane. There was also an email from his relatives letting him know his parents had received his note and were happy to learn he was well. Afi breathed a little easier. The school had informed his parents that they were removing him from the school roster. This was so good.

Now that his own recapture was not an issue, Afi realized he could use the upcoming time in Pago Pago to look into the local fire knife dancing scene. Maybe he could learn a few new moves and even participate. Better yet, if Zane arrived a day or two ahead of all the doctors like he planned, then Afi could show him around and there would be time to get reacquainted.

******

Brenda was nearly frantic with last-minute preparations, and she was struggling with the lack of cooperation she was getting from the school in Samoa. A week before the conference she walked into Zane's office exasperated.

"Zane. You were there. What is it with these people? For God's sake. We leave Pago Pago and sail seven boats into Apia. Then they make us sail around the island and get everybody into little dinghies like we're being taken to some isolated prison? I can't believe they don't have roads in."

"They don't have roads in." Zane's voice was soothing. "Brenda, it is like a prison. This is not a pleasant place no matter what the brochure says. Plus, whatever you think of the school, they can't have kids running away. It's a little like Alcatraz."

Brenda rolled her eyes. "Thank heavens we decided to leave the wives shopping in Apia. What's the lone husband doing?"

"Gil has set him up fishing for the day."

"Thank you Gil. The less people we schlep to this prison school, the better."

"It's going to be a delicate dance, Brenda. We're not there to criticize the school, but the people who run it are not big believers in using drugs. They're more of the fix-things-with-fresh-air-and-tough-love ilk and they see our approach as a last resort. Meanwhile, we're telling doctors that if our approach fails, a school like this is the last resort. So while they're letting us visit, they aren't stupid, and they aren't greeting us with open arms."

"Is this going to be more trouble than it's worth?" Brenda wondered aloud. "I don't have such a good feeling about it."

"It's too late to back out. We used the location of this school as a justification for the trip. Now too much of the itinerary is planned around it. I say we make the best of it and go for the real home run when the conference concludes in Fiji."

"Of course." Brenda took a breath. "You're so sensible Zane. It's why I enjoy having you in this department. God knows this is the most expensive thing we've ever done. It has got to turn into the most successful marketing event ever."

11. The Conference

Zane woke up in Apia feeling irritable. He'd stayed out too late, drank too much, and was running late for breakfast.

Yes, he and Afi did have a wonderful couple of nights together in Pago Pago, when he first arrived in the Pacific and his only duty had been to finalize preparations. Now that his coworkers and all the attendees had shown up, though, the situation was more demanding. He, Brenda, Gil, and two senior sales reps were serving as professional herders. Their first tasks had been to get the group of doctors and spouses to the hotel, made sure everyone liked their dinner, get everyone up in time for breakfast the next morning, and put them all on boats departing for Apia.

Zane's intent was to focus on his job until the conference ended in Fiji. Miss Demeanor would pick him up there, and he would enjoy a week at sea with his friends, and more time with Afi. Until then, his work needed his full attention.

However, the morning the doctors set sail for Apia, Afi heard about a fire dancing event in Apia he wanted to attend. As Penthes' little fleet of chartered boats prepared for the half-day sail from American Samoa to Samoa under a sunny sky, Afi persuaded Toby to sail over to Apia too, so he could perform in the event. Miss Demeanor sailed faster, so Afi was waiting for Zane when he came ashore, inviting him to come party once all the guests were herded off to bed.

Zane should have turned him down, and he knew it. But ….

After the late night partying, he'd been with the baffled Afi at three in the morning when Miss Demeanor was nowhere to be found. Afi's room for the night was aboard the boat, and he couldn't believe Toby would take off and leave him. Zane couldn't believe it either but he was more worried about Toby. Afi could stay with him, borrow fresh clothes, and seek out information the next day. But where was Toby?

In the morning, as the irritable Zane rushed through brushing his teeth, he noticed a slow drizzle outside. Great. Well, Toby had warned him his conference was during the rainy season.

"Look, I've got to go," he said to Afi as he headed out the door, hoping Brenda wouldn't be too annoyed at his tardiness. "Stay here and sleep in, checkout's been handled. You've got our group's satellite phone number, so call me if you can't find Toby. I don't know what else to do. Afi, I'm really sorry, but I'm probably already in trouble with my boss."

Afi still smelled of smoke and fuel from his performance, which had won him plenty of accolades last night. He gave Zane a groggy answer.

"It's okay. Go. I'm sure Toby's back by now and Joy is coming in from Hawaii tonight. We'll work things out."

Zane headed downstairs trying to think of the best thing to say to Brenda. Gil greeted him in the lobby instead.

"Is Brenda with you?"

"Of course not." Zane was confused. "She's not here?"

"Called her room three times. Got a couple of issues I need her to make a decision on. You—I figured I could let you get some beauty sleep, not that you look all that much more beautiful." Gil chuckled.

"I can't imagine where she went," Zane said. Gil agreed. It was so unlike Brenda not to be the first one down for breakfast, make-up perfect, jewelry just right, the smiling face of Penthes as she greeted each doctor personally.

It was then Zane looked up and saw the policemen headed towards them.

******

Joy spent two days visiting with her mother in Honolulu, shopping, seeing sites, and going to beaches. She didn't think the two of them had ever had so much fun together. Joy had been surprised when her mother responded to her email, and even more so when she agreed to this visit. How had she managed it? The woman said she simply left her husband a note saying she was meeting Joy in Hawaii for a few days and left the house with a small bag.

With that single act, Gina seemed to have found the little girl inside herself, and to have rediscovered playtime. Joy noticed her mother's head and back didn't bother her once during their time together.

Before her mother's arrival, Joy had mailed the packets with the photographs and the CDs, along with the letter from Afi introducing himself as a former student who was hoping the recipients would recognize their own children, understand they had been misled, and act to intervene. She had mailed copies to the addresses Afi had found for former attendees of all of the Turn Your Teen Around schools who had gone public on various social-networking sites. She mailed copies to two former girlfriends of her own, asking them to hang onto the materials for safekeeping. Finally, she sent a copy to Zane at his home and at work.

She was now checked out of the hotel and having one last lunch with her mom in the coffee shop, saying goodbye before she headed off to catch the four o'clock flight back to Pago Pago. She and her mother talked a little of her marriage, and she was up front about her affection for Afi and the nature of their arrangement.

Her mother worried INS would hound them and Joy would get into trouble. Joy confided she was prepared to live with Afi to avoid scrutiny and willing to orchestrate a slow and believable divorce. She owed him that much for helping her. Her mother was offering her help when the man at the front desk spotted Joy and came into the restaurant.

"You checked out of Room 425, didn't you?" he asked. She nodded. "I just took a phone call from your husband. He asked me to look for you. He has to talk to you right away."

"Oh dear," Joy said, a little amused. She gave her mom a what's-a-wife-to-do shrug. "Did he say what the problem was?"

"Yes, ma'am." The man swallowed hard. "He said you need to look into getting him a good lawyer. He's been arrested."

Joy thought of Tropical Retreat Academy and the materials she had mailed two days ago. Had some been delivered already? Was the school having them arrested for trespassing? For libel?

"Good grief. What's he been arrested for?"

The man was trying to keep any expression off of his face. "For murder."

******

Lola Zeitman awoke the day after her fiftieth birthday thinking how wonderful her life was. Her husband had hosted the nicest party the night before and her sister and older daughter had traveled to be there. Only Zane had been absent, having flown to Samoa a few days earlier for the conference being hosted by his company.

Lola had missed him, but she was glad he was doing something so interesting. She made her way through the work day, feeling as if nothing could dent her sense of well-being.

It was late afternoon and she was finishing up a small detail of her interpretation when the phone in her office rang. It was Alex and she knew something was wrong.

"Lola, Zane just called. He needs help."

"Oh dear. Is he hurt?"

"No, he's been arrested."

"Oh shit." Lola ran through the list of most likely offenses. Drunk and disorderly? Public indecency for a poorly planned swim in the buff? Surely he hadn't taken marijuana with him. Oh Zane.

"Lola. It's serious." Alex's voice was calm but she sensed his rising panic. "Zane thinks he's being charged with murder."

******

Half the students were tasked with rising early that morning and picking up trash along the beach before the visitors arrived. The boys already knew they weren't to approach the visitors or try to communicate with them in any way. These were doctors from

America, here to meet with Mr. Hadley, and any contact was forbidden, including eye contact. The staff would be watching. The consequences would be severe.

The boys were quiet and discouraged as they made their way along the cloud-covered beach with the usual lightweight cords linking them together. For work like this they were bound by their left ankle so they could use their hands to perform tasks.

They started with the trash nearest to the tree line and were paying little attention to the familiar surroundings of the small bay when one of the boys gasped and pointed to the shore. Twelve young men looked up. Twelve young men stepped forward. Twelve young men opened their mouths and stared at what had floated onto the beach. It was the body of a well-dressed, middle-aged white woman with curly brown hair and lots of makeup and jewelry.

The police in Apia had a helicopter they seldom used. Mark Hadley had donated the vehicle, and Mark Hadley called early that morning and demanded police get there immediately, remove the body, and tend to the problem before his visitors arrived mid-morning. Samoan police were on the beach within the hour.

Meanwhile Va'iga, who had paramedic training, pulled the body further ashore and determined there was no pulse, no warmth, and no possibility of resuscitation. There was also no purse or identification. She appeared to have been a visitor to Samoa.

By the time police arrived, a soft drizzle had begun, making the beach increasingly damp and uncomfortable. A radio check with customs confirmed a group of forty-seven doctors from some U.S. drug company had sailed in yesterday on several charter sailboats from Pago Pago. A woman who fit this description was part of the group. A copy of the passport photo was being sent.

The woman's name was Brenda Mills. Mark reluctantly acknowledged she was none other than the same demanding lady who'd been making the arrangements for today's visit. He reminded the police that he preferred to avoid publicity and let the police know he was not pleased with how long this was taking.

The police assured him he no longer needed to worry about hiding this situation from today's guests. Today's guests, the police informed him, would all be among the suspects.

To start the investigation, one officer was questioning the boys who had found the body on the beach, and was trying to discover why they had been tied together and had to approach the victim in unison. Mark made a mental note to blame the ankle contraption on his assistant headmaster Va'iga as a one-time piece of poor judgment. Perhaps a small gift to the police department could help the officers see the wisdom of not needing to mention it in their report? A nice speedboat perhaps? Surely the department could use a speedboat.

The other officer was talking to several fishermen. They'd seen the helicopter land and came ashore to find out what the commotion was about. Their report was most interesting. With bad weather in the forecast, they hadn't seen other boats, fishing or otherwise, anywhere near the bay early that morning. Two different groups *had* noticed a particular boat in the area in the deepening twilight last night. It was a well-known boat these days, with an orange stripe on the side and a bright orange sun on the main sail. It belonged to the man named Toby, who'd helped several villages after the earthquake. He'd had an I-Kiribati boy and a U.S. girl aboard, and also a young man from a U.S. drug company. The same company as the dead woman maybe?

The police radioed back to Apia. Miss Demeanor had indeed entered the country yesterday afternoon with two people aboard: Toby Axton and an I-Kiribati named Afi Siva.

******

As Mark Hadley listened to the fishermen tell the police about Miss Demeanor, he remembered the I-Kiribati kid he'd been persuaded to admit in exchange for goodwill and PR photos.

He didn't think it was a good idea at the time. The kid was a poor fit, not a troublemaker but the sort of earnest, tender-hearted boy who made the school's methods seem even harsher. Worse yet, before Barantiti somehow fled the grounds, no child had ever escaped from one of his schools. Barantiti's disappearance raised hopes among the kids and concerns among the staff. In the end, Mark Hadley decided the boy's absence was a gift in disguise. He'd given word to stop the search, assume the boy had gone home, and consider it good riddance.

But hadn't the boy supposedly escaped on a boat with orange trim? Then weren't Afi and Barantiti one and the same? Perhaps this escaped troublemaker had hidden an evil side after all. What a shame the school hadn't been able to keep him long enough to help him. He would have to make that point with the press, along with the need for more help from the police if a student tried to escape again. See what they are capable of?

"Officer," Mark interrupted the interview with the fishermen. "I may have some useful information on the I-Kiribati boy these fishermen saw. I've good reason to think he might be dangerous."

******

The police in Apia checked the harbor. Miss Demeanor was nowhere to be found and hadn't been seen since the previous day. Toby, her captain, didn't go into town after he cleared customs, and officials assumed he'd spent the evening on the boat. Afi had been seen shopping and eating dinner, and then later he'd been at some fire dancing show in the company of the same young American male who'd been on the boat last autumn. Zane Zeitman.

A police car was dispatched to locate Zane. He was found at his hotel along with all of the other Americans from the drug company. They were finishing breakfast and about to set sail for the trip to the other side of the island. Afi had stayed at the hotel with Zane. Police were going to pick up both young men.

Meanwhile, an all-points bulletin was issued for Miss Demeanor and her captain. The modern sea is nothing more than a wide-open space; open to planes, helicopters, and satellites. Police assured everyone he'd be found.

******

"Yes Officer. What is this concerning?" Gil was polite, even cooperative, but Zane saw his worry.

"We're sorry to inform you that we believe a member of your party has... uh... has..." the man was looking for a better, softer word but failed to find one. "Has been killed. Brenda Mills."

Zane swallowed the bit of toast in his mouth. After that, he felt like he was hearing and seeing everything through gauze. This didn't happen, not to people you knew. Not really.

Gil set down his coffee cup and asked short questions with a calm that impressed Zane. The officer answered politely. Yes, she was definitely dead. Apparently drowned. No sign of struggle. Found just after dawn on the other side of the island. Yes, it could have been an accident, but then how had she gotten over there, why she wasn't dressed for swimming, and how had she drowned in calm waters near shore. Murder, or at least manslaughter or negligent homicide, was considered most likely.

Then the gauze around Zane grew thicker as the officer turned to him. "Locals report you were seen last night in the company of a crew member of the boat Miss Demeanor. That boat was sighted last night after sundown in the bay where Miss Mills was found. It was the only boat seen there. I'm going to need to take you in for questioning. Do you understand you are a murder suspect? Do you know where your companion is?"

"We were both in Apia all evening. I—"

The officer cut him off. "You'll have a chance to tell your story. Right now, I need to..." They all three looked up to see another cop enter the restaurant with a confused Afi in tow. Afi gave Zane an exaggerated shrug of bafflement. Zane shrugged back. Zane turned to Gil. "I swear neither of us had anything to do with this. This is ridiculous."

"Of course you didn't, Zane." Gil looked baffled as well, but he was fighting to be calm. "I'm going to have to get these doctors moved along. I guess I'll send them over to Fiji, but I promise I'll get you some legal help right after that. And we need to do right by Brenda. By her remains I mean." Gil looked overwhelmed at the thought. "It's going to be okay. We'll get this straightened out. I promise."

"Doc," one of the older cops interrupted, wrongly assuming Gil was one of the doctor's in the group. "I don't think you understand the situation. Basically, we've got a dead lady here. It doesn't look an accident, an assault or a robbery. That means somebody wanted her dead. No one in Samoa knew her, and all of you did." The older cop noticed the restaurant had gone quiet and every soul in the place was listening to him.

"So while I'm not going to take you *all* into custody right now, you need to understand. None of you are leaving this country until we say so. At the moment, your entire conference consists of murder suspects."

******

Zane, like most people, hoped to never spend time in jail. However, if it had to happen, then the facility in Apia could have been as good as it got. Used mostly to detain the drunk and disorderly and the odd drug user, Zane was treated with a minimum of indignity. Upon being questioned he'd outlined his entire itinerary since the moment he set foot in Samoa, and he was confident Afi's story would match his and witnesses would support both versions.

He was allowed to make a phone call before lunch, not a right granted the world over he realized, and he opted for his folks. Thankfully his dad answered from late afternoon in Texas, distraught but promising to help. "Be smart. Stay safe. We're not going to rely on your company to take care of you, son. We'll start looking into bail and a lawyer for you, too."

Zane was surprised when only a couple of hours later Neil showed up at the jail to bail him out in person. The COO told him he'd been in route to Fiji when the whole fiasco happened.

"The more I thought about it, the more I felt the conference was too important for someone in upper management not to make an appearance," Neil said. "I chartered a plane to fly me down from Hawaii. Of course I had them divert here as soon as I heard."

He actually gave Zane a bleak smile. "Could this have been a worse disaster?"

Zane supposed not.

******

Afi gave the police a full and honest account of his past evening, even though he was nervous the police might charge him for public drunkenness or for spending the night in a room with another man. Zane had caught his eye and mouthed "truth" before they'd been separated, and Zane was right. The stories needed to match, even if the drunken carousing or public affection with Zane weren't stories Afi was comfortable telling.

He was also allowed a phone call and tried to reach Joy at her hotel in Hawaii, but she'd checked out already and he missed her by minutes. So instead he poured the story out to an uncomfortable desk clerk, who promised to try to find Joy.

He watched while Zane was freed by his fancy U.S. company, and was surprised when not much later a bail bondsman came for him. Joy, or more specifically Joy's mother, had managed to post his bail from Hawaii. It wasn't such a great way to make the acquaintance of one's mother-in-law, but Afi liked the woman already.

******

After two days of questioning everyone, the missing Toby became the police's prime suspect. He'd apparently left the harbor in Apia shortly before sunset, at a time when Afi and Zane were accounted for elsewhere. To the best of anyone's recollection, the boat hadn't returned to the harbor, and Afi and Zane's alibis continued to be good well into the night. So they were both released, in spite of Mark Hadley's insistence that Afi was potentially dangerous.

No other attendee at the conference appeared to have arranged for or had access to transportation to the south shore, eventually removing them all from the list of suspects. Everyone at the Tropical Retreat Academy, of course, provided alibis for each other, which was always something to be wary of, particularly as the woman had died so near the school. But in this case, no connection to the dead woman could be found, other than the fact that the people who ran the school were irritated with her demands concerning the visit the next day. That hardly seemed motive for murder.

No connection between Toby Axton and Brenda Mills could be found either, and police finally concluded the two had met unnoticed, maybe walking along the harbor, and an ensuing sunset cruise between two bored and maybe lonely adults had followed and ended poorly.

Maybe Brenda wanted to see the bay for herself before going over the next day? Maybe Tony had offered to take her? Maybe… it was hard for the police to fathom what sort of maybe could have happened which would have left a fully-dressed woman drowned with no signs of injury anywhere on her body. But when a man ran, leaving friends behind with no explanation, it was the opinion of the police that the man had a reason for running.

The entire conference was allowed to proceed on to Fiji after a couple of days of thorough questioning, made all the more miserable by the incessant rain and the confinement in the hotel. Neil had already been forced to release the chartered cruise ship after agreeing to a substantial partial payment, and he had sprung for flying charter planes down from Hawaii to get the group on to Fiji, where some of the conference could still be salvaged.

Once in Suva, a rather subdued Penthes staff did the best they could with grumpy and unreceptive doctors who never wanted to hear the name Penthes again. It was, as Neil quipped, the most unsuccessful marketing event ever.

February 2010

12. What a Shame

The day before Brenda's memorial service, Chicago was drenched in a cold drizzle, and as temperatures dropped overnight layers of ice began to coat the sidewalks, cars, and roads. The service was moved to 2:00 p.m. to give the city time to salt and gravel the streets.

At a few minutes before two, a dozen Penthes employees huddled together at the back of the room while two family members and a friend stood in a small group near the front. Word was the two closest of kin were a brother with a drinking problem, whom Brenda had avoided for years, and a cousin she'd been close to who had traveled to Chicago to take charge of the proceedings. The friend from college happened to live in the area.

Gil had done his best to coax the thirty-odd people in Brenda's department to attend, but the last-minute weather provided an easy excuse. Zane wasn't sure if attendance at one's funeral was a fair measure of a person's life, given that fame or even fertility could provide an overflowing chapel, but there was something sad about the lack of grievers.

Executives seldom made emotional connections with those at lower levels, it seemed to Zane. An unmarried woman executive saddled with an unfortunate affair in her past probably had zero potential friends at her company. Zane didn't think it was fair, but he bet it was true.

It wasn't like she'd had time for friends elsewhere, either. He knew Brenda sunk her heart into her job and yet Penthes, Inc. wasn't a human being, even if the courts considered it one. Not only did Penthes not have a heart with which to grieve for Brenda, it didn't even have a butt to put in a seat at the funeral home.

The service began with the cousin saying a few words, followed by a mortuary chaplain with the good taste to keep his remarks short and vague. Then Neil stood up to speak. He assured all in attendance how much Brenda would be missed and how deeply the company regretted she'd died while conducting its affairs. He finished with an awkward conclusion about how the perpetrator and his sailboat would be found soon and brought to justice. At least the remark was awkward for Zane, who remained unconvinced Toby had killed Brenda.

He'd watched Toby deal with emergencies, seen his kindness, and heard the man's response when he thought Zane was a threat to Afi. He couldn't imagine a single encounter between Toby and Brenda that led to murder, and he couldn't even contrive an accident in which Toby didn't do the right thing and seek help. He supposed an innocent Toby might run to protect his own privacy, but even that was far-fetched. Toby was smart enough to know how damning his vanishing would appear.

The whole service took less than twenty minutes. As they walked to their cars, Zane wished Chloe had come so he could talk with her. He didn't think she and her grandfather were in the habit of sharing confidences, but he felt like she'd been avoiding him ever since he'd learned about Joel. Of course, the conference and Brenda's death put the last few weeks well out of the realm of the ordinary, so maybe he was misjudging the situation.

He also wished Peter hadn't cancelled their mentoring session this first week back. For once, Zane felt like he could have used Peter as a therapist.

******

Joy was surprised to discover that, as a U.S. citizen, she had no automatic right to live in American Samoa. To enter the territory, a U.S. citizen had to have a way to leave within thirty days, or proof of employment to stay.

Joy allowed herself to use the credit card she never touched to get Afi back to American Samoa, and to purchase two refundable tickets to Honolulu with a departure date in exactly thirty days. She was hoping they wouldn't need them.

She met Afi at the airport with a long hug. After a day in jail Afi looked as shaken and confused as she felt. Joy still couldn't believe Toby had committed a crime, and she kept expecting to see the now familiar orange and white sail out of the corner of her eye.

But Miss Demeanor was nowhere to be found, and Joy knew if she and Afi were going to be allowed to stay in the region, she needed to find work fast. Am. Sam.'s accommodations for tourists were sparse and pricey, but Joy found cheap lodging in another part of town. Between the credit card, her cash, and the money her mother had insisted on giving her in Hawaii, she knew they could get by until their four weeks ran out.

Afi used most of his remaining cash to buy a used bicycle at a thrift store near their rent-by-the-week apartment. Joy was annoyed at the frivolity of the purchase, and as soon as she saw it, she said so.

"I'll be heading out in a few hours on my useless bike to see if they'll let me perform for tips at one of the tourist places. I had this childish idea that bringing in some cash might be helpful."

Oh. She apologized, and that evening as she watched him head off to towards the nice hotels on his beat up bike with his fire knife dancing supplies on his back, she realized she'd sold Afi short. He was an adult capable of contributing to their survival, and she needed to recognize his talents and ingenuity.

Late that night he returned with money in his pocket, and plans for how to do better the next night. All was forgiven as they shared a mattress and the comfort of worrying together.

"I think Toby could have had other reasons to run," Afi said as he and Joy ate from a single bag of popcorn. "You don't know much about the group he heads, but there are reasons y^1 stays hidden and its leader has to be careful."

"All the secrecy seems odd. Leading an internet group is hardly a dangerous lifestyle."

"Think about what his group advocates for," Afi said. "Toby thinks all people should be paid fairly for their work. He doesn't object to good fortune, or to handouts as a way to help people through bad times. He does object to people living their whole lives off of the money made by another."

"I didn't realize he was such a conservative."

"He's not." Afi laughed. "His enemies are those he targets as the biggest affront to a true meritocracy."

"People who spend their lives on welfare? The cycle of poverty?"

"Definitely not. He thinks that's something we need to fix. The real problem is the cycle of wealth."

"What?" Joy was confused, and then she got it. "He has problems with wealthy people who didn't earn the family fortune?"

"Yup. He believes inherited substantial wealth is the single largest problem in our society. He says anyone is entitled to enjoy money, as long as their own skill and hard work produce it. Toby believes wealth needs to end with the person who earns it."

"But that's ridiculous."

"Why? A human being can only spend so much. After that, you're building a dynasty, hoarding money to give power to a small group of people who've done nothing to earn it. Your offspring."

"But you're talking about people's children." Joy was not convinced.

"Look. Most of the world has figured out that just because someone is a capable ruler doesn't mean their child will be. We go find another competent leader instead of accepting the offspring of the last one. We call this new system democracy. Why shouldn't wielding the power and influence of extreme wealth work in a similar way, where the best are selected anew in each generation?"

"How would you ever enforce a change like that?"

"You not only change laws, you change culture. People have to recognize that leaving behind a fortune is bad for the family and wrong for society."

"You think what Toby writes is controversial enough that some super rich guy came after him? Framed him for murder? It sounds a little crazy."

Afi shook his head. "Think about it, Joy. Toby spent the last ten years of his life making this point often and with eloquence.

Many of the people he discussed it with were quite wealthy. Some agreed with him, and their names might surprise you. Others disagreed, some vehemently so. I know he received threats. Maybe by helping us, someone was able to find him. That makes more sense to me than Toby hurting a stranger and running."

Joy took one last handful of popcorn and pushed the remainder of the bag towards Afi.

"We don't even know that Toby ran," she said. "His boat is gone, but he could have encountered whoever this Brenda lady did and it could have been bad for Toby too." She felt an odd crunch inside her stomach, but she went on. "Maybe someone took his boat. Maybe he's…"

Afi reached out and touched Joy's arm. "He gave both of us a hand when we needed one. Assume he's alive. We need to find and help him."

Joy had reached that conclusion already. She just couldn't figure out how.

******

Jack and Sara Littleton examined the hand-addressed, bubble wrap-lined, large manila envelope for any clue as to its authenticity. Jack was inclined to think it was some sort of sick joke. Sara was disturbed by the photos that showed Ben. She didn't believe they could have been created digitally. The video was disturbing also, but Ben was hard to pick out, as he was one of the kids farthest from the camera. He wasn't in the worst video of all, showing what was being done to the least cooperative of the boys.

The boy who sent it claimed to be a former student, identified himself, and gave his email address.

"What are our options?" Jack said. It's not like we can drive over and make sure things are okay?"

"Let's just call the place."

"We only have a number for the headquarters door, remember? They don't want worried parents calling day and night." Jack hated to make a fuss.

Sara, however, felt differently. She'd spent hours making those cookies, thinking of her son enjoying them, knowing somehow that as he ate them he'd realize his parents loved him in spite of their harsh decision.

"Then let's call the headquarters. I want to talk to Ben."

Jack knew from experience there was no reasoning with the rising anxiety in Sara's voice.

"I don't care about their stupid rules," she said. "I want to know if he got the cookies. I want to talk to him now."

******

Lisa Rosen was a single mom trying to do her best. Her two younger daughters were happy, well adjusted, and so much better now that their older brother was not around to torment them. Lisa looked at the photos, especially the ones of her son being flogged with a belt against bare skin. She studied them closely. "I hope it's doing him some good," she thought.

******

Susie and Dale Carter had never agreed about sending James to the school. It was Susie's family's money and Susie's insistence that somebody better make a man out of James and get him away from that damn music.

Dale caught the innuendo. He wasn't fond of the music James and his band played either, but he thought this school was an extreme response. Still, he'd learned long ago that Susie and her family were going to do what they were going to do.

"The school warned us we might receive trash like this," Susie spat out the words as she threw the photos into the wastebasket. Dale let her go on for a few minutes about the pitfalls of a society that couldn't tolerate discipline. It didn't matter. He'd watched the video clip several times and seen the fear and pain in his son's eyes.

He'd call the Samoan authorities tomorrow from work and lodge a verbal complaint against the school. Then he'd email them one as well and send copies of it to as many United States authorities as he could think of. He was sure he could think of quite a few.

******

Dan and Rachel Whitman had dragged their feet for weeks before agreeing to send Danny to the school in Samoa. Their pastor had been so insistent this was exactly what Danny needed after he was caught sneaking liquor out of their cabinet. The boy, up to now a well-behaved thirteen-year-old, had cried that he'd never done it before. He'd been trying to have a toast with his friends on New Year's Eve.

"This is only the beginning," the pastor warned the Whitmans. "I've seen it before. Act now, before you lose control over him."

They were assured that after a brief period they would be in touch with Danny, and the school would help the family learn to grow together in God. But Danny, a smart boy who'd never responded well to unreasonable rules, seemed unable to make it out of the brief adjustment period. Now these horrible photos had arrived instead. Dan and Rachel looked at each other. They should have trusted their instincts from the beginning.

Within minutes Rachel was online researching organizations that might be able to help them. Dan began composing a letter to be sent, along with copies of the photos and video. They'd start with UNICEF, the United Nations children's fund, and move on to all of the organizations in the Global Movement for Children.

Dan was sure they'd encounter a mass of bureaucracy out there, but somewhere within the collection of people trying to fight poverty, hunger, child prostitution, child conscription, and child labor there had to be someone who could and would help him shine some light on a difficult to reach school that was far from what it claimed to be.

******

Stan Bowden knew that as a single dad he had not made the time for his son he should have. Hell, how was one supposed to be good at their job and handle the home and kid too? Sure he'd made mistakes after his wife died, and so had his son, but judging from the material his personal assistant reluctantly passed along to him, this Tropical Retreat Academy looked like it had been one of his biggest.

Oh yes, he knew how to get the boy back. It was called refusing to pay one more cent of the outlandish tuition. That would work, but it would never regain the boy's trust or affection. For that, Dad had better show up for once in person.

"Book me a flight to Samoa," he called out to his assistant.

"Pago Pago?" she said, surprised.

"No, that's in American Samoa. Book me a flight to Samoa Samoa."

"Hmm…," she said searching online. "I'm not sure anyone flies there."

******

Penthes was a subdued place in February 2010, for many reasons. Brenda's untimely death had been a sharp, unpleasant reminder of mortality that left everyone uncomfortable.

Zane barely acknowledged turning twenty-four as he fought off a depressing sense that life was passing him by. The half-melted and refrozen snow banks lining the streets of Chicago were filthy and grey, while the adjacent sidewalks were slick at night and covered with a cold wet slush by day. The sun wasn't seen a single time during the entire month.

The launch of the new drug was dismal, and the assigning of blame began. No one had anything good to say about anyone.

"Why would someone pick such a remote location where so much could go wrong?"

"Why don't we have innovative new products that don't need a glitzy marketing plan?"

The truth was, many of them feared for their jobs. They knew the revenue from this new product was important, and heads were going to roll. So most heads were kept down, and most mouths grumbled in whispers too soft to hear.

Except for Neil. He was everywhere, talking to people, complimenting them, stepping into the void of leadership with a barely concealed relish. He was livelier and friendlier than he'd ever been. Zane couldn't put his finger on why this bothered him so much, because no reasonable person could quarrel with either Neil's words or his actions. But there was something creepy and even repulsive about the way Neil seemed to be so energized by the company's troubles.

Chloe felt it too. She and Zane finally ran into each other in the copy room in a way that made contact unavoidable. Always blunt, Chloe didn't flinch.

"My grandfather confided that he told you things he promised me he'd never tell anyone." There was anger in her eyes. "I'm furious with him and I don't particularly want to deal with you either."

With that she turned on her heel and headed to the doorway. Then she turned back.

"I'm starting to think Neil's been drinking baby's blood to achieve immortality. Once I calm down about this other shit, we need to figure out what's going on with him."

"You're right," Zane called after her, acknowledging the truth of everything she'd said with one blanket statement.

He spent the afternoon feeling relieved that at least Chloe's avoiding him could be crossed off of his long list of things to figure out.

******

Toby had known for years the day could come when he'd have to disappear. He didn't know when or how, but he'd made preparations to make it easier. His first defense was making his boat easy to identify with a big orange stripe and obvious sun on the main sail. Before long, any search would include all boats of his size and type, of course, but their quick removal would give him a head start.

What a shame. What a damn, damn shame. Could the timing have been worse? What were the odds he would meet three people he liked? Hell, he hardly liked anybody. Three whole people. All at once. And then this. Unbefuckinglievable.

******

Zane sat on his bed with his laptop, preparing for his next meeting with Peter. With the conference, they'd met only twice so far this year. Zane knew he was supposed to be providing the man with an objective look at the pharmaceutical industry, and he'd let this ball drop, figuring nothing happened fast in the world of research.

He was wrong. In January, *Newsweek* had published a bombshell of an article about anti-depressants, reporting on studies that showed dummy pills worked almost as well for people with mild depression. The magazine confessed they faced a moral dilemma by bringing attention to these results. If antidepressants relied on expectations to make them work, would telling the truth leave more people depressed? Why not shut up and let folks be happy?

The magazine concluded that the expense of the drugs, and the possible side effects, justified what they were doing.

The article received immediate push back. Doctors wrote in to point out they had seen antidepressants work with their own eyes. *Of course they have. The patient believes in the pill so the pill works.*

As Zane read the article over a second time, he decided there was another compelling reason to speak the truth. If hunger tells you to eat, and thirst tells you to drink, then maybe temporary or mild depression tells you to make changes in your life. Maybe feeling down is your heart and soul begging for something new.

Isn't it a shame if this call to turn from a caterpillar into a butterfly gets silenced because it's easier to make the unpleasant feelings go away by swallowing a pill?

February 2010

13. The Power of Secrets

The worldwide headquarters of Turn Your Teen Around was located in Vanuatu, and Mark Hadley could not imagine why any business in the world would be headquartered anywhere else. Not only did he not have to pay any income tax, he also managed to avoid all capital gains taxes on his company's sizable investments. But the best part was that, until recently, Vanuatu refused to release any of his account information to any law enforcement agency in the world, and they now did so only when absolutely necessary. Mark appreciated how seriously they took client confidentiality in Vanuatu.

Of course, his actual office wasn't really located there. The country of Vanuatu is a group of small islands west of Fiji. It's capital city of Port Vila has about 30,000 people. The place offered little of interest to Mark Hadley, and it was rife with malaria, sea snakes, poisonous cone shells, and scorpion fish. And hook worm. Ick.

No, Mark Hadley believed it was the business of a smart businessman to find all the exceptions he could to enable him to make as much money as possible. That's what business was, for heaven's sake. Loophole was such an ugly word. It made it sound like he was sneaking around when he was only being savvy.

The functional headquarters of his company was located in Los Angeles, a city Mark did love. There was the whole Hollywood glamour thing, and plenty of people who shared Mark's perspective, and who provided him with lavish praise for the fine work he did with youth and for the fine way he made so much money while doing it. There were great restaurants and museums, and the occasional temptation to keep life interesting. So Mark had never set foot in Vanuatu and would consider himself lucky if he never had to do so.

He did maintain an office there with a staff of three ni-Vanuatu, as the locals insisted on calling themselves. These three young people were all from his church, and their employment gained him more praise. They understood they were to keep the doors open and the place clean, to forward mail and emails as instructed, and to deal with phone calls in as polite and non-committal a way as possible. They were not to bother him, particularly as it was fifteen hours later in Port Vila and there was almost never a convenient common time to conduct business.

He was annoyed when Tini called him on a Thursday night, upset because several parents had called her and insisted they be put in contact immediately with the school on Samoa. For heaven's sake. Why? He'd flown into Samoa after the earthquake last fall and soothed all of the parents by email. Absolutely no one had been injured. Then he'd soothed them again a few weeks ago after the awful news of the murder made its way into the U.S. press. He assured the parents, it had nothing to do with the school, which just happened to be located on the beach where she washed up. So sad.

So what was it this time? Tini wasn't sure. Three sets of parents were demanding contact with their children now, but none would say why.

The next call was from Dick Stafford, the headmaster of the school in Samoa. Against all probability, an angry father had flown into Apia and found a way to call the school directly. He was on his way over on a motorboat, with locals he'd hired to help him find the place. What should Dick do?

Mark calmed both as best he could. He advised Tini to give the parents his personal email address and instructed Dick to greet the man and be as cordial as possible. Then Mark turned to the pile of unopened mail on his desk. Odd. His U.S. headquarters had received letters of inquiry from two international organizations receiving complaints against him.

The kicker came when he checked his email, and found a note from a Samoan official who'd been helpful to him in the past. The man wanted Mark to know the Samoan police had received three credible and documented complaints concerning abuse at his school and they had no choice but to look into it.

Mark really didn't want to have to close a school again. Yet he lived with the knowledge that such might be necessary, so he'd planned for the day. Those hoping to cause him harm inevitably made the assumption he'd put up a fight, but he knew what worked better.

Time to get the students home. Dismiss the help. Put the property up for sale. Get out before it got bad. Minimize the press coverage. He needed to provide officials with a generous thank you for their support and express his deepest regret that some of his employees had apparently acted in ways that abhorred him. The same apology would go out to the parents of course.

The Tropical Retreat Academy would close with no problem and no need for further fuss. All bills would be paid and any outstanding tuition fully refunded. He knew the drill. Mark Hadley would take a nice little break, make sure he didn't need to do any damage control with the other schools, and then he'd find another island home for the new school he'd open.

******

The meeting with Peter Hulson did not go as Zane expected. For starters, although Peter seemed a little thinner than at their last meeting a month ago, his health hadn't deteriorated much. He was feisty and full of questions. He was also unimpressed with Zane's recent research. Peter had read the article in Newsweek right after it came out.

"I didn't think you read popular media."

"I generally don't. But I do listen to the radio, and it was in the news. I follow the studies and journals, you know, and I'm a little disappointed the reporting wasn't more nuanced. There are a lot of individual circumstances, and I believe our medicines do help some and not just the most severe cases like they claim."

He shrugged off the facts in the article as he moved the subject to his bigger area of concern. "I think that disaster of a conference is going to hurt our bottom line more than any set of studies. What the hell happened out there, Zane?"

Zane didn't know. "The most common theory is Brenda showed poor judgment, went for a sail with a man she just met, and somehow ended up dead."

"Jesus Christ. You know they act all business like, but some women are worse than men. I should have found a way to get her out of here years ago. She really did seduce my son. I know that sounds like a father's rationalization, but it isn't. She took advantage of him at a time when no man should have to deal with temptation. Sylvia wasn't, isn't, a bad gal. She and Pete could have made it through everything if Brenda hadn't inserted herself into the family dynamics at the worst moment. Providing comfort, my ass."

Zane didn't say a word. Peter let the silence pass.

"So how did you end up getting arrested?"

This part was easy. Absolute honesty. He suspected Peter knew most of the story by now anyway.

"I was questioned and detained on suspicion but never got charged. I knew the guy who is the prime suspect because it was his charter boat I was on last September when the earthquake hit. I enjoyed him and his crew and had gone out with one of them after the guests headed off to bed. Once witnesses reported seeing the boat over near the school, and others reported seeing me with a crew member, the police picked me up."

"But you weren't on that boat the night Brenda died, were you?"

Zane could tell Peter wanted the chance to ask him these questions in person. Of course. The man had bailed him out and had a right to ask.

"No, not at all. I came over to Apia with the Penthes group, and after everyone was down for the night I spent time with Afi. He's the young I-Kiribati crew member who's really into fire dancing. It's pretty awesome stuff, and we went out to see some of the top Samoans perform."

"I see. And you had no idea where Brenda was?"

Zane had been over this a lot. "No. The only odd thing was that she bailed on having dinner with the group, saying she wanted some time to contact people in Fiji before it got too late. She made sure the other four of us would be in the restaurant keeping the doctors happy. There didn't seem anything suspicious about it. She said she'd see us at breakfast."

"So what do you think happened?"

This was the one question Zane couldn't answer.

"I have no idea, Dr. Hulson. It makes no sense. I don't think Toby, the man with the boat, is capable of murder. But then again I'm not sure I'd recognize if someone was, if you know what I mean."

Peter nodded. "Some people lie so well, even to themselves, it's hard to judge what they could do. Well, add figuring this one out to your list of tasks. I understand you have a personal attachment here, but I'm willing to bet it won't influence your judgment."

With that Peter made a point of laying down a check made out to Zane Zeitman in shaky handwriting for the amount of one million dollars.

"I'll be giving it to my personal attorney today, to get to you when I pass away," he said. "I wanted you to know the check exists. Now, see if you can earn it by getting me facts about what happened at the conference." He paused for effect. "Preferably facts that haven't already been brought to light by other channels."

Zane had to admit he was as susceptible to the power of big whole numbers as the next person, and he was sure Peter knew it. Seeing a check made out to Zane Zeitman for one million dollars had been a thrill, and a fairly motivating experience.

Being asked to play detective, along with his other responsibilities, delighted him. Between the two, Zane felt driven to provide Dr. Hulson with enough information to justify his reputation for problem-solving and the sum of money he was being paid to do it. So he scribbled everyone's names on a big legal pad, and then doodled thick arrows and dialogue boxes of the known links between the people, adding himself in just to be fair. He studied the connections and drew the lines in thicker. Then he remembered reading how sometimes what wasn't there was more important than what was.

Zane stared at his notepad. There was something of a void in his scribbles. One player stood out, having no real links to anyone else.

Mark Hadley. To hear him tell the story, the man was involved because he had the misfortune to run a school with a beach in the wrong place. To be fair, there was a tie between Hadley and Afi. They'd never met, but Afi attended his school and Afi, Joy, and Toby had some plan to shine a public light on the school's less-than-stellar methods. Hadley couldn't possibly have known about this plan at the time of the murder, though, and it in no way involved Brenda. So wasn't Brenda ending up dead on his beach worth thinking about?

Joy mentioned she couldn't find biographical information on Hadley more than about ten years old, so they assumed the man had something unsavory his past. They'd guessed prison. But what if Hadley had somehow known Brenda? Been an ex-lover? Shit. What if Mark Hadley was Pete?

Zane's heart raced a little with this new idea. The timing seemed about right. The man's age seemed close. There was at least a vague similarity in appearance between the old photos Zane had seen of Pete in newspaper clippings and the man he'd met briefly in Samoa.

Yet Peter Sr. had combed the Pacific for years searching for his son and concluded he couldn't be alive. Was the conclusion still valid if, from the beginning, the son had wanted to disappear? Zane needed to go back and look at the timing more carefully.

Wait.

The first problem was the idea made no sense. Why in the world would Pete run away from his life and end up involved in what amounted to teen prisons? Zane was starting to evolve complicated scenarios in his head to explain such a possibility, when another part of his brain said *stop. Go show Mark Hadley's picture to Peter Sr. and ask if the idea is reasonable.*

Ah yes, brain. Good point.

Except, there were no pictures of Hadley on any of his websites. Or anywhere else on the internet. The only pictures of Mark Hadley were… on Zane's phone. He'd given it to Toby to use last October because Toby's old model didn't even have a camera. In spite of the no photo policy, Toby had managed to snap a few pictures of the school through a hole he'd made in the front pocket of his shorts. Zane had never looked closely at the photos, but a good phone would hold them safely until you needed them. Surely there was a picture of Mark.

Zane scrolled through countless worthless photos until he got to the ones on the grounds of the school. They were easy enough to spot, as each picture was rimmed by a fuzzy grey blur made by the inside of khaki shorts.

There was the headmaster, Dick Stafford, or at least half of him sticking out from the grey fuzz. There were a couple of boys off in the far distance. And yes, here was Hadley's head from the back. It made sense that Toby was being discrete and taking pictures when the man was looking away. Wait. There he was kind of from the side. A little blurry, but better than nothing. Zane now had an interesting possibility to raise with Dr. Hulson.

******

Joy was filling out the seven-page application from the American Samoa Department of Education. "Are you now or have you ever been a member of the communist party?" Seriously?

Her cell phone chimed the arrival of a text message. Probably Afi. They'd invested in a cheap local phone for him once it looked like he, his bike, and his fire knife were going to spend a lot of time traveling alone late at night. So far two local hotels were allowing him to perform for tips, and the take wasn't bad. To Afi's delight, the applause was even better.

But no, her old cell phone from Fiji with its new Am. Sam. SIM card had a text message from an unknown number.

"Joy. Afi. I am okay. Innocent. Trying to find a way to straighten this mess out. Still willing to walk thru fire for either of you. Stay safe."

It wasn't signed, but it didn't have to be. Joy's heart was pounding in her chest. She texted back.

"How can we help? Willing to walk thru fire here too."

There was only silence in response, followed, finally, by a message informing her the number she'd attempted to contact to was not accepting messages.

Suddenly the Pacific Ocean seemed huge to Joy, as she had the sense of Toby as a tiny dot of a man out there, so alone.

******

"I certainly wasn't inclined to think Pete ran away of his own volition," Peter said. "It wasn't an option I liked. He did have himself in a mess with Brenda and Sylvia. Not an uncommon mess, mind you, it's one other men deal with. Leave the wife, lose the money, move on. Or lose the mistress, endure the tears, soothe the wife and move on. But Pete was such a softie. He couldn't bear to make anyone cry."

This morning's discussion reminded Zane he was not a trained therapist. They had skills he didn't. He was also aware he was being paid well to pretend to have those skills, and the payer didn't care if he was faking it.

"How guilty do you think Pete felt about Joel's death? Did he hold himself responsible?"

"Probably. It wasn't his idea to put the boy on the medication, but it was his field of expertise. He thought he should've known more about the drug and I felt the same way. I'm the one who forced the issue, so Pete was at least as angry with me as he was with himself."

"How did Sylvia feel about the medication?" Zane asked.

Peter laughed. "She wanted to get the boy into counseling instead. Said it was a better first choice for treatment. Neil said that was nonsense; therapy was slow, expensive and often ineffective. It's why our drugs are better. How could we make claim this to the public when we made other choices for our own loved ones?"

Zane thought about that. "So putting Joel on medication was actually Neil's idea? This was marketing driven?"

Peter shrugged. "Neil was right. Joel and his panic attacks were getting attention. We claimed we'd developed cures for mental issues and we needed to walk the talk."

"This was 1999. Did you have any reason to suspect there was a link between these antidepressants and suicide in teenagers?"

Peter put his head in his hands. "No. I didn't. I wasn't aware of any studies; I don't even think there *were* studies done yet. There was anecdotal evidence, but the doctors didn't understand it. They thought the antidepressants gave the young person a lift, a little more energy, so the kid had the strength to act on his self-destructive impulses. In other words, they thought the suicides were the result of the medication working."

"But that wasn't the case?" Zane encouraged Peter to go on.

"I guess not. Doctors started prescribing the meds for teens who weren't depressed. You know, off-label uses. These kids were obsessive-compulsive, some had PTS, some had never expressed a self-destructive thought in their life. Then… well… you know. Out of the blue."

"Had you heard of these cases in 1999?"

"No, of course not. Not yet. But…"

"But?"

"But Pete found out after the fact that Neil had. Neil was always scouring the press for stories about our products. Our image was part of his job. He decided not to mention the incidents to us because he thought they were a weird coincidence."

Zane decided to charge out on a limb. "You don't think Neil wanted Joel dead, do you?"

"Jesus Christ, Zane. Of course not. Neil may not be the warmest guy in the world, but he's not heartless. Besides, it was a publicity nightmare for us, trying to keep it out of the news. Why would he want to bring that on the company?"

Zane nodded. "Plus it was hardly a sure thing. We're talking a few percent of the time that this happens, right? So it's not exactly a reliable murder weapon. Was Pete angry with Neil?"

"Of course he was. It was irrational; Neil wasn't to blame. But Pete was upset and Sylvia was livid."

"When Pete disappeared, you really didn't consider suicide or running away to be strong possibilities?"

"I considered both, even though I didn't like either idea. Lost at sea had a certain melancholy appeal. Surely you understand."

"I do. But, in the process of trying to sort out this mess, I've come across someone I think could possibly be your son Pete."

"What?" It was a bark of a sound.

"He runs a group of schools in the Pacific, and his history sort of evaporates around the year 2002."

Peter's face had started to become more animated. "I could see Pete gravitating towards running schools for teens. Trying to help kids like Joel, make amends for what happened. It fits, Zane. It sort of fits."

"Not quite so sure that works," Zane cautioned, worried now about getting the man's hopes up. "The schools aren't, well, exactly what I'd call nurturing, although the man has been successful. I suppose they could be an odd response to a son's death. Make these boys tough, so they can last longer in this harsh world? Or maybe punish these boys the way you'd like to punish your son for causing you so much sorrow? It's a stretch, but it's possible."

Zane pulled out his phone. "I couldn't find a photo of the man anywhere in the publicity for his schools, which alone makes me suspicious. But I do have a couple of bad pictures of him here on my phone. Would you take a look and see if it looks to you at all like Pete?"

Peter grabbed the phone from Zane with a force that surprised him. "Hell yes, I'll look." Then, as he saw the fuzzy grey rings around the pictures, "What's this?"

Zane explained the no photo policy and how the captain of the charter boat had come with him when he visited the school. He told Peter about the I-Kiribati crew member who'd been at the school and how the horrible treatment had prompted the captain's concern. So, yes, the photos were taken from inside the man's pants pockets in hope of finding some damning evidence.

"This is the place you were carting all of my best doctors off to as part of my conference?"

Zane nodded. "We were, still are, positioning our new drug as a better alternative. Safer and way less expensive. It was a good pitch, Dr. Hulson. Even I liked it."

"So where is the man you think might be Pete?"

Zane flipped through photos until he found the back of Hadley's head. "Here's one."

"Zane, that could be anybody."

"Here's a better one."

Peter studied the blurry photo. "It doesn't jump out at me as being Pete. It's possible. He could have had a little face work done, I suppose. Probably would have, if he chose to do this." He shook his head. "I'm not sure. It's hard to tell from a single bad photo."

Zane had a thought. "Let's go at this the other way then. I spent an hour with Mark Hadley. Get me some pictures of your son Pete, preferably a lot of them. Maybe some videos. I'll study them and see if I can see a resemblance."

"My wife Darlene was the one who kept our photographs and home movies," Peter said. "After she died, I gave books and cartridges of them to Paula. I'm sure she has them somewhere." He thought for a second. "She's in Milan right now, on her annual clothes-shopping trek with her daughter. Maybe her housekeeper can help us. If not, I'm sure Paula will when she gets back."

"Would anyone else have photos we could see sooner?"

"There are some in the company archives. Chloe has the best access to old newsletters and publications. Hell, you might as well show Chloe these bad photos of this guy and see what she thinks."

"'Chloe is a little upset with me, Peter."

"Oh right. Of course she is." Peter sighed like he hadn't wanted to be reminded. "I've always kind of liked the girl, you know, in spite of the fact that she's not cut out to run a company. Too much of a lone-wolf type. Anyway, I admire her spirit. She demanded to know what I had you working on. I think in her own way she was looking out for you by questioning me. So I told her."

"You told her you had inoperable liver cancer?"

"No, I left out that part. I told her I was impressed with your research skills and had pulled you off of marketing projects and asked you to spend time looking into things I wanted looked into. I told her I thought it was my prerogative as head of this company."

"She had a problem with that?"

"She wanted to know what things and I told her it wasn't her concern, and she told me if the things involved her dad they were her concern. So I fessed up. Told her I had you looking into Penthes drugs, our corporate culture, and some of my personal issues as well. Including her dad's disappearance. She wasn't happy about the last one."

"I suppose not." Zane was trying to respond wisely.

"Then she asked if I had told you about Joel."

Zane waited.

"We're alike, Zane, in some ways. I'm not comfortable lying either. My life might have been easier if I was."

"So," Zane said, "you told her yes."

"I did, and she said that given all the pain we went through to cover it up, I'd made a stupid decision. Less stupid because she thought you were trustworthy, but stupid nonetheless."

"That's why she's so upset with me," Zane said.

"Not completely. Chloe, Chloe hates pity. She's angry because I told you she found Joel. That's a piece of information almost no one knows, and for some reason of privacy or pride, Chloe is sensitive about it. She was right; I didn't have to tell you that detail. It made her furious. What a mess. You must think the whole family is nuts."

"I think you're a group of fairly normal and not particularly bad people who've made some poor choices." It slipped out before Zane could stop it.

"Thank you for that, Zane. Thank you for the truth." The encouragement felt good. Picking up momentum, Zane went on.

"And, I think secrets eat away at people. They can be horrible secrets, or really not that bad when you pull them out into the light of day. As long as we tuck them away like they are the worst things imaginable, and live in fear of their being found out, they fester with a power beyond any of the facts. I think your whole family has an internal pocket of pus, swollen but well hidden, and it sucks the joy out of your lives more thoroughly than that bulging tumor is drawing the life out of you."

There was silence.

"Well then." Peter Hulson stood. "I'll see you next Wednesday morning." Peter began walking towards the door. "Bring photos from Chloe and we'll talk about whether this guy could possibly be my son, and if so, what to do next."

Zane recognized he was being dismissed and even ushered out. It looked like the whole pocket of pus thing had taken the conversation a bit too far.

March 2010

14. Catching a Dream

Zane guessed Chloe had learned exquisite self-control, and she was relying on her best techniques as she responded to him. They were in her small, but well-furnished office, on the far end of same floor as sales and marketing.

"You've decided my father could still be alive?" She allowed her face the slightest of *I can't believe this* looks.

"Chloe, I'm doing what your grandfather asked me to do. I'm looking into possibilities. I've been over the reports and Mark Hadley's location, timing, and general appearance all make this an option. I'm sorry. I know this is a painful thing to bring up, but by the time an all-out search began, an adept sailor could've made it to a port. If he'd prepared in advance, he could've disappeared before your grandfather's dragnet over the area got established."

"You're saying my dad not only left me and my mother by choice, but that he spent time, maybe weeks or months, lying to everyone he loved while he planned to disappear?" Her eyes were hard and cold as she looked at him. "Have you given any thought to what such a scenario implies for me and my family?"

No actually, Zane had not. He was trying to solve a problem, which was what he did well. The problem was figuring out what had happened to Pete Hulson Jr. He hadn't been concerned with the emotional subtext of his theories. Until now.

"Maybe you could look at the photos to eliminate the possibility," he said. It was the best he could do.

"Sure." She spat out the answer. "Let's see them." She laughed aloud at the first. "How were these things taken? Through somebody's knapsack?"

"Through his pocket. The school doesn't allow any photography on campus."

"Wait. This guy you think might be my dad is the person who runs these teen prisons you were talking about?"

"Right." Zane thought he'd been clear about that in the beginning but maybe Chloe had stopped listening to details after she heard her dad's name and the words "still alive".

"No, Zane. Grandfather doesn't know my dad like I do. Did. There is no possible universe in which my dad runs a group of schools like that, unless aliens capture him and replace his brain. Seriously. He was a gentle man, one who preferred to avoid conflicts and see everyone happy. He was good to my mom and good to me and Joel and oh, damnit, get the hell out of here."

Tears were welling up in her eyes. Zane would have offered comfort to another person, but instinct told him that was the worst possible response. He got up and walked to the window and looked outside for a minute.

When he thought she'd regained her composure, he lowered his voice and said "Then look at the second photograph. Show me pictures of him. Chloe, if I can come up with this theory, then other people looking into Brenda's murder can, too. It'd be easiest to figure out the truth here and now."

She didn't respond, but moved on to the second blurry side photo. "I don't think so, Zane. I really don't. Come here." She turned to her computer and opened a folder filled with older, scanned images of a happy family of four all taken within a few years of each other. Pretty, light-blonde mom. Taller, sandy-haired dad. Awkward, preteen boy with glasses. Young, tawny-haired daughter with cute, turned-up nose and contagious smile. It was a smile Zane couldn't recollect having ever seen on the adult Chloe.

He studied several pictures of the man, all of better quality than the ones he'd seen while doing his research. He tried his best to recollect Mark Hadley' face, his jaw line, his features. Zane was pretty good with faces.

"No, I don't think so either." He felt Chloe's relief as every visible muscle in her body relaxed. "I'm sorry, really sorry, I ended up causing you more pain."

"I know you are."

Gil came into Zane's office the next morning with a disturbed look on his face.

"I know Dr. H has got you working on his own stuff, Zane, but I'm going through Brenda's things here trying to make sure no one drops the ball on anything. I wondered if I could maybe hand one thing off to you."

"Sure Gil. I'm willing to do my part. What you got?"

"It's a marketing plan Brenda was working on. Near as I can tell, she thought the new patent for our drug would make it especially well-suited for a particular group. I have her notes and some strategy outlines."

"Let me guess. She wanted to go after counselors in the best private schools where the parents could afford expensive medications. A concerned counselor could suggest parents ask their doctor about our specific cocktail designed for the angry or rebellious teen."

"Good guess." Gil smiled at the bite in Zane's wit. "But you couldn't be more wrong." He handed Zane the packet with a discouraged shrug. "This isn't the kind of marketing I signed up for."

Zane started to read it. *No, it probably wasn't.*

Zane was back in Chloe's office a day later. "Do you think there's a place in this world for an ethically run pharmaceutical company?"

Another person might have been offended, but not Chloe.

"I like to think there is. To be honest, direct-to-consumer marketing makes it hard for a company to survive without pushing the limits. Some of us would be ecstatic to see direct advertising of drugs made illegal, but it's not going to happen. Too many people make way too much money off of it."

"Well, I've been going over the plans for our wonder concoction for troubled teens. Turns out the main target group would have been trickle down from the high-end doctors we were courting."

"I don't understand," Chloe said.

"This particular medication is a prayer answered for the foster care system. All those angry upset children. All that state-funded medication. Kids in foster care are about ten times more likely to be medicated. It looks like prescriptions to make these kids less trouble are an accepted part of the system. It rolls in the bucks for pharmaceutical companies and rolls in the perks for the more heavily prescribing doctors. Some of these kids live for years on high doses of serious shit. Several kinds of serious shit, actually. Chloe, it's like a temporary lobotomy with unpleasant side effects."

"Scary idea, but this isn't a world I know much about."

"Me either. I'm sure there are honest-to-god needs for drugs, but at a rate of ten times that of the general population? Brenda's plan to save the company was to market our new product as the premier one-tablet-does-it-all for kids without a soul in the world to look out for their interests."

"They do have social workers who look out for them, Zane."

"Yes and I'm sure there are fine ones. Just like there are fine foster parents. But there's a problem overall and Brenda was hoping to capitalize on it big-time. By the way, in her notes she called this Neil's big idea. Where exactly is he coming from?"

"I'd say Alpha Centauri, but I don't think that's possible." Chloe shrugged at her own bad joke. "Neil's from some small town in Nebraska and he latched on to my dad back in college. My cynical view is he saw how naive and nice my dad was, and in some ways my grandfather too, and he figured he'd have a meal ticket for life as Dad's best friend. I know he's not close to whatever family he has, and he doesn't have much of a personal life. At least not one we know about here at work. And, well, I don't know how to put this last part nicely."

Zane waited. He was betting this last part would be good.

"Every time there's trouble around here, Neil is at the heart of it. Not in a way he could be blamed, because it's never in a way he could have predicted. He just consistently plants these little seeds, then when they grow he finds a way to capitalize on them."

"Like?"

"Like I know he was the one who encouraged Brenda to give my poor dad a shoulder to cry on after Joel died. Also, I heard him tell Joel," she swallowed and went on, "I heard him tell Joel once to always remember how upset his panic attacks made my grandfather. It put more pressure on Joel, and made things worse." Chloe shrugged without conviction. "It's possible Neil is only guilty of ongoing poor judgment."

"But Neil seems astute, Chloe, like a man who knows exactly what he's doing."

"I know. He does. Speaking of that, do you have any idea why he seems so energized since Brenda died?"

"Maybe he's just a guy who likes trouble. Like you said, he finds ways to use problems to his advantage."

"He could revive his foster care idea now," Chloe said "and singlehandedly save the company after you, Brenda, and Gil bungled our best hope. It's a good plan. Who's going to stop him?"

"Well, Gil could try. He's the one who found the notes about targeting kids in foster care, and he really found the idea distasteful. He gave it to me to see what I thought."

"He's got a teenage daughter," Chloe said. "She's a little high strung; from what I hear she demands a lot of his attention. She's also quite an artist. Works in watercolors. I bet this hit a little too close to home for him. He's a single dad, too. Don't know the rest of the story."

"Well, he's my acting boss at the moment, and near as I can tell, a good man."

Chloe nodded. "I agree. He's also smart enough to keep his head down and stay off of Neil's radar screen. It's going to be interesting to see what happens."

******

Most of the sixty-five-thousand inhabitants of American Samoa live on the main island of Tutuila, where tourism and tuna canneries are main industries. Unemployment is high, but there remains a chronic shortage of trained teachers.

The capital, Pago Pago, looks modern, but the ninety-percent Polynesian population mostly adheres to deep Christian beliefs.

S. R. Cronin

Women wear the local all-gender skirt called the lava-lava down to their ankles with modest tops, in spite of sweltering heat. The aiga, or extended family, is important, and the role of the matai, or family chief, remains significant.

Life in Fiji helped prepare Joy for Samoa. Although Melanesian and Polynesian cultures are different, adapting to one was helpful in learning to adapt to the other. So a demure and modestly dressed Joy tried her best to parlay her U.S. teaching certificate and Fiji experience into a job, before her thirty-day travel visa ran out.

She filled out all the paperwork, but recognized things don't move as fast in the South Pacific as they do in Boston. So, while Afi danced to buy their groceries, Joy made appointments at schools to plead for work in person. Solving her problem in her time frame was going to take luck as well as persistence.

She found that bit of luck when, during an interview, she was allowed to fill in at an understaffed school after a pregnant third grade teacher left suddenly when her contractions began two months early.

The teacher was back and still seven months pregnant the next day, but when she was unable to come in the following day, the children and staff liked Joy so well they called her back in. Joy did her best, and by the following week, when the lady was put on bed rest until the end of the school year, strings were pulled and Joy had her position.

Afi took Joy's laptop with him to hotels during the day when she worked. He'd use the hotel internet to search for information on Tropical Retreat Academy. Hadn't the parents gotten the packets yet? Why was nobody doing anything?

Finally, he found the small paragraph in the Apia newspaper letting him know the packets had been received and acted upon in ways he'd never have guessed. According to the newspaper, the school had shut its doors with little explanation. It was gone. Afi smiled from deep within.

******

Zane knew he needed more information. He wasn't sure what he was after, but it seemed neither he nor his alter ego Ying were likely to uncover it. It was time to become somebody who could go where Zane could not, and who would never be suspected of being him.

Zane seldom altered his shape to appear female, but except for his height there was no particular barrier to doing so. He could approximate breasts and wider hips. A wig worked wonders. He could add years, and a more ambiguous ethnicity. The stooping of age would help. Meanwhile, he needed to learn more about a part of Penthes that he, like most people, had ignored. That was the beauty of the janitorial group. They didn't get a lot of attention.

In his office, Zane began to gather supplies. A janitor's jumpsuit a bit too small, women's sneakers, and an unattractive salt and pepper wig were locked in his bottom left drawer, waiting to help him take his gift to a new level.

Neil was at his desk typing into his computer when the cleaning lady came in to empty the trash. Dressed in the dark blue uniform they all wore, and pushing the yellow cart with cleaning supplies, she only registered in his mind as female, browner and older, and beyond that he paid no attention. She was having trouble making the annoying crinkly plastic liner fit into the wastebasket, and he almost asked her to not bother when he decided this was as good a time as any to go to the can. He headed to the executive washroom without a thought.

Ximena, as her name tag identified her, took a quick look at the computer screen. PowerPoint was open; she examined the slides. Neil was hard at work preparing to market the new product to the foster care community. Okay, that question was answered. She un-minimized Word. Hmmmm. Neil had recently looked at a couple of documents about succession planning for the company. Looking to fill Brenda's slot? Or looking into what would happen if Peter died before naming a new CEO?

She dusted around on the desk, opening the middle draw where people so often stuck small things they did not want to lose. She didn't expect to find anything. It was more of an instinctual peek. But there it was, in plain sight — the rather unusual necklace Brenda had absolutely, positively been wearing in Samoa when she told Zane she would not be joining the group for dinner.

Luckily, Ximena carried her cell phone and kept it close. She snapped a fast picture of the necklace inside its zip-lock bag without disturbing it and had just closed the drawer when an annoyed Neil came back into the room.

"Sorry," she mumbled softly, eyes down as her duster made a last sweep. She moved deferentially to her yellow plastic cart and left with her head down.

Neil let out a derisive puff of air as he returned to his important work.

Back in his office Zane studied the photograph he'd taken. It helped sometimes to have a good memory. On her last night in Samoa, Brenda had been dressed casually, for her, in lightweight black pants and a metallic copper and black top. The necklace was a Native American dream catcher, made out of copper and adorned with black beads. Nice costume jewelry, nothing expensive. Zane noticed it because it was unusual, and because Brenda had fingered it while she talked to him, like it mattered to her.

So the real question was, what was it now doing in Neil's drawer? Had Neil removed it from Brenda's body once he arrived in Samoa? Would they let him do that? Had the police given it to him after the investigation was over? Why? Why keep it in his desk? Zane was willing to bet Neil harbored no secret love for Brenda. Wasn't holding on to something so personal and so connected to a murder victim way too stupid for Neil? Or was it careless arrogance?

Okay, he needed to find out more about Neil's initial few hours in Samoa, and he needed to find out what had happened with Brenda's body while he had been too worried about his own well-being to care.

Zane had another thought. He needed to get a hold of Joy and Afi. They might be able to contact some of the boys who found the body on the beach. Maybe one or two was by nature observant, or for some reason liked dream catchers. It would be useful to know if Brenda was or was not wearing the necklace when her body was found.

******

Joy settled into a routine of taking the bus to school, doing her best with the children, then coming home to share an early dinner with Afi before he headed off to work. Sometimes while he was out she'd go to places with internet access, looking for information to help them, or to help Toby. She now had a friendly email relationship with her mother and had renewed contact with a few friends back in Massachusetts. In spite of all this, and being surrounded by people for most of her day, she was lonely.

She wondered if she was starting to miss the comforts and familiarity of the East Coast. It seemed reasonable, until she realized if Toby somehow came back and asked her to spend the rest of her life with him on his boat, even if they were running from the law, she'd say yes in a heartbeat. Shit. She wasn't lonely. She was in love.

Meanwhile, she'd gathered information on what it would take to make Afi a permanent resident of the United States. It looked like they would need to live together as a married couple for two years. Under other circumstances this wouldn't be a problem, as roommates didn't come much better and her affection for Afi was real. Yet it never could be what she felt for Toby.

Joy began to spend more of her lonely evenings on Toby's website. His organization remained the one thing about him that bothered her. She wanted to know what he really stood for. She found this.

> Governments and those with wealth and power are equally capable of becoming the bully on the playground. For individuals to flourish, or at least keep their lunch money, they must put reasonable restraints on both. Otherwise, they choose one bully over the other.
> No powerful entity is entitled to skew the odds against any individual such that they don't get to dance to the music they hear. We don't all get to run the world. However, every single one of us gets to go to the dance.

Joy saw in her head the images of many individuals rising to dance and she smiled with delight.

Yes, he deserves all the wonderful things I feel for him.

******

While Zane worked his assignment for Peter by day, he took time to socialize with friends or coworkers by night. Britta and her friends were enjoyable, and sometimes he went out with Raven and other coworkers. Yet amid all the people, he often felt alone as his mind wandered back to the peace and beauty of the Pacific and to the excitement of sailing on Miss Demeanor. He hadn't spent that much time there, yet the whole experience continued to pull at his heart. He missed Toby and Joy. He missed the boat. He missed Afi. Damnit, he ought to admit it. He missed Afi and the worst part was he had no idea now of how he was ever going to see Afi again.

He found himself spending more time on Toby's website, reading the philosophies that had appealed to Afi as a boy back on Tarawa. Toby and his group had written pledges for those who wished to join y^1. One of them was this.

As a human who celebrates the individuality of each of us, I will cease expecting others to share my tastes and my interests. No one need hide who they are, or pretend to be like me, in order to be treated fairly.

As a gay man, Zane thought a world practicing that philosophy would be a far friendlier world.

******

Mark Hadley was starting to get pushback from three of his other schools. Not like he had gotten from the Samoan one, where somehow, against all odds, somebody had gotten pictures and managed to get the addresses of the families of the students. These were more general complaints, but Mark could see where it was going. He began to reawaken his more global, more thorough exit strategy, in case he had to use it a second time.

******

Neil had always believed it paid to have people on your side. His friend the headhunter had done him many favors. His buddy Harold, the private detective, was great until something about Zane's family spooked him last fall. That still struck Neil as strange, but it turned out to not matter, because Neil didn't need to make Zane go away after all.

Years ago, he'd taken the time to locate and win over the right medical billing specialist in his doctor's office. He'd been careful. He didn't need an angry, jilted lover. He needed a sophisticated woman who saw herself as his flirtatious friend, someone to whom he could provide gifts and flattery without expectations for a relationship.

He found the right woman, and his time and patience paid off. For, along with the many other carefully calculated decisions Neil had made, he chose to use the same family doctor as his discerning friends, the Penthes family. Dear medical billing specialist Penelope had, over the years, provided him with a wealth of information on Peter and his kin. Most of it paled in comparison to her recent piece of news that Peter Sr. was dying of liver cancer and had at best a few months to live. She thought Neil would want to know.

"The bastard," Neil said. "He's going to conk out without giving me the satisfaction of naming me CEO." Penelope gave him an odd look at this response.

"Oh, of course I'm sorry for the guy, Penelope," he added. Then, in a more conspiratorial tone, "Thanks for telling me. You're a champ." He gave her an affectionate little pat on the butt and a nibble on her ear while she giggled.

Neil prided himself on being someone who could turn misfortune into gold. Okay, so he wasn't going to get the future he wanted. It didn't matter. He was still going to get a hell of a deal.

He checked, and he absolutely, indisputably was in line to be CEO if anything happened to Peter. Of course he was. Given Penelope's assessment of the situation, he might as well start the ball rolling to build up *his* company. Every positive thing he did would benefit him, and would no longer make anyone else look good. He could go for it.

He felt a lightness in himself as he charged ahead with all of his best ideas. There was some concern Peter and others may have had some scruples on the foster care front, but no need to worry now. He'd get everything in place so it was ready to roll once Peter was gone and no one could stop him. Neil felt great.

******

Toby laid low in the outer islands of Fiji, managing to keep well hidden. Although he'd been a happy loner for much of his adult life, he had to face the fact that for the first time in years he was lonely. He missed Afi and, strangely enough, even the kid from Penthes. Most of all, he missed Joy. All these years alone, and then he'd gone and fallen in love.

His more immediate problem, though, was his current situation couldn't go on forever. He needed to get to his island home, and he had no idea whether Samoan officials, U.S. law enforcement, or the powers that ran Kiribati could or would care enough to be waiting for him. Would they find the entrance to his house? Would they go as far as to post someone on the island? Would they bother to be flying overhead, or would they use some sort of satellite surveillance? Could they do that? How expensive was it? How advanced was all this technology?

If they did care enough to chase him down, then his disappearance looked totally damning, and straightening this mess out was, in the best case, going to make a real mess of his life. He didn't even want to think about the worst case.

So he went with the odds. He bet the death of a distant American woman at the apparent hands of a U.S. expat was not a situation likely to compel the Samoans to spend time and resources they didn't have. He bet the I- Kiribati would not get involved or provide information about his generous rental terms unless specifically asked, and he bet that no one would know to ask.

At the end of March, after weeks of hiding, a nervous Toby set sail for home.

y^1
Is
Why

15. A Creative Species

Zane brought a list with him to Peter Hulson's office because he'd made two promises to himself. The first was he would give Peter every scrap of information he had. The second was that under no circumstances would he tell Peter how he'd had gotten the information.

The elderly blue eyes widened at the sight of the list. Zane sat down as Peter winced as he shifted in his seat. Zane suspected the man was trying to stay alert by limiting his dose of painkillers. He appeared as attentive as ever, but was getting more impatient.

"You've got a lot to cover?"

"I don't want to forget anything," Zane said. "First, though, you should know Chloe seems to have calmed down about your sharing information about her. She's not only talking to me, she's helping me. We looked at pictures of her dad and I showed her the ones of Mark Hadley. We both doubt Mark Hadley is your son."

The older man's expression changed, one slight bit at a time, until Zane thought Peter Hulson looked as sad as he had ever seen a man look without tears. He searched for something hopeful to add. "I think Chloe cares about you."

"I know."

Zane waited a few seconds, then moved on.

"Second, Gil is my acting boss now, and he handed off to me a marketing plan Brenda was working on. It involves a heavy push to market our new drug cocktail to physicians who care for kids in foster care."

"Seems sensible," Peter said. "I'm sure there are a lot of messed up kids in that group."

"That's one way to look at it. Gil, Chloe, and I viewed it more as putting kids on prescriptions to make them easier to care for. Like over-prescribing drugs in rest homes. Nobody is there to object and the heavily medicated subject causes less trouble."

"Zane, isn't the idea of foster kids causing less trouble a good one? Seriously? If it's the result of people buying more of Penthes' products, shouldn't you and your coworkers support the idea? We are a business, remember."

Zane was surprised. "I thought because you objected to the idea of ghostwriting for doctors—"

"You thought I had scruples." Peter finished the sentence. "I do. I think misleading doctors is wrong, although there is a grey area where ghostwriting is concerned. None-the-less, I'd rather let other companies cross that fuzzy line. But, please understand, I don't have any moral objections to tapping into a huge market for what we produce. What's your next issue?"

Zane took a second to regroup. It looked like his shocking news that Neil was going to go ahead and run with this horrible marketing approach wasn't going to cause Peter Hulson any concern. *Move on with the conversation.*

"Neil is studying the company's succession planning documents," he said.

"And you know this how?" Peter had developed that uncanny ability common among executives for honing in on the most uncomfortable question he could ask.

"I went into his office and looked at what he had open on his computer screen."

"You'd have looked pretty stupid if he walked in on you."

Zane sighed. "I had an excellent cover story."

"Okay. As my COO he needs to keep abreast of this. He has to fill Brenda's position, for starters. What's your problem with that?"

"The document was open to the section on filling your position if you died without naming a successor. I'm thinking Neil suspects your situation."

Peter nodded. "Do you have anything else for me?"

"One more thing. You asked me to look into Brenda's death. I remembered that the evening she died she came to my door to tell me she wouldn't be at dinner. I assumed it was because Gil's room was on another floor. I noticed she had on this kind of black and copper outfit with a lot of matching copper jewelry and this black dream catcher necklace."

"Who wears jewelry when they are working in their hotel room?"

"Lots of women, probably. Anyway, the necklace stuck in my mind because it was unusual."

Peter's eyes had turned hard. "I know the necklace, Zane, or at least I think I do. It sounds like the one my son bought for Brenda, and she had the poor taste to wear it to a company function. My daughter Paula was there. She helped Pete pick it out from some artsy jeweler, thinking it was a gift for Sylvia. When Paula saw it on Brenda, she guessed what was going on, and went straight to Sylvia. Sylvia confronted Pete and all hell broke loose. I would've hoped Brenda would have the good sense to give the damn necklace to charity after that. So she actually wore it on your trip?"

Zane nodded. "By the time I left Samoa I was less of a suspect and more of a witness who might remember something useful. So I went over everything I could think of for the police and they showed me footage from the hotel lobby of Brenda leaving several minutes after she talked to me. I studied it closely."

"And?"

"As I told them, she looked to me like someone who was headed out somewhere. Not getting air or looking for a spot with better cell phone coverage or something like that, you know. Her hair was fixed, she had on make-up, she looked put together even for Brenda, and she was most definitely wearing the necklace."

"So why are you bringing this necklace up now?" Peter's irritation was growing.

"Because I found it in Neil's desk drawer."

For the first time since the meeting began, Peter looked impressed. "Now that's interesting."

******

Joy knew what all teacher's know. Poor behavior is contagious in the class room. Good behavior is contagious, too, but that's more noticeable on the playground than in class. One person standing up to a bully makes it more likely a second person will. And a third. Teachers know we do catch traits like kindness, and courage, too.

So Joy wasn't surprised that so many heeded the rally cry Afi put forth on social networking sites frequented by former students of the Turn Your Teen Around Academies. Once Tropical Retreat closed its doors in Samoa, Afi reached out to find more ways to get information into the hands of friends and families.

Each school was in a difficult place to access, but local authorities did investigate complaints alleging serious abuse. International organizations could be brought to bear pressure. Friends had friends with friends who lived nearby. The old six degrees of separation concept was put to work, and once Afi issued a call, the movement grew.

There were a fair number of angry families out there who thought they had no recourse but to heal and move on. Individually, that was true, but not if they worked together.

******

Zane stayed in email contact with Afi and Joy, and knew they were continuing to lie low in Am. Sam. Joy had a temporary teaching contract until school let out and she could get a full time job in the fall if she wanted it.

They'd filled out the paperwork to apply for U.S. residency for Afi, but the challenge was the paperwork had to be presented in person, either in the United States or in the country in which they had been married. American Samoa didn't count as either. So once school was out in mid-May, they had to get to Hawaii or Kiribati. Neither could be easily done. Zane was trying to think of a way he could help.

Zane was proud of his friend for shutting the doors of his old school and stirring up accountability for Mark Hadley. Now that Afi had time and incentive to practice his fire knife dancing, he wrote Zane about how he'd improved and kept finding new ways to use his hypermobility to make his performances unique. He was a regular at a hotel three nights a week now, and a local troupe had included him, so he got extra work whenever they got a booking.

Zane knew an email answer to his two friends would have sufficed, but he decided to treat himself to a call to Joy's phone, even though he knew she guarded her minutes closely. Afi and Joy shared dinner around 4:30 p.m. before Afi got ready for work, which meant the best time to catch them would be a cheery 5:30 in the morning Chicago time. Zane set his alarm.

"Joy!"

"Zane? Oh my god! I can't believe it's you." The normally calm voice had risen half an octave.

"Look, I know things are tight and I'll make this quick. Any news?"

Joy knew of course what Zane meant. She hadn't dared mention Toby's text in an email because she feared her email or texts could be so easily monitored but a phone call was safer. So she shared Toby's cryptic text message with Zane and they both reiterated their belief that Toby was innocent.

"I've got news about that," Zane said. "In fact I need Afi's help. Is he there?"

Afi got on phone with a grin and the two young men savored the sounds of each other's voices as the story of the necklace was told. Afi understood how helpful it would be to know if Brenda's body was found with the necklace on it. Or not.

"We're talking half-awake teenage boys cleaning a beach at dawn, then seeing a dead body. I'm not sure any of them would have noticed a necklace, Zane."

"Well, let's find out. You've got the addresses, so why not contact each boy. I'll work the lead from here. It's a whole new world if we can clear Toby's name." Then Zane updated Afi on all the rest of the news from Penthes.

"You know, I think I'd rather be beaten than be one of those foster children so heavily drugged they don't know what's going on," Afi said. "Neither one is living, is it?"

"Not really. You fight the one there, I'll fight the other here."

They signed off with a laughing three-way hug and Joy's insistence Zane should call her cell more often. He would. He absolutely would.

******

Peter Hulson had never been able to explain why he didn't like Neil Bennett. The man was smart, ambitious, and capable, everything Peter professed to admire. He was Pete's friend and had been an asset to Peter's company. He held no unusual or offensive opinions and, except for the one claim of harassment years ago, he'd done nothing to embarrass Penthes. He even lacked odd hobbies or peculiar tastes. Peter knew he should have adored him.

But he didn't. Peter had an inventor's dislike of the predictable, and he could predict Neil's reaction to anything within a percentage point. It was always the reaction most likely to bring the situation to Neil's advantage.

"Go figure." Peter laughed to himself. "He's the ideal employee and I don't like him for it."

In comparison, of course, the people around Neil seemed filled with silly human failings. In fact, Neil had a way of bringing those failings out in others. The longer Neil spent with a group, the more problems everyone else seemed to bring upon themselves.

Going on instinct, Peter requested copies of the specifics of Neil's last-minute trip to Fiji. Neil's story to Peter had been that, upon reflection, he felt it was important for one of the senior executives to be at the close of the conference. Having not taken any personal time for months, Neil decided he would combine a bit of vacation with an appearance in Fiji. The decision was reasonable enough.

The man flew business class to Hawaii, standard procedure for an executive. Then, not wanting to wait for the infrequent scheduled flights across the Pacific, he chartered a plane from Honolulu to Fiji, with a scheduled stop on Christmas Island. The barely populated atoll was about one thousand miles south of Hawaii and a little less than half-way to Fiji. Refueling?

Neil said in his report he requested a day's layover and logged a vacation day into the Penthes system. Well, Neil did like to SCUBA. He also skied well, of course, and played a perfectly fine game of golf. All the right stuff.

Neil provided an expense report for his day on Christmas Island as required. It had no doubt been filled out by his personal assistant. According to the receipts, he had dined alone and there was only one occupant in his hotel room. So this wasn't a hanky-panky excursion. Of course it wasn't.

Perhaps there was a bit of misuse of company funds, Peter thought, but it wasn't outrageous for the COO of a company. Excursions like this were considered acceptable for those at the top.

Neil included a copy of the flight plan filed the morning of January 27 showing the plane leaving Christmas Island for Fiji just after dawn, with Neil intending to arrive in Fiji by late afternoon, a few days before the conference attendees. He probably planned to dive there also. According to the pilot's report, Neil received a phone call from Samoa while they were in route and insisted they divert the plane. They had, arriving in Apia late morning. So the pilot's report basically matched Neil's story.

Neil also provided a curt written report of his own after the incident, detailing how Gil had identified the body earlier that morning, but he had asked to see the body as well and been allowed to do so. Peter's best guess was Neil took the necklace then because it had once been the source of embarrassment and conflict. Perhaps he didn't want it to show up in a photo.

Why had the authorities let him take it? Perhaps Neil made a small contribution to cover any trouble taking it might cause. Maybe he just put it in his pocket when no one was looking. Either way, it was unusual, and Peter realized with some relish that this was the first truly hard-to-explain behavior he'd ever seen Neil Bennett exhibit. Intriguing.

In fact, the information about Brenda's necklace might have been the most useful piece of intelligence Zane had produced so far. It reminded Peter that while Zane was bright and eager, he didn't have the experience for the investigative part of what Peter had asked him to do. Sure he could report to Peter about morale at Penthes and the reputation of the industry and he might even turn up something new about Pete by using fresh and unbiased eyes.

However, Zane wasn't a professional detective and Peter knew he had to face that fact. Good or bad, it looked like there was more to Neil than Peter knew. He needed additional data about the man and he needed it soon, because he didn't have all that much time left to figure out whether Neil ought to be trusted with Penthes' future.

******

Most of Afi's classmates liked him well enough before he escaped, and more than a few felt gratitude for the times Afi had spoken up for them. Once they learned he was responsible for their release, however, his status was elevated to that of hero.

It wasn't surprising he heard back right away from ten of the twelve boys on the beach. Six of them had an opinion. One thought the lady might have been wearing a necklace. Three thought she probably wasn't. But two were positive the dead woman had not had on a necklace of any kind.

"How can you be so sure?" Afi wrote them. "It could have slid around to her back, been hard to see."

No, the boys were sure because they had guessed the lady had been strangled and dared each other to approach a step closer to look for strangle marks on her neck. No strangle marks. No marks at all. The sparkly t-shirt was cut into a V-shape, and the white neck had been eerie and bare. They were positive because they had looked at it so closely.

Afi had not expected such definite information, but he was happy to pass it along to Zane.

******

Although Joy's father had yet to exchange a word with her, by March, Joy's mother was passing along greetings from him too, in stiffly worded phrases like "Your father sends his wishes that you are well." Joy, still angry, ignored the comments until Zane posed his question about the necklace. Her father, with his gift for throwing his weight around with strangers, could possibly be of help if he were willing.

Joy presented the request to her mother. Could a U.S. judge make an inquiry on behalf of a relative to find out if a certain piece of jewelry was found anywhere on or alongside the victim? If the judge was a man with Judge Cabrini's assertiveness, Joy thought he probably could.

She didn't know if her father's speed in helping her was her mother's doing, or if perhaps in his own self-involved way the man wanted to reach out to her. Either way, she had an answer in two days. Apia's police department had a complete log of Brenda's effects. They were more than happy to tell any official anywhere that while the woman was wearing quite a bit of jewelry, no necklace of any sort had been found on or near the body.

******

Zane sat on his bed, the small box of childhood keepsakes open and its contents spread out. There were photos of Balthazar and the Dr. Seuss book and a few of the many math and science fair medals he'd won. He'd even kept a few of his favorite old video games, which of course ran on systems so primitive they no longer could be found.

Zane looked through the childhood treasures with nostalgia. Well, at least he no longer wanted to grow up to be a chameleon. He picked up one of his precious issues of *Professor Xavier and the X-Men*, carefully preserved by an enthralled ten-year-old. Professor Charles Francis Xavier, protector of the odd, had been Zane's greatest childhood hero.

In the end, he thought, one wants to be what one admires.

So what about the thousands of foster kids Penthes was perfectly happy to see put on stronger medication? These children were part of the odd, in that they had no family to claim them, no kin to protect them. Couldn't the outliers always use one more person to look out for them?

******

Mark Hadley liked to play poker. He saw himself as a daring loner who, through no fault of his own, was out of aces at the moment. As he packed up the few items of value in his Los Angeles office, he thought about how good the cards had been since 2001. That, of course, was the year when his cards had turned so bad he had been forced to close everything, change his name, and start over.

Mark knew back then not to fight the charges, even though some of them were wrong and others were blown out of proportion. To stay and fight would bring his schools the kind of publicity he could never recover from, because the fact remained that a few of the charges were true. Things had gotten out of hand at a place or two. A child had died in one case, ended up disabled for life in another. Once that became known, no one would ever trust him with their child again.

So Paul Harris reinvented himself as Mark Hadley and moved on. Mark was older, wiser, and had a tidy sum in the bank to help him with the transition. Now, Mark Hadley would move on as well, legally changing his name to become... who? Mark was still toying with the choices, for both himself and his new set of schools. The last nine years had been lucrative, but maybe the next nine would be even better.

******

Gil had studied public relations years ago, hoping to end up working for a politician or a cause he believed in. Back then, there had been so many. Then along came the child, a surprise from a girlfriend who had problems remembering to take a pill every day. She wanted the baby, so there had been a marriage, after which Gil came to grips with the harsh realities of commitment.

The baby girl was delicate, with health issues from the beginning, so Gil left his barely paid position with a nonprofit for the better pay and health insurance that came with a job in the marketing department of a pharmaceutical company. It turned out the girlfriend, now wife, liked to party more than Gil had realized. Eventually, he was pretty sure there were boyfriends and an increasing taste for party drugs.

Then came the fights and apologies and promises and tears. One day, Gil looked at the cash withdrawals on their bank statement and knew he'd better open a separate account or they weren't going to have money for food and rent. Gil got home from work one evening and found two-year-old daughter Erin sitting on the carpet, playing with a bottle of dish soap by herself. His wife was nowhere to be found.

Gil was an easygoing man, but he knew the time had come for an ultimatum: professional help and a twelve-step program of any sort, or out the door. His wife looked at him like she wondered why it had taken so long. She left the next day while he was at work and at least she left Erin with a neighbor. He never heard from her again.

Gil knew he had choices. He could put Erin into foster care and go back to the life he had wanted for himself. He hadn't wanted this child and he had no family to help him. He gave the option serious consideration and realized his wants had changed. He still hoped to do some good in this world, to have some fun, to find love. But he also loved the delicate little girl who called him daddy, and he wished to remain her daddy. That would require day care and health insurance and the stability his current job provided.

So he had a long talk with himself. If he was going to go this route, becoming a bitter I-gave-up-my-life-for-you parent was not an option. Not for him. He wanted to embrace his life, his work, his daughter, and his choices. He wanted to find fulfillment within all of them. No self-pity. Life doesn't do things to you. You choose.

Which is how Gil became one of the happiest employees of Penthes Pharmaceuticals. He was capable and hardworking and soon found himself in middle management. Because he wasn't terribly ambitious, he threatened no one and people liked him. They wanted to work for him. He was a reasonable boss and a good person, and after a while Gil realized he *was* making a difference in the world. There was a small group of people who had better days and better lives because of him. It wasn't a lot, but it was something.

Of course, there was also his daughter. Cared for with sensible limits and limitless love, she blossomed. Her health improved. She would never be terribly strong, but a dozen years after her mother left her, she was a quiet, caring girl who enjoyed art and had taken to making these amazing watercolor and ink creations that appeared to almost float off the paper. Already Gil was looking into the best colleges for the artistically gifted.

Then had come the new patent on the drug, and the conference and his boss's death and his horrible discovery that the company which had been more or less good to him for the past fourteen years wanted to stay afloat by encouraging the heavy medication of children like his beautiful daughter. Had he made different choices, this group could have included his beautiful daughter. The idea made Gil sick to his stomach.

So he did the most aggressive thing he'd done in his career. He picked up a pen and paper and began to draft an alternate proposal, to take directly to Peter Hulson. He pulled numbers, facts, and analogs. There was more than one way to make money, and he thought he could prove it.

Yes, Neil's way would make more in the short term and so the stockholders would like it better, for now. But Gil wanted to plan for the future, at least the future beyond the next quarterly report. He proposed becoming a niche pharmaceutical company, one which provided more information, assistance, and honesty than any competitor came close to giving. Let the big companies deal with the lawsuits and bad press. Gil had a vision of positioning Penthes to be the provider of choice in a changing world.

******

At twenty-two years old, John von Neumann received his PhD in mathematics and went on to make major contributions to quantum mechanics and computer science. Yet his most well-known creation involved no math at all.

John von Neumann worked at the height of the cold war, and he described a strategy called MAD. Mutually assured destruction. It goes like this. You have a weapon so awful that if you use it against me, I will use my similar weapon against you, and we all die. Therefore, as long as both of us stay fully armed and ready to fight, we never will. Mad, right?

Much of humanity hoped MAD meant we'd finally made war so horrible we'd have to walk away from it. No such luck. Instead, we found ways to have little wars tucked away in places we couldn't nuke because half the civilians there were on our side. We found ways to turn the fight against terrorism into a worldwide activity. We're a creative species. You have to give us that.

These were Toby's dark thoughts as he approached his island home. He hadn't seen a single low-flying plane, and had only sighted one distant freighter, on his entire four-week journey. Granted he'd taken his time, riding out one storm at sea rather than seeking a port and avoiding all known frequented routes.

Any law enforcement scenario Toby could think of involved authorities boarding his boat at this point and taking him in. Yet, as he approached the island, there was no sign of life or of intrusion.

Toby concluded the I-Kiribati hadn't been asked to give up his location, and U.S. authorities hadn't become involved. It looked like Tropical Retreat Academy wasn't asking questions and Brenda Mill's friends, relatives, and coworkers weren't clamoring for answers. In short, as long as he stayed out of sight, and out of Samoa, he was a free man.

Put another way, the doctrine of mutually assured destruction was working on a simple two-man level. Neil Bennett had, from all appearances, kept his word and successfully discouraged follow-up investigations well enough to let Toby get away. He'd promised to keep Toby's name out of any international criminal databases. Sooner or later, Toby would have to get more supplies and he'd find out if Neil had kept his word on that front as well.

Neil probably had, because Toby was armed as well. He had his own weapons that he could never use, so they would both keep their silence. It was mad. And maddening.

April 2010

16. The Smell of Coffee Liqueur

When Zane and Peter met on Wednesday, Zane led off the meeting with his latest research on Mark Hadley. He'd managed to learn about Paul Harris, an entrepreneur in the alternative education field who had run a successful chain of small private schools until several of the schools ran into problems and had to be closed.

Mr. Harris then legally changed his name, address, and appearance. The few photos Zane found showed the newly minted Mark Hadley preferred lighter, longer hair, and the more relaxed business attire reminiscent of Southern California. Mr. Hadley built a second chain of schools, in some cases buying the old schools from his former corporation and re-opening them under his new name. Legal, of course.

Zane brought copies of the mentions in the business press indicating Mark Hadley's second company had closed, all assets were in receivership, and no one could be reached for comment.

"He's going to do it again," Zane said. "Give him a year or two and he'll have a whole new chain of schools going."

"Indeed," Peter said. "An unsavory business, but of no interest to me."

Zane was disappointed. He'd hoped his efforts would be of intellectual curiosity to Peter but reminded himself that in Peter's increasingly uncomfortable shoes he, too, would have less interest in extraneous information.

Besides, it was clear Peter had business of his own he wanted to get out of the way. The man had squirmed in his seat until Zane finished talking. Once Zane was done, Peter explained without a lot of eye contact how he realized Zane could not be expected to produce anything much more useful about Brenda's death.

"It's not personal, Zane. I just think things have gotten complicated and I'd be better served hiring a good private detective, one who specializes in this sort of issue."

He added that Zane could work on getting him more information, of course, and could continue to be his eyes and ears within the company as originally agreed, because Peter still thought Zane could be useful. Their deal still held.

Zane was a bit taken aback and even, in an odd way, a little hurt. He supposed what Peter said made sense and he should have anticipated the move. But he did have sources of his own and he had been learning pertinent information. Zane interrupted to explain about Afi's former fellow students and Joy's father.

"Peter, both of these unrelated sources have established for us that the necklace in Neil's drawer absolutely was not on dead Brenda. Yet I know from my own eyes that it was on live Brenda. This means Neil, or someone he is in contact with, was with live Brenda that night, or at least with dead Brenda before she washed ashore. Whatever. You get what I'm saying."

Peter paused to consider. Zane had once again gotten new and potentially useful information.

"Maybe you're a better detective than I thought." The old man was almost smiling. Peter gave a what-the-hell shrug as he went to his desk to get his copies of the documents from Neil's trip. "Let's see if we can rule out the possibility of Neil being with live Brenda that night."

They pulled their chairs closer and went over the receipts and notes together. The paperwork painted a pretty solid picture of Neil spending two nights on Christmas Island.

"The kicker is the flight plan," Peter said. "This is a good clear copy of the original, and nothing has been altered. You don't mess with this stuff. That plane took off from Christmas Island the morning of the 27th, and on the morning of the 27th Brenda had already washed ashore. There is no Neil in Samoa to take her necklace."

As Peter pondered the implications, Zane thought about a new private investigator, or, in fact, anyone else delving into this. Half-truths found could damage his friends.

"Peter, can I have just one more week at this solo?" he asked, surprising himself. "Someone else poking around will have an effect. Please. If I can't come up with a reasonable scenario for you before our next meeting in a week, I'll back off any way you like and provide all the assistance I can to whomever you want to lead your personal investigation."

Peter liked deals like that and Zane knew it. On some level he found watching a human wrestle with a challenge to be entertaining. What was a week? He still felt strong in spite of the pain.

"Sure, Zane. I'm not going anywhere for a while. With your new information, you've earned yourself one more week as my primary detective. Take your best shot."

Peter popped another pain pill as Zane left the room, and both of them were aware how much Peter could use all the entertaining distractions he could get.

Logic was what Zane did best. Over the next several days he forced himself to work through the necklace problem piece by piece. What were the options? He started with the least incriminating situation and worked forward.

One. The necklace was a different one altogether. Such a strange coincidence was possible. Ridiculous, but possible. Forget that one.

Two. Neil got the necklace from someone else after the fact. It was given to him by the killer. Or stolen by him from the killer. Or from someone who knew the killer. This avenue was probable. But how and why? File that option away, he decided, because once he was thoroughly convinced Neil spent two nights on Christmas Island it would be his only reasonable choice and he would come back to it.

Three. Neil saw Brenda the night she died, saw her dead or alive. He either was the killer, or he knew the killer. Otherwise he would have come forward with the entire story. But door number three only opened if Neil had been in Samoa when he said he was on Christmas Island. Zane spent much of his weekend mulling that over as he made his way through the motions of everyday life.

By Monday morning, something was bothering Zane about the Christmas Island thing. Hadn't someone he knew been prevented from going diving the day before they flew home? He seemed to remember a twenty-four-hour wait period before flights. A few keystrokes showed that while no wait was required after flying, a wait of twelve to twenty-four hours was the accepted guideline for going from the higher pressure of the ocean to the lower pressure of an airplane's cabin.

Neil seemed like a sensible guy, not one for taking random risks with no benefit. Someone of his means had certainly chartered a pressurized plane. So, Zane had trouble believing Neil would sandwich a dive in between two days of flying. Possible. But it didn't ring true. Why else would the man go to Christmas Island?

By Tuesday morning, something else was bothering Zane. Most of the receipts looked like they were in the same handwriting. Probably Neil's. When Zane traveled on business, individuals like cab drivers often gave him blank receipts so he could fill them out himself, thinking they were doing him a favor. You know, skim a little extra. Most of them probably hoped they'd get some of it back as a tip. Zane supposed they often did.

Such a practice could be prevalent on a remote island. If Neil was given blank receipts at most places, no lie was intended on his part. Yet, it gave Neil an easy option of adjusting dates as well as dollar amounts.

When Zane woke up Wednesday morning, there was something else bothering him about Christmas Island. Zane knew he knew it; he just couldn't quite remember what *it* was. He pulled up a world map on his screen.

Christmas Island was one of the easternmost points of Afi's home country. Maybe one of Afi's relatives knew someone there. He made a mental note to ask Afi the next time he called.

The island was barely inhabited. Surely a man flying in alone on a private jet would have been noticed by many. Maybe someone paid attention to when he arrived and left or what he did while he was there.

Zane went to get a cup of coffee. Maybe a little caffeine would help him think. He held the warm drink under his nose, and then wrinkled it in dismay. Someone had made flavored coffee. The stuff smelled like Kahlua, the one liqueur he never drank.

The smell had him dumping the coffee into the sink while he chuckled at the memory of thirteen-year-old Zane lying on his bathroom floor, sick from swallowing heaven knows how much of a concoction called Tia Maria. That was how he had greeted the year 2000. He didn't think his parents had ever missed the bottle. Thankfully. That much vomiting had been punishment enough.

Then Zane remembered *it.* Damn. Kiribati. Dancers in gold headdresses greeting the new millennium, passing torches and blowing in conch shells. Being the first to great the new millennium. Christmas Island was part of Kiribati. Damn. *That* was what he knew.

Half an hour later Zane sat with a globe in Peter's office.

"I know you're going to love this. We were wrong, Peter. Neil did indeed take off from Christmas Island the morning of January 27 with the intention to land in Fiji the evening of January 27. And he was, I am sure of it, in Samoa the night of the 26th."

"You're not making any sense." Peter would have been annoyed but Zane's ear-to-ear grin made it too difficult. The boy had figured out something and he was proud of it.

"Peter, in the late 1990s the country of Kiribati singlehandedly moved the International Date Line so the entire country could be on the same side of it. It was hard doing business when it was Sunday morning in part of the country and Monday morning in the rest of it."

"Seems sensible enough. So?" Peter asked.

"Well, a lot of the world just ignored it and a lot of globes, modern globes, still don't show it, like yours here, because Kiribati made a really big curve in the line, since Kiribati covers a huge area. Granted, most of that area is water, and most of the rest of the world doesn't give a rat's ass where the International Date Line is as long as it isn't in their own back yard, but as far as the Kiribati are concerned, January 27 came to Christmas Island and Millennium Island about twenty-four hours before it came to Samoa, which actually sits at about the same longitude, but is on the other side of the line. My point is that every day comes early to eastern Kiribati.

They see every day first. And every new day comes last to Samoa. If you get what I mean."

"I do." Peter was laughing. "Zane, you're right. I love this. Thanks for not disappointing me. So Neil took off the morning of the 27th just like he claimed and managed to fly south, even a little southwest, for a few hours and still land on the eastern side of the International Date Line, where it was the afternoon of January 26th.

"That's right," Zane said. "His flight plan called for landing the night of the 27th, because he really planned to land in Fiji, which is on the same side of the International Date Line as Kiribati. I don't think he originally intended any deception."

"So what happened?" Peter asked.

"I'm working on why he went to Christmas Island to begin with," Zane said, "because I don't think it was for diving, because mixing all that flying with diving is a bad idea, and I don't think Neil takes dumb risks."

Peter agreed.

"Then, I'm trying to figure out why he diverted from Fiji to Samoa. My guess is Brenda contacted him about something that caused him concern. You could maybe get answers from the charter company about what sort of message he received in-flight. But whatever, he is in Samoa the night of the 26th, he gets the necklace, Brenda dies. Then, I think, it occurs to him that not leaving Christmas Island until the 27th is a great stroke of luck, because who back home pays attention to curves in the International Date Line, right? So Neil latches on to that story, that timing, and he adjusts his receipts to corroborate it. If nothing else, Neil is great at seizing an opportunity.

"Now I'm sure the officials at the airport in Samoa and Samoan immigration could confirm his true arrival date with no problem, and these guys know all about the date line. But I'm thinking maybe no one asked them. Why would they? Neil was clear and confident about his arrival time with the police, and by the time he was on the scene the authorities had already focused on Toby as the killer and accepted Neil as a late-arriving representative of Penthes. I don't think they bothered to ask their own border officials about an American executive who professed to have arrived to claim the body, and who just wanted to get the matter moved along."

"If that's the case, it was quite a bluff," Peter said. "Because if anyone had checked his arrival time, he'd have been without a way to explain it. But you know, I can see Neil being so certain and so… focused… that he pulls something like this off. I have a great deal of respect for what the man can do. So the only part of this I'm having trouble with is the idea of Neil killing anyone. And, why in the world would Neil kill Brenda?"

"I'm working on it. Have I earned myself another week?"

"Take two."

"How about a trip back to Samoa if I need it? Or, better yet, one to Christmas Island and then Samoa?"

Peter's eyebrow went up. He thought for a couple of seconds.

"Use the company jet. I'll okay one trip. Stop wherever you need to, but don't tell anyone here you're going. And Zane, you'd better come back with more than a suntan. Bring answers."

******

When Peter asked Zane to serve as his eyes and ears, he had no way of knowing what an excellent set of ears he'd hired. As far as eyes went, Zane's were average at best, but his eyes had the advantage of not being attached to only one easy-to-identify body. Zane's eyes got to see things that others wanted to hide from Zane.

He decided it was time for Ying to get a drink after work. Ying donned his orange and peach Hawaiian shirt and seated himself at the familiar bar. It was a warm spring day and looked like it would be a slow evening for the pub. Worse yet, an unfamiliar waitress approached. Damn. Looked like a ginger ale today. This might have been a total waste of time.

He was surprised to see Chloe and Raven come in and even more surprised to see them take a table in the dining section. They usually invited him along for drinks and almost never ate here. Well, at least as far as he knew.

Ying didn't want to stare at the girls, who were now seated behind him and some distance away. He was pretty sure Raven looked like she'd been crying. Not good, but it explained Zane's exclusion and the more private dinner table. Serious girl talk about a jerk who had treated Raven poorly?

If Zane hadn't known his friends' voices so well, he wouldn't have been able to tune into them and isolate them like he did. But he knew them and there they were.

"Raven, even if you never do anything about this, it's important you stop saying it was your fault. Okay? Stop it. You are entitled to go out. You are entitled to look nice. You're even entitled to be affectionate and it does not commit you to anything. Repeat after me. This was not my fault."

Raven gave a half-hearted laugh. Chloe persisted.

"I mean it Raven. Say it."

"This was not my fault," Raven said with little conviction.

Hell. Was this what it sounded like?

"He's an asshole." Chloe was adamant. "He knows he's your boss and turning him down for a date is at best uncomfortable. He knows you'll play along up to a point. What kind of douche bag takes advantage of that?"

This was Neil?

"Neil's socially awkward away from work, even naive," Raven said. "He could have misread the situation"

Yup. It was Neil.

"That's ridiculous. Look, I get you don't want to scream rape, even though I think you should, and I understand the fourteen ways doing so fucks up your life way more than it does his."

Raven muttered something back that even Zane couldn't hear.

"Because, Raven, you're my friend, and trust me, even if you don't want to go after him, you've got to look out for yourself. There is no way you deserved to be assaulted. You can hate him, you can forgive him, but you can't pretend it didn't happen."

This time Raven's answer was audible. "You don't get it, Chloe. Pretending it didn't happen is the easiest thing for me."

"No Raven. I do get it. Not because this has ever happened to me, thankfully it hasn't, although it could. But I say this from my heart, because I've got secrets of my own. I've done things that didn't show the best judgement and then, well, my situation is what it is. My point is you can have horrible secrets, or ones that are really not that bad when you pull them out into the daylight, but as long they are tucked away like they are the worst things imaginable, then they fester with a power beyond any of the actual facts involved until finally there is an internal pocket of pus, swollen but well hidden, that sucks the joy out of everything. I don't want that to happen to you. So look at yourself in the mirror. Tell yourself the damn guy is a despicable bastard for doing what he did. You may never confront him about it, but don't rewrite the facts. Please Raven."

Zane didn't think he had ever seen Chloe so passionate about anything. Ying finished his ginger ale and stood to leave. He wanted to give his friends privacy for the rest of their conversation. Plus, three facts already had his brain reeling.

First. Neil was more of a scumbag than Zane realized and there had to be some way of letting Peter know this without involving Raven. No man who would do that should run a company. Wait. This might be way more common than he realized. How about deciding that he did not want to see one *more* man who would do that running a company?

Second fact. Chloe had quoted Zane almost word for word when she was talking about the dangers of secrets. She had quoted words he'd used privately to Peter, who'd seemed miffed at Zane's blunt presumption in speaking so critically of him. It looked like the old man, offended or not, had taken those words to heart. Enough so to repeat them to his granddaughter.

Which brought Zane to the third fact. Chloe had talked about her own well-intended but bad decisions and living with the secrets they'd spawned. Finding your dead brother is a tragedy, but it's not a decision. Was there something else about Joel's death that Chloe was hiding? Zane hoped not, because Chloe was turning into one of the most likeable people at Penthes, and he didn't want that to change.

******

Joy felt like she was living two lives at once. In one, she taught Samoan third graders by day, dressed demurely in lightweight long-sleeved tops and loose colorful skirts to her ankles. She was Afi's wife by night. Given the vast number of options open to humanity in 2010, it wasn't a bad life. She wasn't hungry, she wasn't hurting, she had a friend nearby, and she was doing useful work. Life came a lot worse.

In her other life, she sailed the ocean, barefoot in a tank top and short nylon gym trunks. Her hair blew free while her body moved softly with the thunk of the boat hitting the waves. Toby's hand was on her thigh as he sat at the helm of Miss Demeanor. She would see his hint of a smile as his fingers started to rise higher up her leg and then he would turn to her, with his soft brown eyes asking her a question. She felt herself smiling her answer back and then he always set the sails and they went below deck where life was incredibly good.

Of course, that other life existed only in her mind. Anyone who'd ever been in love, however, knew it was the more important of her two lives.

******

As the weeks wore on and nothing happened, Joy and Afi became bolder in their contact with Zane. By the end of April, the three of them were talking often. Sometimes, Joy left the room and gave Afi a few minutes alone. Other times, the three of them brainstormed about what had happened. Afi still laughed when he thought of Zane's adventures as Ximena the custodian, and he and Joy speculated about the meaning of the dream catcher necklace.

They loved Zane's analysis of how Neil had taken off from Christmas Island the day after he'd arrived in Samoa, and they agreed with Zane that the Samoan police had likely never looked into the arrival time of the prestigious U.S. executive. That could change, of course, with an anonymous tip, but the three of them saw nothing to be gained. Local news sources never mentioned the investigation. Best to leave it that way.

In the y^1 chat areas, Afi asked questions regarding Toby's whereabouts. Although Toby had disappeared before for weeks at a time, other participants agreed it was odd Toby hadn't been heard from for months. No one had a theory. Afi figured that was just as well, also.

Afi threw out tidbits about the threats Toby had received, hoping to learn if Toby's disapproval of inherited wealth had played a role. Others responded that y^1 had become so large that silencing its founder would longer do an opponent much good. Afi thought the point was valid, so he let the issue drop.

One last item caused him concern. In that first week aboard Miss Demeanor, he'd shared toiletries with Toby because he had nothing of his own. Looking for toothpaste, he'd found dark brown hair dye. After the visit to Toby's island home, Afi guessed Toby dyed his hair to keep his identify secret because of the dangers of being y^1's founder. But if the threats no longer mattered, why did Toby still do it? Maybe the dark hair was about wanting to look younger or to better blend in with those around him. Perhaps it was as simple as he'd been doing it for so long he'd become accustomed to the look.

The best phone call ever came from Zane in early May, after he'd surprised his boss with the curved International Date Line. His boss wanted more answers so he was letting Zane go to Christmas Island and Samoa to retrace Neil's path and ask questions. To do this, he had been given his own plane. His own plane? Well, the company's plane, but he was getting to use it.

He would fly to Christmas Island in a couple of weeks, then come to Am. Sam. and Samoa. Then, depending on what he found, he'd go on to Kiribati and possibly to Fiji. Why didn't Joy and Afi join him? School would be out, and they could come with Zane and take care of their immigration paperwork issues while they were on Tarawa. Afi could see his family or not. Zane would have the plane return them to Am. Sam., or they could deplane in Hawaii instead, whichever they preferred. They should start looking into their options now. Were they interested?

"Are we interested? This is a question you have to ask?"

"No, probably not."

Afi closed his eyes as they filled with emotion. With one phone call life had gone from could-be-worse to incredibly good. He would see both Zane and Kiribati in a little over two weeks.

May 2010

17. Regrets

Wednesday, May 5, was a beautiful Chicago spring day, the kind the city has half a dozen of each year between the bouts of thunderstorms and high winds that herald the transition from freezing cold to way too hot.

Peter sat huddled under a blanket, oblivious to the sunshine coming in through the windows and bouncing off of the whitecaps visible on the lake below. Zane took a good hard look at Peter. "Oh," was all he could say.

"No, I don't regret my decision," Peter said hoarsely, "so don't ask. Odds were overwhelming that treatment would only have bought me a few more uncomfortable months. Trust me, I wish the odds had been different."

There was silence. Then Peter asked, "Are you going back to the Pacific?"

"I am. I've reserved the plane and listed you as the approver."

Peter pulled the edges of the blanket tighter over his arms. "I've told Neil I'm experiencing some health issues and having tests run. He looked neither surprised nor sad."

"Should you be worried about a power play from him?" Zane asked.

"I don't think so. I think he knows he doesn't have to bother. What do you have for me today?"

"Minor stuff on the Brenda murder. Friends in Samoa say it's dropped out of the news. My friends wonder if Penthes, or someone speaking for Penthes, let authorities know that would be preferred."

"Interesting. Who might have done that?" Peter couldn't quite manage a smile, but he gave Zane a bit of a wink.

"Indeed who?" Zane played along. Then it occurred to him. Not who Peter was joking about, but why Peter was making the joke.

"You don't particularly like Neil, do you?" Zane asked.

"Like has nothing to do with business."

"Bullshit. With all due respect, it has a lot to do with business. When you lost Pete and Joel you could have let Neil fill in the gap. But you resisted, looking for a better replacement. Neil wouldn't go away and it seems to me he played a part in making sure you never saw a worthy candidate. Yet you never stopped looking. Why not?"

"I've been asking myself the same question, and I'm not sure I can answer it. Not rationally anyway."

"Okay." Zane swallowed hard because when he came in the door he hadn't been sure he was going to do this next part, but it looked like he was. "I know for a fact that Neil, emotionally restrained as he is, is capable of horrible, even criminal, behavior, in another arena. I can't betray specific confidences but no one wants a man who acts in a way he has, to have even more power and prestige to misuse. Maybe if I give you a vague version of what happened, you'll feel better about your instincts."

"Oh no. Did he rape someone again?" Peter's eyes were sad, but not surprised.

"What? This has happened before?"

"So she said. She was sweet girl, a new hire in marketing. It was about seven or eight years ago. She came straight to me crying. I don't know how she got an appointment. Brenda was livid with her for not handling it through appropriate channels. Neil said he'd bought her a drink after work, nothing more, and he accused her of making it up to get money. Said it was the most ridiculous thing he'd ever heard. She wrote me a formal letter a couple of weeks later retracting everything and admitting she had fabricated the incident hoping for a lucrative settlement. She apologized and resigned."

"And?"

"And I had no choice but to agree to her resignation. Neil had never been accused of any misbehavior before. I've tried to keep an eye out ever since as I watched Neil continue to take out all of the prettiest new ones for a drink. I mentioned to Brenda to let me know if she ever suspected a problem. I think she told Neil because he was miffed at me for a while. Anyway, no other stories ever made their way to me, and in every other respect the man is a boy scout. But my instincts, well, my instincts said when that girl came to me crying, she wasn't lying. My instincts also told me that no matter what he did, Neil would make sure I never heard an accusation like that again."

"Yet now you have."

"I know. We don't need to embarrass your friend Raven. It is Raven, right?"

When Zane winced, he added, "She's the newest, she's pretty, and she's the one you know best. I don't have to read minds. So. I believe you, and I know you believe her. I think the issue is what plausible alternative to Neil do I have at this point? How exactly does a dying man go about changing the course of a company?"

"How about I find a way to get him charged with murder?" Zane said.

"Well, yes, that would be good. Quite good. Why don't you work on that, and I'll work on putting together a decent alternative we can turn to in case you're successful."

Peter did smile then, a weak but happy smile. "I wish you and I'd had the chance to start plotting like this years ago. What fun we could've had. Well, we'll just have to move quickly now, won't we?"

Zane left to get started.

******

Toby enjoyed the quiet of his island home, and after a few days he started to feel safe again. Not safe enough to turn on the satellite providing him with internet access, but safe enough to go for walks on the beach, to make cooking fires, and to light lanterns. It made for a huge improvement over hiding in the dark for weeks in the outer islands of Fiji.

Better yet, his well-insulated vault still held a precious bit of dry ice and his last two Argentine beef tenderloins. He savored both of them the first week home and opened a treasured Malbec as well. His basket tomatoes had been producing lavishly, and after cleaning up the rotten ones he picked the ripest. Fortunately, oil and vinegar don't spoil if one can keep the bugs out. After two such meals, he felt human again.

What a mess, what an incredible mess, he told himself. It was his own fault, in so many ways. He'd broken every rule he'd made for himself by taking Afi aboard, and then turned around and done it again with Joy. His great idea of helping them earn money so they could move on had been just stupid. What had he been thinking?

Then there was the kid from Penthes. Zane. Nice kid. Toby had no business whatsoever agreeing to have him back on the boat. But, there'd been the work together in Samoa after the earthquake, and that goofy walk through hot coals, and somehow they were all best buddies. Friendship after all these years had felt good.

Then, as a final act of hopeless idiocy, he'd agreed to sail alongside the Penthes regatta over to Samoa so Afi could fire dance. *Stupid, stupid, stupid.* What was the matter with him?

What *was* the matter with him? Finally, after two weeks at home where he kicked himself each day for every stupid choice, Toby woke up and asked the question with different intonations.

What was the *matter* with him? He was innocent. He'd lived a law-abiding and good life. To pay for his stupid but well-intended decisions with a lifetime of hiding was too high a price to pay.

What was the matter with *him*? Nothing. He had people who cared for him. He could change his life if he chose. He fired up the satellite dish and started to make contact.

******

Joy saw the email from Toby, and suddenly she could hear her own heartbeat. There it was, with no disguise, no preamble.

"Joy dear. Dear Afi. Am home safe and think I can remain so as long as I choose, but this is no way to live. Would like to explain what happened to you in person. Any travel plans? Will sail to meet you anywhere without Samoa in the name. Let me know if we have options."

It was unsigned, but obviously from Toby.

******

Toby saw the email reply from Joy and he could hear his own heart beating in his chest.

"Toby dear. Am teaching and done with school in a week. Zane is coming to the Pacific to look into things on his company plane. He'll pick us up and take us to Kiribati to handle paperwork for Afi. Can you meet us there around May 20? Will Tarawa be okay? Yes, we know you're innocent but in trouble. We want to help."

******

Gil had a vision for a new Penthes, and he was sure it could work because people didn't buy things based solely on cost. Prizes in economics had been won demonstrating people would pay more not to buy a product from someone they disliked. Economists found that surprising, but no one else did. Because a person's best interest wasn't always a matter of dollars and cents, a pharmaceutical company like the one he was envisioning had a chance.

The problem was the stockholders. Their need for profits was insatiable, and Gil understood. He owned stocks in his 401K and he wanted them to be in companies that made lots of money fast and paid him huge dividends when they did.

So, the only way the new Penthes became possible was if it was no longer a publicly traded company. Not because free enterprise didn't work, but because it did.

Gil had watched friends run their own small companies and seen his buddies make it as consultants. People worked harder when they worked for themselves, or when they had an interest in the outcome. They would take chances. They would sink their heart and soul into what they were doing. They were ethical and even compassionate, if they were that way to begin with. They cared in a way they couldn't as an employee collecting a paycheck and certainly not as a stockholder hoping to collect the cash.

The way to create this new company was for the employees to buy it. Then the workers could find it in their own best interest to accept less pay and more employment risk, for a while, in return for more flexible working conditions, more involvement in the operation of the company, and possibly greater economic rewards down the road. There would be a bonus in working to find desperately needed medicines, and in working to see the medicines were used appropriately. Gil's theory was that if it was *their* company, the employees would care.

Caring employees could build an amazing pharmaceutical company that was one of the good guys. Medical professionals would prefer to rely on a company known to set high ethical standards as opposed to cynically accepting large fines for improperly pushing their drugs. If this new company had the kind of time stockholders could never be expected to give, Gil could market products to a growing group of customers who would ask their doctor about what Penthes recommended. Because they trusted Penthes.

******

Later that week, Chloe dropped by to see Zane, mostly because she was worried about Raven, who was now talking about quitting. Chloe was hoping she could find a way to get Zane's help without telling Zane what the problem was. Tricky business, but she was good at waltzing around secrets without raising suspicions.

Zane wasn't in his office, so Chloe reached for a pad of sticky notes by his computer, and as she glanced up she felt her insides turn ice cold. There, right there on Zane's computer screen, was one of the dozens of photos which flashed around in his absence.

She'd found his screen saver kind of cute, getting a kick out of the endless parade of college life, family, friends, and vacations. This last photo, available for three seconds, was taken on a sailboat, and it showed an Asian boy laughing alongside a girl with a thick black ponytail. A man was standing behind the two of them, looking straight at the camera.

The screen then flashed to the five Zeitmans standing in front of a Christmas tree. Chloe took a deep breath and turned around to see Zane in the doorway watching her.

******

Zane looked at Chloe's face and he knew. He said nothing as he brushed past her, typed in his password, and went to his photos. He opened the one that had been on the screen when he walked in.

"It's him, isn't it? Your dad? I can't believe I didn't see it before."

Chloe nodded. Her voice was a whisper. "I think so. It's hard to tell with only one photo, the dark hair, tanner, older skin. But yes, I think so."

Chloe had shown pictures of her dad to Zane only a couple of weeks ago to help him try to determine if the Turn Your Teen Around guru Mark Hadley might have been Pete years after he disappeared. Zane remembered studying the few still shots she'd shown him, and was amazed at how often people don't see what they don't expect.

"Chloe, I don't know why I didn't notice the resemblance. I guess I was so focused on is-this-man-Mark-Hadley that I didn't think about other possibilities. But when I saw you staring at my screen, I saw it. I'm so sorry. This must be an awful shock. To find out after all these years that he might be still alive…"

"Zane, you idiot." Chloe said it with affection in her voice. "I know damn well he's alive. I helped him get away." She closed Zane's door, sat down in his guest chair, smoothed her jacket with composure, and then burst into tears, sobbing as hard and as loud as Zane had ever seen a human cry.

Zane was afraid the noise might bring knocks on his door, but fortunately his nearest neighbors all appeared to have snuck out early for lunch. He sat offering tissues, and by the time she'd gone through half a box, Chloe was laughing at her own noise.

Zane hadn't said a word. He was trying to craft that perfect remark but settled on "You were only fourteen?"

"I was." She laughed in a way Zane thought could turn to tears at any second. "I loved my daddy very much. He was hurting so bad. Mom hated him and his whole family after Joel died. She loved me, but she hardly saw me she was so broken up. Grandfather was at his worst—defensive and angry and pulling Dad in closer and suffocating him because he thought Dad was all he had left. Then there was Brenda. Dad felt awful about what he'd done with her, and he just wanted out and to pay Brenda lots of money to go away, but she'd been so crucial in covering up how the drugs probably caused Joel's death. Like, really crucial. She made it clear she didn't want money. She wanted to be important at Penthes, and she wanted Dad. He didn't see a way out of that last part without bringing the whole company down."

Chloe stopped to blow her nose one last time. "Can you imagine how much the press would have enjoyed the entire suicide-drug-infidelity-cover-up story?" she said. "Dad placated her and pretended to like her and looked for a way out. Finally, he came up with one."

"Why did he turn to a child, to you?"

"Well, he didn't turn to me. He involved me. He didn't have a lot of options and he needed help. Some of my grandmother's money went straight to him when she died, and as things with Brenda got weirder he hid that away and added to the stash. He couldn't access it all without raising suspicions after the fact, so he put it in various places where I could retrieve it without much scrutiny. Plus, he had this idea that we would stay in contact that way, so he'd always…," a sob escaped, "he'd always be my dad."

"But you lost contact?" Zane asked.

"We talked online at first, a lot. Then when I was sixteen Mom found an email from him and thought it was from some creep on the internet being affectionate with a young girl. She freaked out and started to monitor all my internet use, then Dad freaked out and decided we had to break off contact." Chloe gave Zane one of the saddest looks he'd seen. "I haven't heard a word since."

"So you didn't know for sure if he was alive now?"

She shook her head. "I almost hoped he'd turned into this Mark Hadley, because it would have meant he was okay. Or sort of okay, given the guy sounds like a creep."

Zane decided to change tack. "Does anyone else here know? Your aunt, your cousin? Employees? Friends?"

"Zane, think about it. Secrets like this don't get kept. Everyone around me has some kind of agenda. The only people I thought about contacting were Nicolas' people, in Greece. They might've known how Dad was doing, but of course they're protecting Nicolas and his side of the deal."

"So Nicolas knew?"

"Nicolas was key to the whole thing. He got Dad the second sail boat, got him cash in local currencies, and planned out how they would sail north toward Christmas Island, because everyone would start by looking for them to the south towards Tahiti. Nicolas helped Dad head off to an uninhabited atoll where he could lay low while my grandfather combed the pacific like Dad knew he would.

"Dad considered bringing grandfather in on the whole plan," Chloe added. "It would have make it easier, and Dad was sort of saving grandfather's company. But the more Dad thought about it the more he liked the idea of a clean break with no obligations."

She dabbed at her eyes and took a long sip of water.

"What happened to poor Nicholas?" Zane asked.

"Dad found ways to ensure he got back to Greece and was well rewarded for his discretion."

"So what did your dad live on?"

"Oh, he'd funneled enough money to where he could get to it, and I helped with that both before and after. A teenager can handle a lot of business if she's told exactly what to do, and if she cultivates a certain brusqueness about her that wards off interference. I got good at that. It took Dad about six months to plan this. He was so proud of the millennium sail idea. It was goofy and so much like him that no one questioned it."

"Once he was gone? Wasn't that hard for you?" Zane was trying to pick his questions with tact.

"I missed him more than I thought I would, yes. Mom got even angrier at him for dying, which surprised me. I wanted to tell her so bad. But I'd promised and I knew the shit would hit the fan if I even gave her a hint. I couldn't do that to my dad. Grandfather seemed numb after Dad was gone. Neil stepped in to take more responsibility, just like Dad predicted he would. Over the years I think Dad had started to see Neil as less of a friend. Brenda kept insisting with these dewy eyes that Dad must still be alive somehow, which started to annoy everyone and really annoyed me. She wasn't one of my favorite people to begin with obviously."

"So now what, Chloe?" Zane asked the question without thinking.

"Technically I guess I have to kill you…" He thought she was joking, but up to that point the precariousness of his situation hadn't sunk in. He now knew a multi-million dollar secret. People who knew such things often didn't fare well.

Now what, indeed.

It occurred to both of them at the same time.

"People who know secrets they shouldn't often don't fare well," Zane said.

"They sure don't," Chloe agreed.

"How the hell could Brenda have found out about your Dad?"

Chloe laughed. "Maybe she came in to talk to you and saw your screen saver."

******

As Toby sailed his way to Kiribati in calm weather, he forced himself to stay calm inside as well. No more regrets. No more self-flagellation. The only stupid mistake he allowed himself to dwell on was the way he'd let his understanding of technology slip away while he lived at sea.

For starters, at that moment he hadn't even understood Zane was using his phone to take a picture, or he would have looked away. Of course he knew phones could take photos, because he'd used Zane's phone to snap pictures of that teen prison school. It was just that when someone pulled out a phone, his first assumption was they were going to make a call. So he'd stared at Zane, wondering why the boy thought he could get reception in the middle of ocean.

Once he realized his mistake, he didn't want to make a big deal of it. He figured Zane wasn't the kind of person to bring a roll of photos into the office, so it was safer to say nothing. But, apparently, no one developed a roll of photos anymore. One downloaded them and had them flashing around in plain sight. Not the way it had been in 1999, when screen savers had been points of light pretending to be stars.

How was he supposed to have guessed Zane would display Miss Demeanor's voyage, and Toby's face would appear in three of those shots, along with his boat? How was he supposed to guess that Brenda, of all people, would see those photos flash by and study them and become certain?

More to the point, who would've thought the years would teach Brenda restraint? Instead of shrieking her discovery to the world, she'd grown shrewd enough to keep her own counsel. She'd become clever enough to plan to confront Toby in person.

No, even if he'd understood the advances in technology, he couldn't have predicted the awful way in which all of this would combine.

******

Chloe and Zane left for lunch to continue the conversation outside of the office. As they rode down in the crowded elevator, Zane thought of Peter. This was exactly the reason he made an awful spy: mixed loyalties and lies.

He owed Peter Hulson the truth and the whole truth. He owed his friend Chloe his loyalty and discretion. He had no idea what actions would produce the best outcome for all concerned. Including himself.

"Let's focus on Brenda's death," Chloe suggested as they left the building and started walking. "I know you have a tough decision to make. I have one too. I'm not sure I'm willing to impede a murder investigation to keep a secret my dad no longer needs kept. Do you have a way to contact him?"

"My friends in American Samoa are in communication with him. He's technically on the run from the Samoan police, but they think no one is pursuing this and as long as he stays out of their jurisdiction, he's fine." Zane said.

Chloe thought a minute. "Don't take this wrong, but I'm not sure I'd hold it against my dad if he had killed Brenda. She screwed up his entire life. I'm interested in helping him, not catching him."

"Well, lucky for you, Toby insists he's innocent. And…"

S. R. Cronin

Zane felt his loyalties shifting to his friend. The trick here, he decided, was remembering that ultimately Chloe and Peter Sr. were on the same side. Or at least not on opposite sides.

"Chloe, your grandfather has had me looking into this murder from the beginning, as well as looking into anything else that passes his fancy."

She raised an eyebrow but said nothing.

"I know about Raven. Don't ask how. Your grandfather knows Neil has done something like this before, but honestly he's probably done it more often than that. Don't ask how I know that either. Your grandfather is trying to come up with sensible business reasons to give his board of directors to not turn the reins of Penthes over to Neil because your grandfather truly doesn't like the man, even if Neil is the obvious choice. Don't ask why he's so motivated to fix this now.

"Lastly, I know there is high probability Neil was somehow in Samoa the night Brenda died, in spite of his own word and the evidence he offered to the contrary. I know he has a necklace Brenda wore the night she was killed and the necklace was not found with her body. I have pictures of it lying in Neil's desk drawer. Don't ask how. In short, I know there are reasons to think Neil killed Brenda, and I know proving it would solve a lot of problems for a lot of people."

"Bit too much of the man of mystery thing, Zane," Chloe said, sounding more like her old self. "But given I accept your facts, what exactly were you planning to do about all this before you found me in your office?"

"I was going to get on the Penthes plane tomorrow and, with your grandfather's permission, go talk to people on Christmas Island where Neil made contact and at the airport where he landed in Samoa. I was going to give Joy and Afi a lift to Kiribati, where, according to an email I got a couple of nights ago, Toby is sailing to meet us because he thinks it is a safe place for him. I was going to look Toby in the eye and get answers about Brenda's death. Then I was going to bring it all back here and, if my suspicions turned out to be correct, find a way to get a U.S. citizen named Neil charged with murder. Your grandfather agreed to look into that while I was gone, so I suspect his personal attorney will be part of this too."

"Your scenario makes more sense, doesn't it, if the man on the boat already had deep emotional ties to the both the murderer and the victim?" Chloe said.

"Sure it does. Look, I'd rather have answers than theories before I go to your grandfather a second time and tell him I think I've found his son. So I will, at the least, wait until I get back from this trip before I speak with him. Do you think, if confronted, Toby will admit to me who he really is? If he's your dad?"

"Admit to you?" Chloe said. "I don't know. He might be trying to hang on to a hope of keeping his current life. But I do know he sure as hell isn't going to be able lie to me about it."

"You won't be there."

"Don't be ridiculous. Of course I will. What time do we leave in the morning?"

May 2010

18. Takeoff

Chloe and Zane met at the corporate hangar at Midway Airport the next morning.

"I spoke to my grandfather last night. He was baffled I wanted to go along but he okayed it and even offered to provide a cover story for both of our absences."

"That's good." Chloe only had half Zane's attention as he watched the lavish catered food being loaded. She laughed.

"You didn't expect standard airline food, did you?"

The small jet held six passengers and would be roomy for the two of them. Done in tasteful tan leather and thick beige carpet, its massive amount of polished teak was reminiscent of a fine yacht. Zane noticed the ample electrical outlets and the well-stocked bar.

The copilot, who doubled as cabin steward, informed them they'd be stopping around 7:00 p.m. local time in Honolulu, where the crew would need to rest overnight. Hotel rooms awaited them. They'd takeoff early the next morning for the four-hour flight to the town of Banana on Christmas Island.

"Banana? Really?" the man said. "This is one isolated piece of real estate. What about it interests a pharmaceutical company?"

Chloe and Zane both laughed, but neither answered.

Zane stretched out on a leather couch and opened an imported beer. He sipped as he played computer games, marveling that he was being paid for this. He shrugged and opened a bag of gourmet chips. Sea salt and vinegar. Nice.

Thanks to the wandering of the International Date Line, the Penthes jet landed outside of Banana on late Saturday morning, four hours after their take off early Friday. Zane avoided discussing the purpose of their trip during the flight as the pilots were in easy earshot, and one didn't know where loyalties would lie. Chloe was mostly silent, too, and Zane guessed she'd reached the same conclusion.

Once they landed, the copilot stuck close to them, making it difficult to ask questions of anyone at the airport. All four visitors had to make the five mile drive into town to present their passports in person, and as they crammed into the car Zane took the front seat. At least he could talk to the driver and use the travel time to learn more about Christmas Island.

No, he didn't know the island was the world's largest coral atoll. Zane learned five-thousand people, mostly Polynesians, lived and fished in four towns on Christmas Island. They grew coconuts and sold the copra. They provided for the tourists who came to dive, surf, fish, or bird-watch. What did most tourists do? Most fished. Some came with special permission to tour the bird sanctuaries. Zane could hear another conversation in the back seat. Chloe was asking the copilot about instrument flying. Well done, Chloe.

"So," Zane asked in almost a whisper "what did the previous man from Penthes enjoy most when he was here a few months ago?"

The driver remembered the man had done very little. He'd rented his own car and traveled around the island where he questioned locals. Nothing more. Then he left.

"What is the matter with you people?" the driver asked, gesturing to the wide expanse of open beaches and the beautiful surf in every direction as far as the eye could see. "We have hotels here. Friendly people. Excellent fishing. Why wouldn't you want to stay and enjoy?"

Zane agreed. He would have stayed a dozen nights there under the stars if he could have. But he couldn't.

After paperwork was complete, Chloe instructed the two pilots to stay put while she and Zane took care of business. Zane had to admit there was an advantage to having a companion who was used to ordering people around. As the driver took the two of them to the small hotel where Neil claimed to have stayed for two nights, Zane got his first real chance to think out loud with Chloe.

"How do you suppose Neil figured out to come to Christmas Island? Your dad and Nicolas were supposed to be headed south to Tahiti, remember?"

"I know," Chloe said. "Because they weren't found, I'm sure Neil realized they must have gone in an unexpected direction. Look at a map. There aren't good options to the east or the west. "

"Better yet," Zane said "they'd just come from here, too. They probably spent time on their first stop setting things up."

"They did. Christmas Island was hosting an unusual number of tourists due to the whole millennium thing, and the activity and confusion worked well for them."

"Why did they bother sailing down to Caroline Island?"

"Being seen down there, making satellite calls from there, set the whole search to the south in motion. Plus, I think Dad wanted to sail along the date line before he let his entire life go. He was funny like that." She looked wistful for a second. "Maybe he still is."

"So coming here was a safe guess on Neil's part." Zane tried to turn the conversation back to less emotional topics "I noticed he had a few extra days before he had to be in Fiji. Maybe checking on less likely scenarios was his plan B, in case his guess about Christmas Island didn't pan out."

By this time they were at the hotel and hoping for answers. But no, the clerk at the hotel did not remember Neil. No diving shop recalled him. Nor did anyone at the restaurant where he claimed to have eaten two meals. Except for their driver, it looked like Neil had come and gone without a single soul on Christmas Island remembering him.

"This is ridiculous," a frustrated Zane complained as they ordered their own lunch at one of the little restaurants. "How many lone Americans flying in on a private jet do they get here in a month?" As they ate, a local man approached. Like the driver, the people at the airport, and the man at customs, he spoke English for tourists as his second language.

"You're Afi's friends?" he asked. Zane nodded with a mouth full of food, glad to be asked the question. *Thank you Afi.*

"You should have found me first," he said. "I'm his mother's cousin's husband's cousin. My cousin on Tarawa contacted me because Afi was looking for someone here to help you."

Zane checked his phone for a message from Afi. No reception, of course.

"We'd be grateful for your help," Chloe said.

"You need it. If you're going to go around asking questions about one of your own people, the people here will be confused. Was he a bad man? Are you bad people looking for him? Will harm come to them if they help you? If they don't? You are stirring up worry. It doesn't make anyone want to answer you."

"Right." *That actually made sense.*

"The man is not why we are asking," Chloe said. "We're trying to help another friend in trouble, and learning about this man's visit can help him. No trouble will come to anyone who answers us."

"I know. Afi's mother's cousin's husband explained it all. Finish your food. Then we'll go back and ask again." They did, but this time Afi's relative did the talking in the local Polynesian dialect and it made all the difference.

Zane and Chloe were able to leave Christmas Island by early afternoon, after establishing how Neil, well-armed with Australian dollars, had traversed the island four months ago, asking questions about the year 2000. He'd shown pictures of a friend of his, and of him and the man together. He'd described what he thought happened: one nice boat for arrival, another smaller one for departure and a second man who left separately by air. All he wanted was a confirmation. Please. After all these years. He offered money to compensate for time spent trying to remember. A good bit of money, if needed.

Most people on Christmas Island had no idea what Neil was talking about. But some did. Several of them took their promise to forget forever seriously, and they said nothing. Not everyone was so inflexible, however. There were a few who had knowledge, or at least indirect knowledge, and they'd been persuaded to speak up.

The man Neil seemed satisfied with their information. He left the next day for Fiji. It was true he asked a couple of well-meaning business people to provide him with extra receipts, in case he needed them to keep things simpler with his employer. Yes, he'd left on January 27. His plane had taken off at dawn.

Zane was almost giddy heading back to the plane. So it was true. Neil had guessed his old friend Pete was still alive. How? Brenda probably came to him with the news. Maybe Neil hadn't been sure if he should believe her, prompting his fact-finding mission.

Zane turned to Chloe to ask her what she thought, and he stopped short when he saw the pensive look on her face. Of course. She didn't share his exuberance at having the puzzle pieces fall into place.

"You don't have to do this," he said. "You can stay right here and we can pick you up on the way back."

"Don't be ridiculous."

"Okay then. Neil has known for four months now that your dad's alive. For whatever reason, he's chosen to keep it to himself. That's important. Would Neil know we're on this trip?"

"The plane gets used all the time." She shrugged. "As long as he doesn't need it, he'd have no business monitoring who goes where. But if the COO asks anyone else in the company a direct question, he will get answers."

"So let's assume at some point Neil finds out we've gone to Christmas Island. He's bright enough to know that if he could get answers, so can we," Zane said.

"So basically, he knows about my dad, we know he knows about my dad, and soon, he will know that we know he knows." She laughed in spite of herself. "What now?"

"We probably should minimize our conversation on the plane. Also, let's shorten our trip. We can make the stop in Samoa to confirm Neil's arrival date on our way back if we need to. I say we get ourselves to Am. Sam. as fast as we can. I think we can make it before dusk, and use the satellite phone to call ahead and have Afi and Joy at the airport ready to go. We can refuel, and try to make it to Tarawa tonight. The sooner we meet up with Toby, with your dad, the better."

******

Neil read the text message from the company's copilot with growing frustration. What the hell? He was COO of this damn company. How had two kids taken off in the company plane without him knowing it, apparently on a mission to snoop into his behavior? Of course, they couldn't have done it without approval from the one man who still outranked him.

There had been a time when Neil and Peter Sr. shared a cordial, even a friendly relationship. Peter had appreciated the skills Neil brought to the company. Back in the day, before... well... before it all.

For a decade now, they'd remained polite to each other, and seldom spoke of any matter that wasn't business. However, when they did talk of business, there was respect and cooperation. Only over the last six months or so had Neil noticed Peter's formerly courteous behavior turning curt, though never quite rude. None-the-less the small sense of business camaraderie was gone.

Which raised the question. Did Peter Sr. know about his son? Worse yet, did he know Neil knew? Neil was confident the answer was no or all hell would surely have broken loose around the office. So probably Chloe had gone along on the trip to confirm her friend Zane's suspicions of Toby's real identity. It made sense to do that before getting the old man's hopes up, given his delicate health condition. Neil realized that meant he still had time to rectify things before all was lost.

His best bet was to feign ignorance and continue on as normal, like he had for the last four months. Peter's cancer was finally progressing faster, and the man was on more pain medication every day. It couldn't be much longer. If Peter would die before word got back to him, it would all be so simple.

Of course, Chloe, Zane, and even Pete might still make trouble after Peter's death, but once Neil was named CEO he'd have momentum on his side. Stockholders wouldn't like a lot of drama. All the employees would bend over backwards to help him.

Some had already, of course. Josh, the shy PowerPoint kid in marketing, had turned out to be of some use. He knew Zane's password. Good observant eyes. Josh had opened up the photo file for him and Brenda so they could study the pictures. They stared at the sailboat, and the weathered man at the helm. Was it or wasn't it?

Brenda was sure, but she'd never had a lot of sense in matters involving Pete.

Going to Christmas Island for answers had been Neil's brilliant idea. It had to be where Pete and Nicolas had gone. After a day there, Neil knew exactly how his old college friend had managed to run away. Kudos to Pete. It was nicely done and benefitted everyone.

Brenda could mourn instead of seethe at her lover's rejection. Pete could stop being the "Jr." he'd always hated being, and could escape from several other nasty situations as well. Neil, well Neil had to be the one who benefitted most of all, because there was nothing in this world Neil wanted more than to be Pete. He was happy to admit it. He was born to inherit an empire from a rich, clever father. Unfortunately, life had provided him with an ignorant, uneducated pig farmer for a dad. But with Pete out of the way, Neil moved up in the world

Then, months ago, the photos were seen and stupid Brenda decided Pete would want to be found. She ignored Neil's attempts to reason with her, to convince her the man was happy where he was and no one benefitted from his resurrection. Of course someone did, she said. She still loved him and she wanted to tell him. For God's sake…

Once she learned Zane was planning to join his friends in Fiji after the conference, she decided to insist on meeting Zane's friends there and thanking them in person for their help months ago. Zane would have no reason to object.

She told all this to Neil, told him how she would know in an instant when she saw Pete if he still loved her and was ready to be found. If he wasn't, she promised she'd leave him be and take his secret to her grave. Neil could tell she was betting Pete's eyes would light up when he saw her.

So of course Neil made arrangements to join them in Fiji. It was at the last minute and he had so much else going on at work, but what else could he do? He wasn't sure how he was going to talk some sense into Brenda, but he had to be present when she and Pete met. He wasn't willing to let ten years of hard work go down the drain.

Then, while sailing from Pago Pago to Apia, Brenda had seen the boat with the bright orange sun on its sail. It was heading from

Am. Sam. over to Samoa along with the Penthes fleet! She'd called Neil on her satellite phone to say "Forget Fiji." She was absolutely, positively going to find and have dinner with the captain of the Miss Demeanor that night in Apia. She giggled like a teenager.

An angry Neil had forced two charter pilots to ignore their flight plan and take him to Apia ASAP. It had cost him plenty of his own money, but he managed to persuade the men to arrive discretely, and to stay put on the plane while he took care of an urgent personal matter.

Then he'd managed to get to the boat before Brenda. The look on her face when she boarded Pete's boat and saw Neil there had been priceless. Because in that minute she realized it didn't matter what Pete wanted. It didn't matter what Brenda Mills wanted. What mattered was what Neil Bennett wanted, and he favored keeping things the way they were. So that night the three of them had gone for a sail and had a little talk.

******

Chloe and Zane's pilots would have preferred to spend the night in American Samoa and not push their limits for consecutive hours in the cockpit. Chloe, however, was insistent they move on. There was a tired, shrill undercurrent to her instructions, and its effect was to make others comply.

A quick check on the pilots' part showed the weather to be clear into Tarawa. With modern GPS equipment, a night flight over the Pacific posed no more dangers than one anywhere else. So arrangements were made for the Penthes jet to be allowed to land in Am. Sam., refuel, pick up passengers, and push on.

At the hanger for private aircraft, Joy and Afi were rushed on board. Dressed in their casual island clothes with the day's dust and sweat still on them, they looked out of place in the immaculate air-conditioned cabin. They stared at a well-groomed Zane like he had come in from another world.

They'd been warned to expect Chloe on board, but not told why, and had been asked not to relay word of her presence on to Toby. They looked confused as they stashed their ragged backpacks, and Chloe stared back at them as the copilot insisted on commandeering the floor to review his safety procedures. Zane wondered if the feelings between him and Afi had been only in his own head. At the least, this mix of people could have been a bad idea.

Minutes later, when the copilot stopped talking and they were in the air, Afi broke the strained greeting by getting out of his seat and grasping Zane in a firm hug. Zane smiled with relief, and hugged back. Then Joy joined in and then Afi and Joy greeted Chloe and the uneasiness of it began to dissolve into a mutual understanding of the awkwardness of it for everyone.

"Do you think we can talk freely now?" Zane mouthed to Chloe.

"I think we have to." Chloe turned to Afi and Joy. "I'm here with Zane because we think we've put together a pretty good idea of who your friend Toby really is. I asked Zane to wait and let me tell you about it in person."

Joy sucked in a deep breath. She was afraid Toby had been hiding something. Now at Chloe's ominous tone, horrible scenarios ranging from drug lord to war criminal danced through her head. "Who is he really?" she asked.

"My dad." Chloe said.

Joy felt the oddest mixture of relief and surprise.

Afi started the questions going, and as more of the story was told, Zane watched as Chloe soaked up all she could about Toby from the others.

"I can't believe we'll be there tonight and I'll talk to my dad after all these years."

"Your dad's in Samoa? I thought Toby couldn't go there?" Afi asked.

"We're not going to Samoa; we've been in the air almost an hour," Chloe said. "I thought you guys knew. We threw Samoa out of the itinerary so we could get to my dad fast, make sure it's him, and see how we can help him. We're flying on to Tarawa tonight."

"Tonight? Why didn't anyone tell me? They're not expecting us until tomorrow." Afi was not happy about the change of plans. "I show up at night with no warning, seeing my family for the first time in years? For the first time since they sent me away?"

"They were supposed to tell you at the hanger," Chloe said. "I understand this has got to be intense for you. Use the satellite phone and call your family now. Surely they can come meet you tonight."

Afi moved away from the others to make the call, and Chloe turned to Joy.

"So. I understand you and my father developed a friendship," Chloe said. Her tone managed the delicate tightrope walk between unkind and warm.

"'I don't know what you'd call it," Joy admitted, thinking that here was Toby's daughter, a half-dozen years younger than she was. "I'm expected to go to Afi's home to meet his family as soon as we arrive. Unless Toby needs us right away, we'll spend the first day with Afi's relatives. It's a courtesy to Afi and his family. As it turns out, well, you could probably use the private time with your dad, too."

A bit of a smile made its way on to Chloe's face. "Thank you for that."

Zane felt out of place. "Look Chloe, maybe I should tag along with Afi and Joy."

She shook her head. "They've got enough to deal with, Zane. Come with me for moral support, and if I pass out or start crying again you can be my medic or tissue provider." When Zane looked hesitant, she laughed. "It's okay, really. I know you can make yourself scarce and give Dad and me time once we're there. But you're the one Dad is expecting, not me, so you should at least go out to the boat with me tonight. I'd honestly rather not go alone."

So they had a plan. Until Afi got off the phone.

"Problems with the early arrival?" Joy asked when she saw his face.

"Not as far as my family is concerned," he said. "But you should know they've had problems with people stealing the lights off of the runway at Bonriki Airport. They got these theft proof ones installed a few years ago, but some locals found a way to disconnect them, and word is they've been missing the runway lights for the last several days."

"There are no lights on the runway?" Zane asked.

"They may know where to find a couple of them. I guess our pilots reached somebody who's going to come open the airport and handle our entry. They told us to come on in. They're working now to find runway lights."

"We go back to Samoa now," Joy said, and Zane agreed.

"No." Chloe and Afi said in unison.

"We have ways of dealing with problems like this," Afi said.

"Name one," Zane said.

"Well, worst case we do what they used to do. Relatives with pick-up trucks would drive out to the airport and park at the edge of the runway and turn on their headlights. I know it sounds stupid, but it works. My family doesn't have a truck, but our church has several."

Joy spoke up. "Afi, I know your mom will be happy to see you, but are you sure members of your church would help you out like this? I mean, well…"

"I know…" Afi said. "I didn't exactly have a warm send-off from them, did I? The thing is, Joy, my relatives aren't mean. They've known me since I was a child. I think they will help."

Chloe thought *it's okay. After ten years I am finally going to get to see my dad.*

Joy thought *it's okay. After four months I am finally going to get to see the man I love and never told.*

Zane thought *no runway lights? This is nuts.*

Zane persuaded Afi to alert the pilots to possible irregularities in runway lighting, so they could at least be mentally prepared. Nervous for the rest of the ride, the group joked about anything they could think of. Amid the laughter, Joy and Afi learned more about the man Toby once had been. Chloe learned more of the man he was now. She was interested in the y[1] organization he'd founded.

"Sounds nothing like my dad," she said. "No matter how he handles his future, there's going to be some catching up to do."

Afi became quieter as the journey neared its end. What if the missing runway lights couldn't be found? What if his parents couldn't persuade the church to send the trucks? Would someone else help? Surely they would.

What if no one wanted him back on the island as he now was? Maybe Joy was right. What if no one was willing to let their vehicle be used to usher a man like him to safety? Could his people be that closed-minded?

Zane gave his arm a squeeze. They were descending, and on this cloudless night, the lights and fires of Tarawa could be seen as tiny pieces of sparkle against the massive black ocean. The airfield, which sat near the town of Bonriki in the far southeast corner of the atoll, appeared to have lights on nearby.

Four faces pressed against the windows of the plane as it came in lower. "I'll be damned," the pilot said over the PA. "I've never landed in the middle of something like this before."

Below them the short, east-west airstrip was visible, surrounded by fifty or sixty trucks, cars, and motor scooters, each with its lights on bright, shining directly onto the runway. As they came in lower and the pilot circled once to study the situation, they could see dozens of individual people as well, holding flashlights and lanterns, and waving at the plane.

"Guess they found a few people who were happy to see you come home," Zane said.

Afi blinked back a tear. "Guess they did."

19. Landing

The welcome couldn't have been more joyful. Afi's father told anyone who would listen how the decision to send Afi to that horrible school was one of the worst choices of his life. Now that the school was closed in disgrace, Joy found it amusing how Afi's entire community derided it and shared in Afi's anger at his mistreatment as if it was their own.

Joy was included from the moment she stepped off of the plane, even though she was certain much of the family recognized her affiliation with Afi as odd. She guessed an I-Kiribati, preferably one of the same faith, would have been a more desirable wife, but there appeared to be a silent agreement to accept both her and the situation with unquestioning good cheer. Family. You had to love them.

A cousin with a truck offered to drive Zane and Chloe the ten miles out to the harbor. After a quick greeting, Chloe was sitting in the truck ready to leave. Zane took his cue, wished Afi and Joy luck and made arrangements to meet the next day.

"He'll need to bring his dingy in to get us," Zane said. "Do you want to call ahead to him or do you want me to?"

"He could see the plane land. He's expecting you. We don't need to call."

She was right. Toby had come ashore and was standing on the dock as they got out of the truck with their travel bags. Zane waved the driver off with thanks, and Chloe took a few steps toward the dark-haired stranger squinting at her in the faint moonlight.

"Dad?"

"Chloe??"

Zane watched them both. *Oh yeah, no question.* Chloe took a tentative step closer. Toby did the same.

"You're alive," she said.

"You've grown up," he responded.

"You've gotten older." She took another step closer.

"You're looking well." He moved towards her.

Then it came. Hugs. Tears. Giggles. Apologies. Assurances.

Eventually, when the emotions subsided, Toby turned to Zane.

"This is your fault, you know." He said it with no trace of blame. "If I'd any idea the U.S. company I was ferrying two businessmen for was going to be Penthes, there is no way in hell I would have taken that job. The guy I filled in for couldn't remember the name of the damn firm."

"Yet when you found out who I worked for you handled it without a trace of surprise," Zane said.

"No, my mouth dropped open. Lucky it was dark by then, and Joy and Afi were so upset to find out you were visiting that school in Samoa that it completely covered up my panic. So if Brenda hadn't twisted her ankle she'd have actually walked right onto my boat that day!"

Chloe was processing the information. "That's right. Brenda was supposed to go on that trip."

"Yup," Zane said. "A lot would have gone differently if we'd both arrived that day."

"I'll say," Toby said. "Among other things, she'd be alive,"

"Speaking of which, Dad, what the hell happened?"

Toby shook his head and motioned to the dingy. "Let's talk while we head out to Miss Demeanor, where we can be comfortable. Chloe, you're going to love my boat."

Zane rowed while Toby talked.

"Brenda was one of those people who could be plenty smart in one arena and stupid in another," Toby said. "She recognized me from photos Zane put on his computer. First thing she did was tell Neil, figuring he'd be delighted."

Zane and Chloe exchanged a knowing look, acknowledging they'd been right in their guess about that. Toby went on.

"Even I knew by the time I left that Neil was one of the most effective sociopaths I'd ever met. Here was a man who looked out for his own interest day and night without the least regard for ethics, the truth, or the feelings or wellbeing of anyone else. Yet he acted like he was a caring friend to anyone who mattered. Those that didn't affect his wellbeing, of course, he ignored.

"He had his claws entwined into so many parts of Penthes, including my dad, that I knew there was no effective way to stop him. For those last few years I tolerated him. God knows I didn't want to fight him for control of the company, or for my dad's affection. I was positive no one could have been happier to see me disappear. In fact, I was counting on him to tone down the search for me as much as he could. I expect he obliged."

"He did." Chloe confirmed it as Zane pulled the little dingy up alongside Miss Demeanor. Toby secured it and welcomed them aboard.

"Wow, Dad. So this has been home? Very nice."

"One of two homes," Toby explained. "I have a beach house on a little atoll I rent. I'll show it to you; you'll like it, too."

"I'm sure I will."

Toby turned on lanterns and pulled out beverages. "I'm a little low on supplies. Beer or bottled water?" It was beer all around.

"Anyway, rather than try to contact me or tell Zane who I was, Brenda decided to surprise me and show up in person. She thought by seeing my reaction she'd be able to tell if I still loved her. According to Neil, she expected I'd welcome her back into my life. I don't know what she thought would happen after that.

"She had this encounter set up for Fiji, after the conference. Then Afi talks me into sailing him over to this fire dancing thing. There are boats full of Penthes people sailing too, but I stupidly agree to do it, thinking I can stay aboard Miss Demeanor and out of sight. I mean, why not? No one expects the dark-haired, older man on a random sailboat is going to turn out to be the son who was lost at sea, right? So I send Afi ashore in the dingy and hunker down for the night."

Toby paused for a long gulp of beer. Zane and Chloe both waited, neither one wanting to stop the narration.

"Only what I don't know is Zane not only took photos of me, he took them of my boat. My sails." Zane groaned. "Brenda sees my boat and recognizes it. Guess what? She can't contain herself. She grabs the company satellite phone and calls Neil, who is on his way to Fiji. She thinks he is going to be happy for her that by the time he sees her next she'll be reunited with her long lost love."

"Neil was not pleased," Chloe guessed.

"I think not. I don't know what he told Brenda, but he did tell me he managed to divert his flight, land somewhere discretely, whatever that means, get himself to the harbor, and pay a local boy to row him out to my vessel. I was having a snack in the galley, waiting for Afi to come back when, imagine my surprise, I see Neil out on my deck."

"You didn't, I don't know, yell for help?" Zane asked.

"Zane, this guy was supposed to be my friend. I had no clue how he got there or what his plans were, but there seemed no reason to panic. He came below deck, accepted a cold beer, and he and I went on to have a fairly civil conversation. The nice thing was there was no need for bullshit anymore. He gave me the facts about how I was found and made it clear he wanted me to stay away. The good news was I wanted to do the same. He suggested I tell Brenda how glad I was to be rid of her, and this could all end well for everybody. I agreed. It might have worked."

"But?" Zane and Chloe said it in unison.

"But I didn't trust Neil. Zane, you know I can't keep a gun on board, every port I enter checks for firearms and confiscates them. So I have my own security devices. I keep things in arms reach to defend myself."

Zane nodded. "The stun guns in the flashlights."

"Yeah, and the drugs in the first-aid kit. Fishing knives. There's not a huge problem with pirates in this part of the world, but I keep things handy. So, just in case, I reached for one of my special flashlights. Neil's a bright man. He saw me reach for something, and he grabbed it first. Didn't matter what it was.

"My first thought was *Oh shit*. Then Brenda stepped on board, shooing away a boy in a dingy. She looked below deck and saw the relief on my face. She ran down the steps into my arms, muttering something about how much she missed me too. I was trying to push her away when I felt like I had stuck my elbow in a light socket."

"Guess Neil figured out what he was holding," Chloe said.

"Guess so. Brenda and I both came to, bound and gagged below deck. Neil had taken Miss Demeanor's helm and had us out of the harbor. He'd seen the first-aid kit and found the ketamine, which I carry legally.

"That's an anesthetic, right?" Chloe asked.

"Among other things. I carry it for emergency surgery. At any rate, Neil had done his homework. He had a plan B. He was sailing around the island in the moonlight while he explained to us how sometimes the weak have to die to protect the strong. He lectured us—well, I guess he technically lectured Brenda—about being a slow gazelle, and how slow gazelles get eaten to keep the herd strong. He peeled the duct tape off of my mouth, not a pleasant experience by the way, and started in with me about some war strategy called mutually assured destruction. He said it was going to look like I had committed this murder, which was going to be Neil's way of being sure I'd never try to reclaim my life as Pete Hulson.

"I guess he'd zapped me first, and as I fell I must have grabbed at Brenda's necklace. He was all excited about how my fingerprints were on it and it would be the final piece of evidence used to convict me if I tried to come forth with the truth."

Toby took a second long swallow of his beer. "I almost told him that framing people for murder seldom works, but then I thought, *don't be stupid. If he doesn't think you're scared, he kills you.* So I assured him I was frightened enough by his plan to go away and stay away. It seemed to make him happy."

Toby closed his eyes for two or three seconds before he went on. "Then he took the needle and walked up to Brenda and stuck her in the arm while she lay there with the tape over her mouth, giving me these wild, pleading eyes. Damn if I didn't feel sorry for her because no one, *no one*, deserves a finish like that and I couldn't do a damn thing. She went limp. He untied her and took off the duct tape and carried her to the edge of the boat. He dumped her unconscious body in the water. I've never felt so helpless in my life. Then he turned to me, and you know what he said?"

Zane thought he did, but he didn't want to say it.

"You're welcome. He looked me in the eye told me I'd never have the life I wanted with Brenda alive and I'd never have the balls to take care of it like he just did."

Toby let out a deep breath. "I didn't say anything, couldn't say anything, and he looked at me and laughed."

"Then he sailed us on to some place he'd picked to let himself off. I don't know what arrangements he'd made, but he anchored the boat, he gave me a knife I could use to work myself free, and suggested I get out of there fast, because in several hours they'd be looking for me. He told me to lie low long enough for him to get the investigation put on low priority. Then he dove into the water and came up swimming toward shore."

Toby paused, and got a second round of beers from the icebox while Chloe went to use the head. Once she had closed the door, he turned to Zane and whispered, "I had a choice then, and I made a bad one. I should have gotten myself free and gone straight to the authorities and told them every word I told you. It would have ruined the life I'd built for myself, and, to be honest, I knew it would ruin a life I'd hoped to start with Joy. But it would have been the right thing to do, and the best thing."

As Chloe rejoined them at the little kitchen table, Toby turned to her. "You should know that after seeing Joy, Afi, and Zane, and giving them my apologies and explanations in person, it was my plan to turn myself in. Chloe, it still is. I'm so sorry for all the pain I caused you once, and now for all the pain this whole thing is going to cause again, but I can't make a life hiding."

Chloe was nodding. "I'm fine, Dad. I feel sorry for you, and I even feel sorry for Brenda. If I committed any sort of fraud as a kid, I doubt I'm liable for it now. The only tough thing is going to be Mom and how angry she'll be with me. And grandfather too. At some point they may understand. If not, I'll live with what I did. I did it out of love."

"You know," Toby said, "of all the things I got that I didn't deserve, one of the best was having you for a daughter."

The three of them talked for another hour. Toby was curious about how Penthes had faired and disturbed by Chloe's reports of the firm's marketing strategy. He tried to be delicate when asking if his sister and former wife were well.

Chloe had no trouble reporting on her Aunt Paula, of whom Chloe was not that fond, but Zane could feel the strain as she spoke to her father of her mother's life. *She loves both of her parents. This is hard.* It helped that Toby was glad to hear Sylvia had remarried a few years ago, and had become involved in several charities that mattered to her.

The most sensitive moment of all, however, was when Toby asked about his own dad. As Peter Sr. had mellowed with the years, he and Chloe had grown closer, and it was apparent to Zane Chloe felt that closeness was a private matter. Even with her dad. Maybe especially with her dad.

It was also apparent to Zane that Peter Sr. had failed to tell Chloe how much his health was declining. She described her grandfather as clearly aging while Zane knew him to be clearly dying. Zane considered bringing the matter up, but decided he still owed Peter Sr. the discretion he'd once promised, no matter how unpredictable the current set of circumstances had been when he made the promise.

The only other odd moment came as the three of them were finally bedding down for the night, in relatively good humor in spite of the challenges of the evening. Chloe found one of those straw bags older women liked to carry to the beach and moved it off the foot of her bunk. It had a pink and yellow yarn flower on it.

"Not really your style, Dad," she laughed, but Zane was staring at it. He'd seen the bag before. Brenda had brought it along to Fiji. Toby caught Zane's expression and nodded.

"Brenda brought it on board with her when she came to surprise me in Samoa that night. I've been afraid to throw it away. I didn't want to make any more evidence against myself, so I just pushed in it the corner and thought I'd deal with it once this whole thing was settled."

"Dad." Chloe rolled her eyes. "She could have had a sandwich in there or a piece of fruit. It could be sealed so you don't smell it, but it be really gross by now. You should see what's in that bag before you let it sit any longer on your boat."

"Go right ahead," her dad said. "I'm not touching it." Of course he wasn't thinking when he said it.

First Chloe pulled out a middle-aged woman's flowery, one-piece swimsuit. Then a pair of matching flip-flops with squiggly plastic flowers that matched the bag. Then a pink and yellow beach towel with more matching flowers.

"Did she buy all these things together at some shop?"

Zane realized Brenda had probably bought them all together, hoping to wear the little matched set as she and Toby went for a walk on the beach and maybe even had a swim.

They all realized a couple of seconds too late where this was going. Next came a sheer hot pink nightie, followed by a healthy sized tube of personal lubricant, and a package of condoms. Chloe looked as if she would have preferred a rotting sandwich.

"Eww," was all she said as she dumped the contents back into the bag.

******

Neil fumed as his hired driver sat idly in the snarl of traffic that appeared to cover the entire U.S. Marshall Islands. He didn't want to spend the night in this particular Pacific hellhole, yet he had no choice.

How could any airport using "international" as part of its name have a problem keeping its runway lights from being stolen? Apparently Bonriki International Airport in Kiribati did, and thanks to the resourcefulness of local thieves, he'd been diverted here to delay his entry into the country until morning.

Last he'd heard from the co-pilot, the Penthes plane with Chloe and Zane was going to spend the night in Samoa. He'd still get to Toby first. That's all that mattered.

******

Toby was a light sleeper when he was docked in port, even more so than while at sea. He was the only one of the three to hear the little dingy approaching shortly after dawn. He shook a baffled Chloe awake and, holding his fingers to his lips, shoved her toward the head with whispered instructions to go inside and keep the door locked. He'd turned to rouse Zane when he heard the dingy knock against Miss Demeanor's side. He hesitated, then decided to leave the stun gun be and go above to meet the intruder unarmed. He was pretty sure he knew who it was.

"Aren't you getting a little tired of secret flights across the Pacific?" he asked Neil.

"I am. These islands are one fucking long way from each other. But I'm thinking there won't be a need to come back."

Toby saw that bringing a weapon up on deck would have been useless. This time Neil had managed to bring a handgun.

"It was naive of me to think this situation was — what's that word everybody loves now? — sustainable. It was naive to think our arrangement was sustainable, Pete. It never was. It was always you against me. I don't know what I was thinking. There's only room for one of us on this planet, and let's face it, it's going to be me."

"You can't shoot me here," Toby said, wondering if Neil had crossed the boundary into living in some fantasy world.

"Actually, I can, as long as I'm quick about it. Because I'm not here. This time, I relied on transportation from a company that, shall we say, considers discretion to be its number one advantage. That, and their ability to provide customers with personal weapons, including a silencer if needed. I've killed before, Pete, as you probably do remember. Since then, I've come to realize I'm one of the hunters of this world, and I have no problem with that. Lest you are worried about my welfare, let me assure you I've left some excellent alibis in place."

Toby tried another approach. "I thought you were my friend?"

"Oh I am. I'm doing this the way a friend should. Quick and painless. You don't know this, but not only are your boating friends flying in to meet you this morning, they are bringing your daughter Chloe along to surprise you. And identify you."

Toby was startled to realize Neil didn't know the Penthes plane had landed last night. Of course he didn't. The flight plan had called for a morning arrival.

Neil saw Toby's startled look. "Yes, I thought the news about Chloe would surprise you. So what are the options? I show up after the awkward reunion? Then she and your friends get to watch me shoot you, which means of course I shoot them, too. What a mess. What an investigation. So much better if I make my pilots leave at the first glimmer of light and get here first, right? That way we let the young people live. I go home with no fuss, and you look like you were murdered by anyone with a grudge against you who tracked you here."

Toby couldn't believe this. "You landed in a plane, Neil. They are going to have a record of the aircraft, the people on board. It can be traced. You'll get caught. Don't be crazy."

"Right on the first. Right on the second. Wrong on the rest. Not a soul on that plane's manifest really exists, and my plane carries the registration of one that crashed in the ocean years ago. They'll find all this out when they look into it. I didn't mess around this time, Toby. No date line sleight-of-hand or fake receipts. That stuff is amateur hour. This is going to look like a professional hit on a man who must have made a plethora of enemies over the years. There were his political leanings—oh yes, I've learned about those—and his penchant for murder. We all know you're wanted for at least one in Samoa and who knows what other trouble you got into over the years as you sank into the intrigues of the islands? It will be so sad, of course, when all of Penthes learns how low you slid. I hope your father lives long enough to hear of it."

"My dad is dying?"

"Oh right. No one would have told you that. Technically no one knows, although I think Zane may. He and your dad have become close buddies here at the end. Did he mention that to you?"

No, Zane hadn't mentioned that. Speaking of Zane, was he actually sleeping through this? Was Chloe still sitting in the head with the door locked? Toby looked around for a way to get himself out of this mess before either of the young people emerged from the cabin behind him. Even armed with his boat's tools of self-defense, they'd be no match for Neil, who was mentally prepared to shoot. Worse than that, Neil appeared to be done talking.

"Toby, the best man won. I hope you understand that."

Neil raised the gun. Toby could feel his mouth go dry and was about to lunge at Neil, figuring it would bring on the gunshot but he had no better idea and nothing to lose. Then he saw Neil's eyes widen at the sight of something behind him. Damnit. Why couldn't those kids have stayed below deck and lived.

******

Zane awoke to the sound of Neil's voice. "These islands are one fucking long way from each other. But I'm thinking there won't be a need to come back." Chloe wasn't in her bunk. Where was she? He rubbed his eyes.

Neil was certainly on board. As he sat up, Zane could see part of him, standing near the stern, facing and pointing a gun at Toby with great intent. Toby had his back to Zane and to the steps down into the cabin, and he was largely blocking Neil's view of what was below. Zane tried to make neither sound nor movement as he looked around the cabin for any weapon, anything that would result in his being able to immobilize Neil for a few seconds, long enough for Toby to grab the gun. There seemed to be nothing helpful around.

Then Zane saw Brenda's bag. He laughed to himself. The idea had merit. There would be no way to hide his hairy arms and legs but he could wrap the flowered towel around his head the way women did when their hair was wet, and he bet the illusion would not have to be terribly good to create a moment of shock. He concentrated as hard as he could on Brenda's face.

******

Chloe opened the bathroom door. She'd been able to hear some, but not all, of the conversation from inside the head. Her dad was closer and his voice had carried better. She could tell he was in mortal danger. She didn't really have a plan, but it was becoming apparent she had to do something.

She pushed open the bathroom door and saw... Brenda.

Well, it was kind of Brenda. A little too tall and skinny, but wearing the flowered swimsuit and flip-flops. She had the towel around her head, and her skin was a deathly pale, light blue grey that would have been at home in a haunted house. The woman, the apparition, turned to Chloe and held a finger up to her lips. Shhh. Okay. Chloe stepped back into the head and tried to breathe deeply.

******

"You can't kill *me* a second time, you asshole," a ghostly pale Brenda hissed as she pushed by Toby and stepped toward Neil's left side. She held a bloody fishing knife in her hand. "But I can and will gut you with this thing."

It was all the opening Toby needed. He had the gun out of a horrified Neil's limp hand in a second, and Chloe, bounding up the stairs now with clear purpose, pushed the stun gun deep into Neil's flesh. As he hit the deck, Toby grabbed a roll of duct tape and went to work.

"Going to be hard to claim you weren't here, you heartless son of a bitch. Particularly as I intend to deliver you to the Tarawa police myself."

"I'll call Afi's people and see if I can get us some transportation over to the police station," Chloe said. "That way you don't have to have people crawling all over your boat." She turned to face Brenda, but Brenda had turned away. "Let's get Neil in custody and then sort the rest out."

"I agree," her dad said. Then, to the twenty-something young man who had turned back around in a middle-aged woman's flowered bathing suit, "You might want to change, Zane, before we leave."

Chloe raised an eyebrow and muttered "What the hell?" as Zane went into the cabin to find his clothes.

******

The plane Neil had chartered took off from Bonriki less than an hour later without permission, and Zane never did figure out how the pilots knew to go. Neil had not lied about one thing. No one was able to trace the pilots or the plane that brought him into Kiribati.

For the next two days Afi's family helped all they could to straighten out the aftermath, and in the end they agreed to care for Miss Demeanor while Toby, or Pete, traveled home on the Penthes plane with his friends to have some long and not particularly easy conversations with people he hadn't seen in many years.

They took off at dusk on the second day. Afi and Joy asked to be dropped off during the refueling stop in Hawaii so Joy could look into teaching jobs there. Joy also knew it would make for a shorter trip back to Chicago and now that Toby knew about his dad's rapidly declining health, he was anxious to get back.

Joy and Toby had precious little time to talk privately during their forty-eight hours on Kiribati, but the looks they exchanged were full of information. So Joy wasn't surprised when Toby suggested he come back to Honolulu soon and help them get settled, once he had taken care of his personal matters.

Then, as an afterthought, he suggested he could bring Zane too. Zane and Afi exchanged a look of delight as Toby reminded them all they did still have some sailing to do together.

Even Chloe had to smile. She was starting to enjoy being around the happy man her father had become.

May 2010

20. No Regrets

While Chloe, Toby, and Zane waved goodbye to the cab taking Joy and Afi to their hotel in Honolulu, Peter Sr. was making arrangements to be cared for in his home by the staff of a local hospice. His doctor had told him yesterday the time would be soon, and so a composed Peter cleared his calendar.

He was proud of himself. He had managed his exit from this world with all the dignity he could hope for. He gave a long look around the plush office with the beautiful cherry wood and the expansive view of the lake, and sighed. He loved this office. He didn't care what anyone thought. It had been a great place to spend a good chunk of his life. It was what he had wanted.

The sunlight was glistening on the water as sailboats made their way down from Belmont Harbor, adorned with swimsuit-clad young people soaking up the newly arrived summer sun. He watched them for a moment from his high perch as they laughed and played and flirted with each other, and he tried to feel the sense of freedom and hope he imagined they must feel. Then he wondered if, instead, each of them was too busy worrying about some petty problem to be enjoying their moment. Didn't they realize they were lucky? That they were happy? He hoped they did.

He called in his personal assistant and explained to her today would be his last day in the office and detailed how she was to handle various aspects of his life over the next days or weeks. He couldn't be sure which. To the woman's credit she was calm and helpful, but he knew her well enough to know there would be tears later.

This evening, he and his housekeeper would have much the same conversation, and it would probably go much the same way. Both women must have suspected he was sick, yet both had been nothing but discrete and kind. Maybe he did have a few friends.

When Gil called and asked to meet with him, Peter gave his okay. The man had emailed him a few days ago explaining he wanted to discuss a potential scenario for Penthes' future. *Just under the wire here, Gil. You're going to need to create that future fast.*

Gil entered the office nervous, filled with the energy of a man who's become too engrossed in an idea to sleep. Gil's numbers were tentative, but, he told Peter, it looked like between the shares Peter held and the shares held by the employees in aggregate, an employee buyout might be possible. Gil wanted Peter to consider facilitating such upon his retirement, after which Gil proposed a retooling of the company from the bottom up. He believed Penthes could turn itself into a zealous group dedicated to honest research on using drugs sparingly and appropriately, and could market not only their products, but their reliability and good name.

"Do you have any idea how much money you are going to lose marketing a good name?" Peter had to chuckled.

"Do you have any idea how much money we pay a year wining, dining, and treating doctors right so they'll push our products? Any idea how much we've paid out in fines the last few years for pushing our drugs to be prescribed for non-approved uses?"

"It's the cost of doing business," Peter replied, his voice growing weaker. "Neil used to insist it was investing a dime to make a dollar."

"Well, we'll start by keeping those dimes while we tighten our belts. Do you know what our biggest single sales expenditure was last year?"

Peter shook his head. He probably did know but between the pain that was now everywhere and the fogginess from the medication, he didn't want to try to guess.

"Penthes is now the largest funder of lobbyists pushing legislation to allow removing children from the custody of parents who refuse to adequately medicate them for mental health reasons. You follow where this goes, right? I either comply and medicate my kid, or I stand to lose my child altogether."

Gil swallowed hard before he went on. "Even the threat of it would have me buying Penthes products. Peter, this is not the company you set out to run. I know it's not."

And it wasn't. Peter had known for years that somewhere along the way, for reasons he couldn't fathom, Penthes had grown a mission statement of its own that bore no resemblance to what he'd hoped to accomplish when he founded it.

"Damn. Maybe it has become a person," he said.

He turned to Gil. "You know, I wasn't happy about it when Neil talked me into going public, and I haven't been happy about it since. Get my attorney. And my accountants. You may have to speak on my behalf. Gil, I've got a lot to do in the little time I've got left."

"Little time left, sir?" Gil suspected Peter wasn't doing well, but had no idea it was serious. Peter filled him in.

"Should you be handling business now, sir? Would you like me to get your daughter Paula? Chloe?" Gil hesitated. "Neil?"

"Thanks, but any business I'm going handle needs to be done by me, and done soon. Besides, Neil said he's taking a long weekend up on the Upper Peninsula and can't be reached. Chloe, well Chloe is traveling too. I should have heard from her by now, but she should be here soon. When I head home tonight, I'll settle in and call Paula. She can be difficult, but it's time I told her what's going on. So let's get those numbers firmed up and legal people in here and see if this idea of yours can fly."

Although they started their work in his office, Peter felt so poorly he had to leave before lunch. By mid-afternoon his housekeeper had been informed and instructed, and the hospice caregivers had arrived and begun to set up equipment to keep Peter comfortable. Paula was found, and she made a show of rushing to his side, astounded her father could be failing so fast.

She was even more surprised when he told her he had known of his condition for months and chosen the style of his exit. Anger followed. Who the hell had let him do that? The hospice caregivers advised her discord would only cause her father more discomfort, and suggested she focus on providing support. She glared but said no more.

Paula had intended to not permit her father any visitors other than family, but although he'd settled into the bed, Peter overrode that instruction. He insisted on being given a phone to stay in touch with his personal assistant and cleared Gil and anyone with him for admittance. When Gil showed up with four of Penthes' vice-presidents and the corporation's chief counsel, Peter asked Paula to leave and send in his personal financial advisor and his own attorney when they arrived.

The group gathered around his bed. "Time to pull the plug on this entity," he said.

The hospice nurse looked up. "You're not on life support, sir. Please. There is no plug to pull."

"Not on me. I've got a work to do. I'm pulling the plug on the corporation I made."

Peter's financial advisor was shaking his head. "I knew you kept a lot of shares from the beginning, but you really have been buying up Penthes stock, haven't you? If you weren't dying, you'd be in a hell of a pickle. Except for all of these shares, you're almost broke."

Peter shrugged. "All I wanted was for it to be my company."

"Well, you didn't get to fifty percent, but you came closer than I'd have guessed," he said, as they all heard Paula's shrill voice rising in volume in the hallway.

"I am the one who forbids a bunch of strangers from walking into my father's room when he's this sick. That's who. You, Chloe, you have every right to go in. But you are not bringing these, these people in with you. He's dying. Show some respect." Paula sounded nearly hysterical. Then there was silence.

They heard Zane's voice, loud and clear. "It's okay. She's fainted. I'll stay here and make sure she's alright."

Peter looked up, expecting to see Chloe walk through the door. Instead, there was a man with a great deal of resemblance to his son. At first he thought it was a trick of the medication. Or maybe he'd died. Surely it wasn't that easy. More likely he was mistaken. The hair was dark and the face was weathered, and it wore a different expression than the one he remembered. It was the face of a man who smiled often.

"'Pete, is that you?" Hell, Peter thought. He'd just ask.

"Yes, Dad. It's me. I know I have some explaining to do, and I suppose some apologizing as well."

"Good Lord. Did you actually come to my death bed so I'd write you back into my will?" Toby winced. Looked like the old man hadn't changed that much over the years.

"No Dad. I didn't. I came to tell you I'm sorry I brought Neil into this family and this firm. You need to know he murdered Brenda and he framed me for it, and he's being held in custody in a place you probably never heard of called Kiribati, and he won't ever be returning to his role as chief operations officer for Penthes. I think he told you he was in Michigan. I thought you might want to know."

"Oh." Peter was confused. "You don't want to be in my will?"

"Actually Dad, being in your will would cause me no end of embarrassment. What I would like is to tell you why I left and tell you I've missed you. If you've got time to listen."

Peter saw Chloe behind Pete. "You've talked to your dad?" he asked.

"The whole way home. Grandfather, he came back with Zane and me from the Pacific. I wanted to call you, but Dad thought it would be easier on you in person. We had no idea." She gestured around at the IV and the monitors. "We had no idea things had gotten so bad."

"Yeah, well, they aren't going to improve, so I thought I may as well get comfortable. We're finishing up some business and you both should hear it. It involves you."

The housekeeper brought in a chair for Chloe and left to get one for Pete. "Should I get Aunt Paula?" Chloe asked.

"Not quite yet," her grandfather replied. He turned to his financial advisor. "Give them the short version."

"Of course. Basically Penthes is worth about 1.2 billion dollars, give or take 100 million on any given day. There are about 10 million shares. Peter here insisted on keeping ten percent of them from the beginning, and he made it his goal to acquire at least a hundred-thousand more each year. As of a year ago, he owned a third of his company. No other investor comes close, but of course other investors could gang up on him. After his diagnosis, it looks like my client went on a buying binge."

"I wanted to die with it being my company again," Peter said.

"As a result, Peter isn't broke, but all he has left is this house, his car and some personal possessions, and a few hundred-thousand in the bank to cover his medical bills. Oh and his Penthes' stock, but he has something specific he wants done with that."

"I want you people to sell the company to the employees," Peter said. "I need to give them my shares, so they can afford to buy the others. They can build the sort of research-oriented pharmaceutical company I wanted this to be all along. You guys." He waved a hand at the attorneys. "Why aren't you generating paperwork for me to sign while I can sign it?"

He turned to his granddaughter. "Chloe, you're young, but you're smart, and more than capable of listening to good advice. And I trust you. So, you guys," he motioned back to the attorneys "you get all my shares to Chloe now and Chloe, you make this deal happen. Act on my behalf, until it's done. And then, get the hell out of the pharmaceutical business and go do something you want to do. Okay?"

Chloe laughed. "You've got yourself a deal, grandfather."

Peter looked at his son. "I wish I'd been wise enough to give that advice years ago." In response, Toby put his hand on his father's withered arm and left it there, saying nothing. Peter closed his eyes a moment and let himself enjoy the warmth of his son's touch. Damnit. He was going to have to up the pain medication soon or he wouldn't be able to focus.

"Gil," he barked. Gil jumped, startled at the sound of his own name at such an emotional moment. "You don't know nearly enough about the biochemistry of the brain and you're no whiz with money. But I worked for two bosses like you early in my career and you know what? No one ever forgets a boss like you. What you do is look your employees in the eye, ask them questions, and actually listen to their answers. You greet them in the morning like they matter. You let them advise you because you value what they know. You can see through people's bullshit and you don't worry about looking weak when you give respect to one beneath you who deserves it. Gil, you know how to lead people."

Peter inhaled deeply. "It took me a long time to realize leadership is not about ordering people around. It's the most important skill of all for running a company. So I'm naming you as my successor. Make this employee-owned thing happen and make it happen well. I want you guys to cure cancer." He gave a little laugh. "Or cure something big. I want you to fire up eight-hundred people to do something that matters. Will you do that for me?"

Gil didn't hesitate. Of course he'd hoped for a leadership role in the new firm, although this rather exceeded his expectations. "With pleasure, Dr. H. We'll cure something big for you, I promise." Peter could see the tears in Gil's eyes, and the sight reassured him. Damnit if he hadn't found himself a worthy successor after all.

"Okay, bring in my daughter. Let's get all this done. Then I want some serious morphine."

Paula was nearly hysterical at having been kept out of the room. "You can't give him everything just because he's your son. I've been here for you for the last ten years. You think I don't know what's happening in here? I'm not stupid."

"Paula, you're not stupid and you get half my estate. Chloe and your own daughter will split the other half."

"Oh."

At a nod from Peter, his personal financial advisor took over. "Ma'am, for planning purposes it's best you know that after we liquidate the assets your share of the estate will be around a million dollars."

"A million dollars! I can't live the rest of my life on a million dollars. You're worth at least a couple of hundred of million, Dad. What happened to the rest?"

"I spent it."

"But what am I supposed to do now?"

"Paula, do you remember once when you were young we walked by a homeless man and you told him to get a job, and then you looked at me, expecting praise."

"I do, because instead of praising me, you told me life was more complicated than I realized."

"Exactly. It's still more complicated than you realize. That's my fault, for sheltering you so much. I'm now trying to fix that, with a parent's love."

Paula started to respond, but Peter's low whisper cut her off. "My time is short, and there's one more thing I want. Pete here wants to tell us a story while my meds kick in." He turned to the nurse. "I'm at a nine out of ten, but give it to me slowly. I want to listen for a while."

He turned to Pete.

"Let me hear about running away. Tell me about sailing ships and tropical sunsets and the wind on your back and doing all the things you wanted to do in life... It's okay... I'm happy for you." His voice was fading. "So tell me the story..."

******

Dr. Peter Hulson Sr. never regained consciousness, although his body lived for another four days. As Zane stood by Dr. Hulson's bedside the next day, having been allowed in to say his good-byes, he recognized there was no one left to say goodbye to.

He was impressed at how, through sheer strength of will, Dr. Hulson had managed to remain functional as long as he'd needed. Yet once his work was done, his brain checked out and gave his body the time it required to conclude its own business.

Zane studied the man who'd made such strides in understanding the brain. *The link between the human mind and body baffles even those who understand it best, doesn't it? Maybe especially those who understand it best.*

Chloe entered the room. "Guess you'll have to find another time to bring joy to someone on their deathbed."

"What are you talking about?"

"Come on Zane. You imagined delighting him with news of his living son, and alerting him to the full creepiness of his COO, didn't you?"

"I suppose," Zane said. "He was no saint, but I liked your grandfather. I wanted to do the job he gave me and have him be happy with my work."

"You did your part well," Chloe said. "Because of you, he had a more peaceful end. You earned your fee, and the thanks he never got to give you."

"I wondered about the fee. With all this employee buyout stuff I thought my arrangement with your grandfather was collateral damage."

"No," she said, "he put your money aside before all that happened, but he did screw you a little, with the best of intentions."

Great. "So what did I get?"

"You got a trust fund for a million dollars administered by his financial advisor, Ted. For the next ten years it can be used only for education, then what's left in it is yours with no strings attached. Ted says he's willing to define educational needs broadly: sumptuous living conditions, excellent personal transportation, you get the idea. Ted thinks he can get you a nice lifestyle, but you have to work with him and go back to school."

"You asshole." Zane muttered it to Peter with a mix of irritation and affection. "You knew damn well I didn't want to be a lab rat."

"Then don't be one," Chloe said. "Nothing in the arrangement specifies what you have to study. Look around, Zane. Find something you want to do and do it. Nothing would make my grandfather happier."

"Yeah. Yeah I will." He brushed his hand against Peter's arm. "You clever son of a bitch. I hope you can hear me. Thanks."

June 2010

21. Glowing

After the funeral, Zane took a few days and headed back to Texas. He planned to work at Penthes for another year while he started applying for grad school. Though he was glad he wouldn't need his folks' financial support, he realized he'd always benefit from their moral support. The last few months had been a study in the ways families could mess things up, most often by not communicating. It was time to communicate.

His mom was on the porch, enjoying the sunset as she planted a few last flowers into pretty ceramic pots. She was sipping on red wine.

"Got a minute?" He pulled out a cigarette as he joined her. "I'm down to just two a day."

"That's good news." She gestured him into a seat.

"I've decided to go back to school in a year and I'm pretty sure I know what I want to study."

"That's even better." She waited.

"There are master's programs in medical ethics, and that's the direction I want to go. My background in neuroscience is perfect but more importantly, this fascinates me. You know, I only got interested in neuroscience to begin with because I was trying to understand myself."

"That makes sense," his mom said.

"Actually, you don't fully understand. Not yet." Zane took a deep breath and concentrated on his father's face, because it was an easy one for him to do. "Watch this."

Lola stared while the muscles on her son's face twitched and morphed until she was looking at a remarkably close facsimile of her husband Alex, down to his clear blue eyes and faded freckles.

"Good Lord, Zane. Where'd you learn to do that?"

"Mostly in English class. I was bored."

The real Alex walked out on the porch. "Can I join you guys?" Much to Lola's relief, Zane turned away.

"Please do." Lola said it in a heartfelt whisper.

When Zane turned around he looked normal. "Dad. I'm talking to Mom about how different I am."

His dad looked a little sad.

"Zane, I know we should've had more conversations about your being gay, but, well, I never want to make you uncomfortable, and …"

"Dad." Zane cut his father off. "I know. We're not talking about that. We're talking about this."

Zane studied his mother's face for a few seconds. Women were harder, but he focused. He wanted to get this demonstration right.

Alex watched wordlessly as his son's facial features tweaked and twisted in ways he couldn't possibly move the muscles on his own face. In the end, the thick male eyebrows and Zane's hint of facial hair remained, but Zane's eyes were Lola's deep brown and his face was close to that of Lola's.

"Holy shit. That is some incredible muscle control."

"Yeah," Zane said, letting his muscles relax back into the familiar comfort of Zane Zeitman. He grinned. "It's way more effective with a wig. It's amazing how much we judge appearance by hair, which I can't alter. I can do this though."

His parents both watched with their mouths slightly open as Zane's face turned from his normal pale tan to a bright red, then to a very deep brown, then on to a pale grey, and then finally back to the tan beige of Zane.

"Can't do green. Don't have the right pigments." He let out a long happy sigh. After all these years, it felt good to be himself.

"Zane." His mother sounded hurt. "How could you have kept this from us?"

"Because you were both always so damn proud of everything I did. I was afraid you'd tell people and researchers would take me away and cut me up in a lab."

"You spent too much time as a kid reading science fiction," his dad said.

"I'm still not comfortable having this known outside the family. Life as a freak doesn't interest me." Zane looked to his parents for understanding. They both nodded.

"We'll keep this to ourselves," his dad agreed.

His mom understood. "So instead of cutting things up in a lab, you want to enter a field where you can protect the freaks of the world."

"Yup. I'd like to help unusual children not be afraid."

"Wait, Zane's changing jobs?" Ariel made her way onto the porch carrying a fresh beer for her dad, a couple more glasses, and the rest of the bottle of wine. She sat down with a grin. Curious, Teddie followed her sister outside. Alex looked at Lola with a question mark on his face. It looked like he'd missed an important piece of the earlier conversation.

"He's going back to school, dear," Lola said.

"Zane, I don't know if we can help you much." His dad looked worried.

"Oh, that's right." Zane chuckled. "Have I got a story to tell you."

His parents both raised their eyebrows. "There's more?" his dad asked.

"Ariel, best pour out that wine," Zane said. "Have a seat Teddie. Believe me, you're going to love this story. It's about sailing ships and vast fortunes and dying old men and murderers and love and most of all, it's about people getting to do the things they really want in life. Including me."

******

It took several more weeks before Zane and Toby were able to meet Joy and Afi in Hawaii. The foursome flew on to Kiribati, and after a couple of days as guests of Afi's family they boarded Miss Demeanor and set sail for Toby's island. It felt good to be back at sea.

Afi and Zane were sitting up on the front of the boat, sharing stories. Toby was at the helm, talking to Joy about his decision to dock Miss Demeanor in Honolulu as he planned to visit Hawaii often next year while he was working for Gil at Penthes.

Joy stood next to Toby, sipping a bottle of water while she listened to him, comfortably barefoot in her swimsuit top and little running shorts. Toby stopped talking, reached his hand out and ran it slowly up her thigh.

Shit. This is my fantasy. The hand gently skimmed her skin under the running shorts.

"Do you and your husband have some sort of understanding?" he asked.

She smiled. "We do. He told me if you ever made a move towards me and I was dumb enough to decline, he'd divorce me."

Toby smiled back.

"So do you think if we go below deck..." he began.

"We won't be disturbed..." she finished.

They weren't, not for a long while.

Over the next several days at sea, private time below deck for Toby and Joy, and then for Zane and Afi, became an important part of the voyage. Each couple did their best to give the other privacy.

One afternoon Joy took the helm while Toby made minor repairs to the sound system. As he shut down the music, the inevitable noises came from the two men below deck. Joy giggled.

"Weirdest double date you've ever been on?" Toby asked.

"Maybe," she said, laughing. "I'm just marveling life can be this wonderful."

"I agree." He switched the music back on and stood with his arm around her as she steered the boat in silence and the two of them watched the late afternoon sunlight glisten on the ocean.

News of all sorts was exchanged during the voyage. Zane and Toby told of Neil's evolving legal status, as it appeared both island nations would turn the high-profile case over to the United States where the press had already dived into the story with expected glee.

It was no surprise Neil was using his amassed fortune to hire an expensive team of attorneys. Word was he hoped to use an insanity defense, in hopes of netting a stay in a high-end mental care facility.

"I thought that had become hard to do," Joy said.

"I looked into it," Toby said. "You're right. Misusing the insanity defense requires a defendant who is highly intelligent, knows a lot about mental health, and is an adept liar with strong sociopathic tendencies."

"Sounds exactly like Neil," Zane said.

"Yeah, that's what I thought."

There was news in other legal arenas, too. Joy and Afi had filed paperwork to allow Afi to live in Hawaii, and several local establishments were happy to include Afi's dancing in their entertainment venues. For the short term, Joy and Afi were happy with their odd marriage and had committed to a life together until Afi's application for permanent residency would move out of its tentative status.

"I love my family, and Kiribati," he told them, "and I appreciate the support my people showed me. But cultures change slowly. I could go back and live there, but I'd never be able to live as honestly as I'd like. The U.S. will be my new home, a place where I am welcome exactly as I am."

It was a sign of the affection between them that Joy seemed as glad as Afi was. "My dad already sent a letter to authorities assuring them this is a legitimate marriage, so I don't think we'll have trouble with INS."

"It also sounds like you won't have any more trouble with your dad," Zane said.

"I guess not. Once my dad figures out he can't control a situation, he finds another way to be important. That's him."

"They're going to come visit us in October," Afi said. "I get to meet both of my in-laws." He grinned. "It should be interesting."

Zane shared how he'd shown his parents his unique shape-shifting skills and how they'd agreed to keep his abilities a private matter.

"What about you and my daughter Chloe?" Toby asked.

"Oh, there's nothing between us."

Toby laughed. "I get that. I meant what about the fact that she's seen you shape shift? Have you talked to her about it?"

"Oh yes. After your dad's death. I even gave her a demo, so she wouldn't think she was crazy. We talked about her testimony in court and she agreed to say I came out dressed in Brenda's swimsuit, which is true, and my clever distraction shocked Neil enough for you to be able to grab the gun. Anyway, she told me she would keep it to herself." He gave Toby a meaningful look. "She assured me she has a great resume for keeping secrets. I acknowledged her credentials were impeccable."

Toby smiled. His friends understood he was struggling to be both Pete and Toby. He planned to start the process by making a second name change to become Peter Tobias Hulson, so he could still go by Toby, but be part of the Hulson family too.

He admitted it was difficult coming out to his followers in y^1. Toby tried to explain to them why he'd made the choices he had, and why he'd chosen to be truthful now. Some followers booed him for the deception while others derided his choice to reclaim his roots. Even Afi seemed hurt at being lied to.

"A software engineer from California?" he asked.

Toby answered with the truth. "Afi, by the time I met you I had told that particular lie so often it felt like the truth."

"Then it was time you stopped telling it," Afi said.

Toby was grateful that many, maybe most, of y^1 listened and accepted his difficult choices. They acknowledged he had a unique perspective as a man who'd stood to inherit much of a two-hundred million dollar fortune and decided he'd be happier doing something else.

Toby's other piece of emotional business involved striking a deal with Gil. For although Toby could have claimed some position of ongoing influence in the new company, he only wanted to work there a while to help the new company get on its feet. He wanted no permanent place at Penthes, but he did want one permanent thing.

He wanted a memorial. He wanted it in the middle of the lobby of the Penthes building. He wanted it to be tasteful, but not small or discrete. It was to be a life-sized bronze statue of a boy, laughing and playing. In large, easy-to-read script it was to say: "The safety and wellbeing of every one of our children is worth far more than anyone's profit." It was to be a monument to Joel

Hulson, with Joel's name and date of birth and death clearly visible.

Gil had been happy to agree.

After an uneventful week and a half at sea, they reached Toby's island a little after dawn and stretched their legs with a long walk on the beach. Toby had decided to keep the place, but he thought it wise to scale back the island's processes so he didn't have to visit so often. Zane, Afi, and Joy spent the day helping him dismantle the hydroponic gardening apparatus and securing the house, and its energy and water gathering capabilities, to better exist without a caretaker.

As the afternoon wound down, they prepared for a feast out on the sand. The coals glistened while the fish were cleaned and cooked. Wine was poured. A salad was made. Amid stories and jokes, they ate the last of the food. As they cleared the plates Afi gave them a questioning look.

"Is now the time for fire?" he asked.

"Definitely."

"Of course."

"Why the hell not?"

A stretch of clouds in the west provided a flame-like show of color while Afi arranged the embers into a small orange and grey rectangle in the sand. Then, one by one, each member of Miss Demeanor's crew improvised a jolly bow to the others, and took a calm yet purposeful walk over the glowing coals.

Afterglow

22. The Correct Answer

The timing was horrible. Thirty-nine-year-old Zane Zeitman was a month into his medical internship, trying to pretend he had the energy of kids fifteen years younger, which he did not. The physical demands of med school were worse than expected, *and* he'd probably never practice medicine. But Afi was right, as usual. Having those initials MD after his name would lend credibility to his work that couldn't be had any other way, and there was no better time to do this than now. Or so it had seemed, until he heard from Ariel.

If there was anyone in this world he would do anything for, it was his fiery-haired sister. All his life she'd been there for him, encouraging him under the guise of sharing a beer and a few laughs. Plus, he still owed her for kicking over her blocks as a kid.

Here she was, crying her eyes out, asking for his help. The correct answer was yes. Of course it was yes.

"I know about atrial septal defects, Ariel," he'd assured her four months earlier, when doctors detected the tiny opening in the heart of the growing fetus. "Lots of people have this and lead normal lives. It's not a big deal. I promise"

Which is why one shouldn't make promises.

In Zane's newborn nephew, the abnormality was larger than usual. While not immediately life threatening, if John was to live into childhood, he'd need open-heart surgery. That left Ariel with the most gut-wrenching decision of her life, for where she lived, no such surgery was possible.

"We can do this." Afi didn't hesitate, as he placed his hand on Zane's arm.

"Teddie would take him," Ariel said, "but she can't right now."

"Teddie needs to keep doing what she is. It's important work. Mom and Dad too."

"I just talked to them, " Ariel said. "If you can take him, they'll help every way they can."

"I know they will."

"They even offered to split care giving with you, but I don't want that. He needs one home. Even if lots of people love him from different places." The last comment brought a fresh burst of tears. Zane wished he could hand Ariel a tissue and comfort her.

"Send him to us. He'll be fine." Zane stepped forward and hugged the screen as hard as he could because he didn't know what else to do.

******

Eight months later John arrived and Zane became a dad at the age of forty. Afi decided it was time to give up his fire knife dancing, as his body stiffened and his reflexes slowed down. Plus, he wanted to be John's primary care-giver. After the surgery, John grew stronger, thriving with all the love.

As Afi fed John, swooping the spoon into his little mouth like an airplane, making noises that made John giggle, Afi considered how his hypermobility was a birth defect too. Granted, his defect provided him with upside, but nonetheless he identified with the little child whose physical oddity had given him such a strange start in life.

Afi wiped up the cereal mess on the floor while John fussed to get out of his high chair. The timing had worked out well. Zane would finish medical school soon, after living on the most generous of stipends. Then he and Zane hoped to settle down, maybe buy a house.

As Afi let the squirming baby down onto the rug, he thanked his ex-wife Joy for sticking with him until he was well on his way to U.S. citizenship. Afi wondered if he and Zane would be together now if Afi had only been able to make short visits instead of living in the same country as the man he loved.

He blew Joy a mental kiss, hoping she and Toby were happy in their home in Hawaii. It would be good to see them next week in Chicago as they all met to celebrate Penthes' unique annual holiday.

The occasion had begun a year after the successful employee buyout. On the company's one-year anniversary, Gil had laughingly called it the Peter-Hulson-was-a-hell-of-a-great-guy day. The idea stuck.

Now, every year on July 26, employees of Penthes gathered together to tell stories as they ate, drank and celebrated. There was reflection on how far they'd come. The new antibiotic for resistant tuberculosis would be part of this year's festivities, as would the ever-more successful dementia treatments and the inroads against liver cancer.

There would be tributes to Dr. Hulson, as a few thousand people raised a glass and cheered for a man many of them had never met. He'd hardly been a saint, and no one pretended he was, but when faced with a burning desire to leave a legacy in this world, Dr. Hulson had found a way to make a difference.

"Here, here. To Peter Hulson, who turned out to be a hell of a guy."

Certainly one of the most talked about topics this year would be how former COO Neil Bennett was back in the news after spending sixteen years at the most lavish mental health care facility his lawyers could find. Turned out this particular luxury hospital prescribed more anti-psychotic drugs in higher doses and more untested combinations than most, and Neil was one of many patients whose health had suffered from the cocktails of drugs forced on him daily for over a decade. He was now part of a group of plaintiffs suing the hospital for overmedicating, and several news outlets had pounced on the irony of Neil's situation.

Reality jerked Afi's attention away from his thoughts. How had John gotten so damn fast at crawling? Afi reached down and scooped up the little guy before he made it to one of the electrical outlets. Why did babies always head for the most dangerous thing in sight?

He plopped the youngster in his playpen filled with toys, and then shook his head as the boy screamed with indignation.

255

"I know, I know. There's nothing fun in there you can hurt yourself with." Afi laughed. "Wait until you get a few years older. Then I'll teach you how to dance with fire and knives. I can tell already; you're going to love that!"

July 2045

23. A Graceful Exit

Zane knew something was up. As he and Afi packed for the annual trip to Chicago to toast Dr. Peter Hulson, he'd heard from his folks, then Teddie, and then John, who was in college in Chicago and would be at some of the festivities.

Then Gil called. He'd retired ten years ago, but still handled the party and wanted to make *sure* Zane and Afi would be at the smaller dinner held the night before, for folks who were with the new Penthes at the start. Of course they'd be there.

Even Afi, who moved slowly these days because of the aches his condition caused, seemed to have a lightness in his step as they arrived in the windy city. As Afi handled the check-in, Zane looked at the hotel's marquee and saw the small dinner was scheduled in the large ballroom. Why was Afi grinning as he watched Zane's face?

Then Zane looked across the lobby and his eye caught the open glass escalator. Wasn't that his dad riding the stairs between the second and third floor? It couldn't be. His dad was in his mid-eighties and hardly traveled anywhere any more. But there was his mom on the step behind him, laughing and gesturing with the animation of a young girl. She looked over and saw Zane watching them and her eyes widened. Busted.

S. R. Cronin

Zane had grabbed an old shirt when he packed for the evening, but as they dressed Afi pulled out a nicer silk one in a shade of deep teal matching the resting color of Zane's eyes.

"This would look nice."

Zane almost argued, then thought, what's the point? Put on the nice shirt. He was glad he did.

When he walked in for dinner, he saw Teddie, escorted by her oldest son, a fourteen-year-old looking uncomfortable in his own dress clothes. He saw his mom and dad and John, and a lovely young lady that had to be John's new girlfriend. Joy and Toby had made the trip, too, in spite of Toby's declining health.

Chloe was there with her husband and children. Her oldest daughter was visiting with Raven, whose diminutive delicateness might have given a stranger the mistaken impression she was fragile. Zane knew better. Raven had spent decades fighting corporate interests as she found ways to offer more natural food options to a hungry world. Her fierceness had won more of those battles than Zane would've thought possible.

The real surprise, though, was the size of the group filling the banquet room. Who were all these people and why were they here?

Gil stood up and spoke into a microphone.

"We're doing something a little different this year," he said, getting the chatter in the room to quiet down. "Tonight we celebrate two people behind our successful founding. Toby Hulson, will you join me at the podium?"

Although Toby had consulted off and on for Penthes, he'd mostly kept his distance from his father's company, choosing instead to turn his hobby of theorizing about economics into a full-time occupation. In thirty-five years, y^1 had gone from a small internet site to a worldwide think tank and consulting firm. While Toby made his way to the front of the room, Gil began.

"We probably wouldn't exist as a company if the man who was heir apparent hadn't chosen another path. But he didn't just pick a different road. His path helped to build ours."

Gil smiled at Toby. "His group y^1 is credited with shaping policy the world over as they advocate for economic approaches designed to yield a happier and healthier world. Today, smaller companies and employee-owned businesses like ours are encouraged by laws and by culture. The gargantuan megaliths that were the way of business in the early part of this century have been shown to be best at one thing, making a lot of money for a few. They're going the way of the dinosaur, to the benefit of almost everyone.

"What's more, inheritance laws are changing. Focusing one's life, company or culture on wealth preservation is thought to be the waste of time it always was. I think we have Toby and y^1 to thank for the greater number of people today who are enjoying their lives."

As the room applauded, Zane thought it was obvious much of the crowd was affiliated with y^1. Then, as Toby took the microphone, Zane realized he had to be part two of this. Shit. He hated public speaking, especially with no time to prepare.

Calm down. This is supposed to be a compliment.

Toby's remarks faded into a distant buzz as Zane tried to figure out what he could possibly say. This was a giant room full of people.

When Toby sat down to enthusiastic applause, Joy stepped up to the podium. Her thick black hair was streaked with gray and worn in a softer style, but after her years in the classroom, she could speak to a room full of people with authority. She began.

"Thirty-five years ago when I met the man who just spoke, I was one of four people on a boat who were all running away from something. Luckily, one of the places Toby and I ran was into each other's arms." There were soft chuckles.

"Over the years, our two fellow travelers also found wonderful things to run toward. Each other, for starters. A life of doing what they loved. Given what Zane Zeitman chose to do, that decision was lucky for many people in this room."

Zane looked around and saw a lot of the room nodding. Didn't some of those faces look familiar?

"Zane." Joy looked right at him as she said it. "There are some people here tonight who want to say thank you, and I'm going to let them do so in their own words."

While the salads were served, two dozen people took the microphone, each telling a short antidote. Each speaker had two things in common.

The first was they were unusual. Some had rare diseases. Others had common ones, but responded strangely to treatment.

Some had unusual physical skills akin to Zane's own. A few had conditions like Afi's. Some had birth defects that had presented nothing but challenges, while several had genetic mutations providing them with what seemed like only advantages. For a few, their oddities were more mental than physical. More, Zane noted, like his own mother's situation. The group was, in the original sense of the word, queer. Every single person in it.

The second thing they had in common was that each had been somehow protected by Zane. His efforts to secure ethics in medicine, his championing of policies that would protect the unusual, legislation he'd helped draft and the tolerance he'd spent his career fighting for had made a difference in their lives. For in this world of almost instant communication and sometimes frighteningly adept technology, so much of what was different could easily have been eradicated, if Zane and others like him had let it.

When the last speaker finished, Zane looked around and saw the whole Zeitman clan beaming with pride. Guess he was the only one who hadn't known about this. Light-headed and knees spongy, he made his way to the front of the room. What other choice did he have?

He muttered his thanks and added a few more vague words. The crowd quieted, straining to hear, and he realized they wanted more. Actually, coming all this way, they deserved more. Zane began to speak from the heart. The room sensed it and went silent.

"When you're a little kid, you have no idea how your life will turn out. You don't even know how you want it to. You have no clue what you want to be." Zane noticed his father laughing.

"When I was a young boy, I wanted to be a chameleon. Seriously. I was different in a *lot* of ways. It took me years to realize everyone is weird, no matter how hard we pretend otherwise. While the strangeness in others can be disturbing, I believe our strength as a species lies in our variety."

That seemed a good ending to Zane, but the crowd kept looking at him, expecting more. He needed a graceful exit. He saw his father lift his water glass into the air, and it gave Zane an idea. He reached for a nearby glass and raised it high.

"To each and every human being getting to do the dance of life." He paused and smiled. "I don't mean a couple of quiet toe taps, people. I mean twirl-around-in-circles-while-pumping-your-fists-in-the-air dancing. Get your feet moving, because whether you dance with fire or polka bands, with drums or a full orchestra, no one can do your dance better than you. So dance it with joy."

To Zane's surprise, the applause started and grew until it was loud. *This is it. This is the happily-ever-after moment. This is the way every story should end.*

March 2064

24. How Every Story Ends

The gurgling and beeping of the equipment in the hospital room was getting to Zane. He knew the machines were keeping his mother comfortable, but he'd spent too much time here and been in this situation too often. His dad. Then Afi, taken too soon. Now his mom, at the end of her life.

He reached to call Teddie again, to make sure she was on her way. He saw his mother wince with pain.

"Mom? Do you need more meds? Nod if you do." He didn't want her to suffer. She looked at him and sorrow crossed her face.

"Zane?"

He couldn't remember the last time she'd spoken.

"Have you had a good life?" The words were hoarse, but intelligible. *Did she want reassurance she'd been a good mom? She had.*

"Yes, I've had a great life." As Zane said it to reassure her, he realized it was true. He knew sometimes there was a final spark of energy at the end. If that's what was going on, he hoped Teddie got here fast.

"Mom? Teddie will be here any minute. Please Mom. You know Teddie will be upset if, uh, if you don't ask her that, too."

Zane was pretty sure Teddie and his mom had been saying goodbye for months now, but she wanted to be here at the end. His mom nodded and closed her eyes with a look of peace on her face.

This is it. This is how every human story ends. Anything else is just a pause, only the end of a chapter. At least she was exhausted and ready. He reached for her hand and held it.

Teddie picked that second to come through the door.

"Mom. I have to talk to you." Lola's eyes opened back up with a start.

"I can't believe you disturbed her. She was so content."

"Kids. Don't fight." Teddie and Zane both patted their mother on the arm while they glared at each other.

Lola whispered with a sudden urgency. "Where's your dad? I need to tell him something." She shifted a little in discomfort.

Zane didn't know what to say. This didn't seem like the time to remind her their dad had died years ago.

Teddie answered right away.

"He's on his way, Mom. He'll be here any minute." She turned to Zane and gave him a meaningful look.

"You know I don't do that anymore," Zane said under his breath to Teddie as they moved away from the bed so their mother couldn't hear. "It's harder for me than it used to be, and the doctors say it's bad for me, too."

"Yeah, well, this isn't exactly a common occurrence," Teddie whispered back, gesturing at their mom's bed. "You know. Maybe it could be a one-time exception?"

Zane sighed. Teddie was right.

"Okay. But turn around and don't watch. It's harder if somebody's watching me. "

"So go into the bathroom and come out as Dad."

"Yeah, okay." As he closed the bathroom door behind him, he couldn't resist one last argument. "All I ever wanted was to be myself."

"I know." He heard her response as the door clicked closed.

As he willed his aging muscles to shift, Zane's memory flashed back to the first time he'd stood at the side of someone dying. Dr. Peter Hulson had been too far gone to acknowledge the last-minute good news Zane had brought him. Later, Dr. Hulson's granddaughter had told Zane he'd have to wait for another time to bring closure to someone on their deathbed. Turned out the wait had been fifty-four years

A few minutes later, a man who looked like an elderly Alex Zeitman walked out of the bathroom. Lola's eyes lit up.

"Alex, you came!" She said it as if he'd shown up for a last minute lunch invitation. "I'm so glad."

As Zane leaned forward to give his mom a gentle brush on check, Teddie whispered "You are being yourself, you know. Right now."

Zane acknowledged Teddie's wisdom with a wink. Then he savored his mother's joy as she began to tell his dad what had been so important to her.

More

Shape of Secrets is part of the 46. Ascending collection of interrelated novels about five family members who each discover they can do the extraordinary when circumstances require it. These books are designed to be read as stand-alone stories or in any order.

If you enjoyed *Shape of Secrets*, consider *Flickers of Fortune*, the story of Zane's sister Ariel as she learns how difficult it is to be precognitive. You might also enjoy *Layers of Light,* the story of Zane's youngest sister Teddie, as she uses her innate skills for out of body experiences to save her friends from a human trafficking ring.

You may prefer to start with *Twists of Time*, the tale of Zane's father as he learns to use his ability to warp time to protect the students at his high school or *One of One,* the story of Zane's telepathic mother as she finds herself the unlikely hero in a rescue mission in Nigeria.

You can also go directly to *One of Two*, the last book in this collection, in which the Zeitman family combines their skills to prevail over the most dangerous threat they will ever face.

Thanks

I would like to thank my husband Kevin, my daughters Shenandoah and Emerald, my sister June Hanson, cousin Marianne Oxenhorn, and friend Jane DeLong for their help and encouragement. You are wonderful! Thanks also to Joel Handley for his editing, Kate Reid for her information on sailing, Anthony Reisch for his Samoan perspective and John Ryan for information on the pharmaceutical industry.

A special thank you goes to my son Casey, who helped with and inspired this story in so many different ways.

Additional Information

Although this book is work of fiction, where news items, cultural information, and scientific facts are included, it was my intent to be accurate. I would like to express my thanks to the following sources for information and background material used in this book. Any misrepresentations of information from these sources is unintentional and regretted.

Links to websites I used in my research and the nine songs woven into the original story can be found at my blog *Fire Dancing for Fun and Profit* at http://ytothepowerof1.org.

The Economist Pocket World in Figures, 2011 Edition. Published by Profile Books Ltd.

Landfalls of Paradise: Cruising Guide to the Pacific Islands by Earl R. Hinz

Flaming Sword of Samoa: The Story of the Fire Knife Dance by Freddie Letuli

Biomimicry: Innovation Inspired by Nature by Janine M. Benyus

Pacific Lady: The First Woman to Sail Solo across the World's Largest Ocean by Sharon Sites Adams and Karen Coates

We Chose the Islands by Arthur Grimble

The Sex Lives of Cannibals: Adrift in the Equatorial Pacific by J. Maarten Troost

About the Author

Sherrie Roth grew up in Western Kansas thinking there was no place in the universe more fascinating than outer space. After her mother vetoed astronaut as a career ambition, she went on to study journalism and physics in hopes of becoming a science writer.

She published her first science fiction short story and then waited a lot of tables while she looked for inspiration for the next tale. When it finally came, it declared to her it had to be a whole book, nothing less. One night, while digesting this disturbing piece of news, she drank way too many shots of ouzo with her boyfriend. She woke up thirty-one years later demanding to know what was going on.

The boyfriend, who she had apparently long since married, asked her to calm down. He explained that, in a fit of practicality, she had gone back to school and gotten a degree in geophysics and had spent the last 28 years interpreting seismic data in the oil industry. The good news, according to Mr. Cronin, was she had found it at least mildly entertaining and ridiculously well-paying. The bad news was the two of them had still managed to spend almost all of the money.

She was now Mrs. Cronin, and the further good news was they had produced three wonderful children whom they loved dearly, even though to be honest that is where a lot of the money had gone. Even better news was that Mr. Cronin turned out to be a warm-hearted, encouraging sort who was happy to see her awake and ready to write. "It's about time," were his exact words.

Sherrie Cronin discovered that over the ensuing decades Sally Ride had already managed to become the first woman in space and done a fine job of it. No one, however, had written the book that had been in Sherrie's head for decades. The only problem was, the book informed her it had now grown into a six book collection. Sherrie decided she better start writing it before it got any longer. She's been wide awake ever since, and writing away.

Places

American Samoa: a group of islands in the South Pacific east of Samoa, also called Am. Sam.

Apia: the capital of Samoa

Boston: a city in the northeast U.S. and Joy's hometown

Caroline Island: the easternmost island on earth, renamed Millennium Island for 2000

Chicago: a city in the north central U.S. and home to Penthes Pharmaceuticals

Christmas Island: a barely populated atoll about one thousand miles south of Hawaii

Fiji: an island country in the western South Pacific

Gilbert Islands: the westernmost and most populated islands in Kiribati

Hawaii: an island state of the U.S. and a common entry point for visiting Oceania

Kiribati: the only country to straddle all four hemispheres, pronounced Keer ee bas

Kiritimati: the local spelling of Christmas Island, "ti" is pronounced "s"

Line Islands: the easternmost part of Kiribati

Millennium Island: the name given to Caroline Island to celebrate the year 2000

Pago Pago: the capital of American Samoa, an unincorporated territory of the U.S.

Phoenix Islands: the middle group of islands in Kiribati

Samoa: an independent island nation in the South Pacific

Savusavu: the town in Fiji where Joy works as a teacher

Suva: the capital of Fiji

Tarawa: an atoll in Kiribati with the nation's capital city and most of its population

Texas: a southern state in the U.S. where Zane grew up

People

Afi: fire dancer from Kiribati
Alex: Zane's dad
Ariel: Zane's sister
Aunt Summer: Zane's closest aunt
Balthazar: Zane's pet chameleon
Barantiti: Afi's birth name
Biribo: Afi's father
Brenda Mills: head of marketing at Penthes Pharmaceuticals
Britta: Zane's college friend and roommate
Chloe: Zane's friend at work and Peter Hulson's granddaughter
Darlene Hulson: Peter Hulson's deceased wife
Doug: Joy's ex-fiancé
Gil: a mid-level manager at Penthes
Gina Cabrini: Joy's mother
I-Kiribati: people from Kiribati
I-Matang: people not from Kiribati
Joel: Chloe's brother, Peter Hulson's grandson
Josh: the Penthes go-to guy for attractive PowerPoint presentations
Joy Cabrini: Peace Corps volunteer teaching in Fiji
Judge Joseph Cabrini: Joy's father
Lola: Zane's mother
Mark Hadley: head of "Turn Your Teen Around in the Tropics"
Miss Demeanor: Toby's boat
Neil Bennet: COO of Penthes Pharmaceuticals
Nikolas: employee and friend of Pete
Paula: Peter Hulson's daughter, Chloe's aunt
Pete: Peter Hulson's son
Peter Hulson Sr.: founder of Penthes Pharmaceuticals
Raju: head of research at Penthes
Raven: new employee in marketing at Penthes and Zane's friend
Ruti: Afi's mother
Sylvia: Chloe's mother

Teddie: Zane's youngest sister
Tiemti: Toby's friend in Kiribati
Toby Axton: Single-handed sailor who lives on Miss Demeanor
Va'iga: assistant at a Turn Your Teen Around school
Zane: a young man with an unusual ability to alter his appearance

www.ingramcontent.com/pod-product-compliance
Lightning Source LLC
Chambersburg PA
CBHW050015180626
46810CB00002B/425